CITIES OF NIGHT

A SMORGASBORD OF STORIES

PHILIP NUTMAN

ChiZine Publications

FIRST EDITION

Cities of Night © 2010 by Philip Nutman
Frontispiece illustration © 2010 by Mark Maddox
Jacket design © 2010 by Erik Mohr
All Rights Reserved.

LIBRARY AND ARCHIVES CANADA CATALOGUING IN PUBLICATION

Nutman, Philip, 1963-
            Cities of night / Philip Nutman.

Short stories.
ISBN 978-0-9812978-8-0

            I. Title.

PR6064.U75C57 2010   823'.914   C2010-900687-9

CHIZINE PUBLICATIONS
Toronto, Canada
www.chizinepub.com
info@chizinepub.com

Edited, copyedited, and proofread by Helen Marshall

In Memoriam

Lindsay Anderson
(1923–1994)

"Never apologize . . ."

&

Mick Travis
(1968–1982)

Special thanks to Malcolm McDowell for constant inspiration.

"If you have a reason to live on and not to die,
you are a lucky man . . ."

*

But this book is dedicated to my three Muses:

Melpomene, for the shadows and the pain;

Clio, for history and the city lights;

But ultimately for Terpsichore for reminding me
how to dance on fire.

Table of Contents

CITIES OF NIGHT

OF

NIGHT

A SMORGASBORD OF STORIES

All men dream: but not equally. Those who dream by night in the dusty recesses of their minds wake in the day to find that it was vanity: but the dreamers of the day are dangerous men, for they may act their dream with open eyes, to make it possible.
—T. E. Lawrence

UNEARTHLY POWERS

PRELUDE TO A NOCTURNE

It was the afternoon of the day of my death, and I was in bed with my Japanese concubine when Haiyan, my housekeeper, announced that the archbishop had come to see me.

"Take him to the bar and get him a drink," I quavered in Mandarin, trying not to laugh because Paul Pope was no more an archbishop than I was a Sufi. Prescient I may often be, but I had not foreseen the arrival of the Pope of Perversity on this most auspicious of days; not only was it the day of my death, but I knew with terrible clarity, that it was the day of The Big One: California was about submerge like Atlantis, and Nevada was about to become beachfront property.

I may have retired fifteen years ago from the professions of novelist and screenwriter; nevertheless you will be constrained to consider, if you know my work at all and take the trouble now to reread that first sentence, that I have lost none of my old cunning in the contrivance of what is known as an arresting opening. But there is really nothing fake about it. Reality often plays into the hands of art. That I had celebrated my ninety third birthday two months earlier was a fact; the living room was still festooned with old-fashioned birthday cards. That Paul had come, albeit unexpectedly, to visit was a fact. But only I knew what the rest of the day had in store for the pestilent millions who swarmed over the West Coast like red ants picking clean a carcass.

I caressed Tomomi's beautiful buttocks beneath the 310-count cotton sheets. Sighing, she positioned her head on my shoulder. She was twenty seven. I did not deserve a beautiful young blossom beside me. We had never exchanged carnal knowledge, but we had shared an intimacy known only to true lovers. She understood that

9

even at my still tumescent antiquarian age that Eros had flown the coop when my beloved Tess passed away seven years previously. Tomo knew I had been faithful to my last wife, the greatest lover of my life, the only woman who had truly embraced my soul. My faithful Tomo saw the shadows and the pain surround me every day. She knew how much I desired paying the Ferryman to cross the river to be reunited with the Angel God had sent me when I tried to kill myself.

But that was then, and this was now. Tess was gone, and I needed to get my lazy arse out of bed.

"I wish you would come with me," Tomo whispered.

"I'm too old to spend nearly a dozen hours on a plane to Paris, and it's time you visited your parents. It has been six months," I wheezed, reaching for my inhaler. Tomo took the tube from my shaking hand and inserted the mouthpiece lovingly between my lips. Although both her parents were from Tokyo, Tomo's family lived in France, her father being part of the Japanese Trade Commission. I was glad they were there because the seismic shift which would destroy the West Coast would send shock waves across the Pacific and trigger severe quakes in Japan. I inhaled, feeling my lungs open like sun-kissed flowers. Tomo snuggled against me. I lay a hand on her back, stroking her spine. I had outlived three wives, and here I was on my deathbed cuddling with a girl young enough to be my great-great granddaughter. It had been an interesting life, but I was now tired of it.

"Go," I said, kissing the top of her head. "Give yourself plenty of time to get to the airport." I playfully slapped her bum. Tomo kissed my cheek and swung out of bed, unaware this would be the last time I saw her lithe, naked body and marvelled in her physical perfection. And perfection in my old, tired eyes she was: her form and contours were precisely proportioned to her five-three height; her weight a tad too skinny for my personal taste, but a wonderful reflection on Japanese genetics nevertheless. As I grew older and more emaciated, I discovered I wanted more to hold onto in a woman. But she was Tomo, and she had given herself totally to me—secretary, confidant, majordomo, nurse—platonic lover, because she knew how I hated sleeping alone.

I slid from the bed naked, sallow, emaciated . . . old. I still worked out a little every day and practised T'ai Chi and Qui Gong, but age had ravaged my muscles no matter how healthy I ate or exercised or meditated and focused on staying young at heart. That wasn't difficult with a carefree sprite such as Tomo as my constant companion. Young in mind was tougher; I simply could not relate to the average twenty-something and the ice-sheet thin facileness of their preoccupations. It wasn't just age telling me this; I had seen in my forties, when Obama took office, a sea change in the generation twenty years younger than me. Generations X and Y-me? had been eclipsed by generations Why Not? and Yes We Can. And then, life being an endless cycle, the hopes, idealism, commitment of those generations were replaced by the apathy and ennui of their offspring, who embraced the most mindless, empty aspects of life. I was too tired for this shit, and standing exposed before a God I didn't believe existed, merely my own pathetic, drained visage reflecting back at me in a mirror (which, after all, is nothing more than a negative space in a frame), I craved the caress of death.

Then Tomo pinched my sagging right ass cheek, and I couldn't help laugh.

"Don't you have something better to do?"

She kissed my stubbled, gray chin. "Yes, take care of you. I won't see you for two weeks, Hurst-san. A lot can happen in fourteen days."

She had no idea.

"Some Banchai tea would be nice."

"As you wish," she replied, helping me slip into a purple kimono. Then she was gone: as silent as a geisha, as nimble as a field mouse.

I closed my eyes. Why, on this of all days, had Paul come to visit? We had been colleagues once, many decades ago, who, like moths, had transmuted into butterflies and, although we had flown off in different directions, had ultimately became friends. Yet like many friendships birthed by the cunt of commerce, our bond had

ultimately soured, tainted by the virus of ego and greed and need—
well, at least as far as he was concerned. My ego was the inverse
of my penis: small and un-needing of worship. When I had been
making a meagre thirty thousand pounds a year as a provincial
journalist in England, I had been happy. And as for my needs, I had
always met them face to face, hand to hand. I had never lacked a
girlfriend nor a roof over my head. Food on the table? I had always
eaten. And back in the day when I'd loved the Nectar of the Gods,
there had been Guinness, Irish single malt, and good wine aplenty.
Perhaps because I had, to invoke that hoary old Campbellian quote,
followed my bliss—writing—the money and Uncle Tom Cobley and
all which came with it had always followed. I had never wanted, nor
had I needed. Perhaps because want and need cancelled each other
out, that's why my wants were met by my needs and vice versa. In
my mind, I began to hum a favourite old Stones song: "You Can't
Always Get What You Want" ("But Sometimes You Get What You
Need").

Paul Pope had always wanted something, and his needs were
many. As I heard Tomo leave the bathroom, I decided to discover
what those wants and needs were.

He slouched at the bar like some old beast in search of Bethlehem.
Pope was six years younger than me but looked half a dozen older.
Despite a congenital hip problem which made itself manifest in his
mid-thirties, he had always been a sporting man, robust, fit, trim—
particularly in his forties when he'd adopted the look of Larry
Mullen, Jr. the U2 drummer: short hair, matching earrings, broad
powerful shoulders, strong arms, a tapered waist. Back then, four
decades ago, he'd looked a picture of health. Only I knew the truth.
Herpes. Liver problems. Erectile dysfunction (the child he believed
he'd fathered was not his). The hip, which prevented him from
playing his beloved football (the British version you Americans
insist on calling "soccer"). Serious depression. The list went on. To
the wide world, Paul Pope was a major Hollywood success; in reality,
a self-confessed failure. I and his second wife knew this only too

well; I had been fucking her in his bed for over eight months before I broke off the liaison (revenge, as the old saying goes, is a dessert best eaten cold; I disagree: there's nothing like eating an enemy's wife's hot pussy day after day while the stupid, arrogant bastard is completely oblivious).

The Pope of Perversity looked up from his cut-glass tumbler of Dewars. "Jamie!" he cried in mock-loving bonhomie. "How are you?!" He tried to slip off the bar stool and nearly spilled his drink, which made me happy, remembering good, expensive single malt was wasted on him, and grateful Haiyan had served him the standby for the unexpected. "Thank you so much for seeing me at short notice."

"Not at all, Paul. But I am curious: what brings you all the way up to Mulholland Drive? Last I heard you were living on a boat down in Laguna Beach."

I sat in my favourite burgundy leather armchair beside the ornate fireplace which had originally appeared in Whale's *Bride of Frankenstein*. The piece was for show, one of the many set dressings from beloved movies I'd acquired over the years. Pope hovered beside his barstool, clearly already liquored up. He swayed, struggling to find his words.

"I know you can do these things," he mumbled; then: "She's disappeared. Wendy. My daughter. I know you can find her, Jamie. I need to find her." A pause; a sip of scotch. "Please help me. And then, when you do, there's something else I want you to do."

"Really?" I raised an eyebrow. "That's rather presumptuous."

He blinked—his dark eyes were still like piss holes in the snow—and downed the Dewars. "Then I want you to . . . to kill me."

Paul was one of those annoying people who could frequently steal a potentially witty response from your mouth by the sheer inanity or audacity of the shit he frequently shat out of his orifice. This comment, though, was a true gob-smacker.

"Are you serious?" I leaned forward. The leather creaked.

"Yes," he said with the voice of a condemned man.

I sat back in my chair and stroked my chin. Well, this was interesting: my illegitimate daughter had disappeared, and her fake father wanted me to kill him. Suddenly, the day of my death and Armageddon time for Los Angeles took on a whole new aspect.

"Tell me more," I smiled.

FULL
THROTTLE

Travel is less about a specific destination as a certain state of mind.
—Henry Miller

Speed Kills—and so do I.
—Anonymous graffiti

"I want to kill the bastard," Rivers said as he pulled the trigger.

The tall teenager was standing still by the open window, and in that instant it occurred to Hurst that he always thought of Rivers in terms of movement: racing their customized sports bicycles, pushing whatever motorbike he could get his hands on to the limit, or running from the law. It was as if Rivers was afraid of stasis, aware that to stay in one position too long was to invite a state of mind akin to living death. Like his surname, Stafford Rivers flowed ever onward, eroding everything around him with ceaseless energy. It was, Hurst acknowledged, what had attracted him to the working-class youth the first day they met, as two eleven-year-olds garbed in uncomfortable black school uniforms standing in the playground of Ralph Taylor Comprehensive—like inmates freshly arrived at a maximum security prison. At the time, he'd thought it was Rivers's punch-first-ask-questions-later attitude, but now he had to admit it: the guy *flowed*. There was no other word for him.

Except right now.

"Shit," Rivers said. "Missed."

Hurst got up from the bed to look out into the garden as "Wish You Were Here" came to an end on the cheap stereo system. Rivers hadn't missed; he just hadn't killed the crow with one shot, and the bird lay twitching on the weed-infested ground. Alex said nothing—Staff was too angry for small talk—and went to change the record.

"That two-timing bitch deserves a smack in the mouth. Fucking slut."

Hurst selected Motorhead's "Overkill" from the untidy pile of albums, deciding it was a more suitable accompaniment to the room's tension than the lush hallucinogen of Pink Floyd. Rivers reloaded the .22 air rifle.

"If the cow was going to cheat on me, why pick a prick like Tully?"

The question was unanswerable. Andy Tully *was* a dickhead.

So much for a fun evening. Staff had learned about Phillippa and Tully on his way home from work, his last day as an apprentice plumber it turned out, fired for habitual lateness. Things always come in threes, Hurst thought as he looked at the Page Three calendar hanging over the bookcase containing several girlie mags and Sven Hassel war novels. Miss September 1979 grinned vacuously while holding her size thirty-eight breasts. What next? Maybe he should have stayed home listening to Jimi Hendrix while getting stoned. Nah, that was no option; Jamie, his snot-nosed younger brother, would be in his room pounding away on his typewriter pretending to be Ernest fucking Hemingway while listening to Rush ad nauseam. No, Friday nights meant one thing—the Rivers and Hurst Hellraising Show—two seventeen-year-olds on a one-way ticket to oblivion, drinking, smoking dope, crashing parties, boosting a car for a ride, sometimes catching the late show at the cinema if a horror movie was playing, and often committing vandalism as the night's festivities drew to a close.

Rivers began pacing, waving the gun around as the dying autumn sun cast an auburn hue across the room, his breathing deepening as his anger increased. Hurst had never seen Staff so pissed off, not even after losing that fight to Barry Rogers. He'd already punched a hole in the bedroom door and the air rifle was making Alex nervous.

"Take it easy, Staff. You were going to dump her anyway."

"Fuck off." A pause. "Bitch! Tully!" He spat the name out like a wad of phlegm.

Rivers strode to the door and disappeared into the gloomy hallway. Hurst heard him clatter down the linoleum-covered stairs, his size-eleven Doc Martens pounding the creaking wood. When he realized Staff wasn't coming back, he followed.

The Rivers house was an old terraced ruin crying out for repair. Half of the light fixtures were without bulbs, there was no central heating, the dry-rotted front door drooped on its hinges, and the plaster was coated with a layer of dirt. The stairs groaned as he descended, a damp smell leaking from the walls.

"Turn that bleedin' racket down," Mrs. Rivers said as he rounded the corner. If the house needed a ghost to add to its charm, she was it. She seldom left the place and always tried to engage him in conversation, a rare commodity in the slum Staff called home. He smiled as she saw him; Mrs. Rivers, seemingly older than her forty-seven years, had a soft spot for Hurst and was pleased that her son had a friend from the better side of town.

"Hello, Alex, luv, how are yer?"

"Fine, Mrs. R."

She stood in the living room doorway, a cigarette in her yellowed fingers, pink plastic curlers in her hair. Same old Mrs. R., irredeemably tacky: food stains on her blouse, smudged mascara around her eyes, and cheap sherry on her breath.

Staff stamped out through the tiny, cluttered kitchen at the hall's end, ignoring his mother as he headed for the garden.

"What are you up to?"

"Shut up, you old cow," he muttered under his breath.

Alex smiled with practiced ease. If Mrs. R. had heard her son, she took no notice and shuffled back into the living room to return her attention to *Crossroads* and her bottle.

As Alex emerged from the kitchen into the garden, Staff was bent over the still-moving crow, pulling a lighter from the pocket of his ripped jeans. He flicked the Bic as Alex neared, burning the bird's feet. The crow cawed in pain, trying to push itself away from the flame. After a minute of this, Staff stood, placed the gun to the bird's head and pulled the trigger, a tight grin on his face, his blue eyes glaring from beneath his mane of long, greasy hair. An off-white liquid shot from the bird's blasted cranium, splattering the soil like semen flecked with blood.

"What do you want to do?" Staff was calmer now, his attention focused on the crow's corpse.

"Score some weed from Dawson. Have a pint or two at The Five Bells. Maybe go see the late show. I think it's *Straw Dogs* tonight. You know, Peckinpah."

Staff snorted, turning to Alex, a leer on his lips. "I've got a better idea." He brought his right foot down on the bird's body, the twiglike bones breaking under the onslaught of the steel-toed Martens as he slowly ground the crow into the frozen soil. "Let's crash Tully's party."

Jamie Hurst looked at the Arthur Rackham illustration of Poe's "The Raven" above his desk for inspiration.

Nothing.

His mind was empty, the unfinished essay on Hardy's *Jude The Obscure* lay in front of him slashed with red ink marks, and the silence in the house did nothing to relieve the tension, squeezing him like a sumo wrestler. Anxiety gouged his concentration. He'd been feeling weird all day since waking drenched with sweat and dread from a nightmare he couldn't clearly recall. Just a sense of speed, of being out of control, the bright orange eyes of a huge beast rushing towards him through blackness. He'd assumed it was an anxiety dream rather than a venting dream, his subconscious responding to preexamination pressures, yet the idea of his life out of control was stupid. The next few years were carefully mapped out, and all was going to plan: get his "O" Levels, then Sixth Form and "A" Levels, leading to University and a degree in English. Beyond that he was confident that a promising career as a journalist lay ahead, and maybe—just maybe—a novel or two. But as he poured over the lit essay, he couldn't dispel the sensation of doom hanging over the room like musty drapes in a gothic mansion.

He shivered.

Stop it.

The only thing wrong with him was a slight temperature—the start of a cold he'd been fighting all week—and an overactive imagination.

Time for a change of scenery.

He got up from the desk. The mundane activity of putting away groceries might help. Friday was his mother's bridge night, and she'd dropped the shopping off in the hallway because she was running late. Friday also signalled Alex's weekend disappearing act with Stafford Rivers, whom Jamie didn't like.

There was something unsettling about Rivers's blue eyes. Their slow, suspicious movements indicated to him the cerulean irises concealed secrets. But the effect Rivers had on his brother bothered Jamie more.

Alex, the distant, erratically dutiful son, turned into a shit in Rivers's company, prompting Jamie to feel like Abel faced with Cain whenever their mother was absent, which was often. Despite a company pension, their late father's only legacy, bringing up two young sons with another about to start university had been a tremendous struggle for Mrs. Hurst. She had sacrificed a social life and borne the burden of two jobs, leaving the boys to spend their after-school hours with neighbours indifferent to their needs. Time alone was nothing new to Jamie; in fact, he preferred it to the sullen presence of Alex, who, as soon as Mother appeared, played upon her sympathies. Like Rivers, there was something cold behind Alex's eyes, a barrier Jamie couldn't penetrate. Right now he wished Alex was home playing Hendrix records loudly in his room. Anything was better than the preternatural silence.

He picked up the shopping bags in the hall and headed for the tidy kitchen. The silence seemed louder, emptier as he began to unload the food, and he hummed an Aerosmith tune to break the terrible sense of nothingness. He wished it wasn't bridge night, wished Mother was home so they could watch TV together. Why, he couldn't rationalize. He was fifteen, for cryin' out loud, not a little kid. A sense of a reassurance had warmed him when she returned with the groceries, although she only stayed a moment because Dot Wicking, her bridge partner, waited in the car outside. How could he have told her he was afraid?

(of what?)

That he didn't want her to go, couldn't face the evening alone? The unnatural feeling smothering the house rubbed away at his nerves like sandpaper on skin.

"Nobody here but us spooks," he said aloud and forced a laugh as he placed a leg of lamb in the refrigerator.

He picked up a carton of eggs.

Then it happened.

One minute he was standing in the middle of the kitchen, the next he felt cold wind hitting his face, and he couldn't see. Blackness. Then a smell of exhaust fumes, a rapid acceleration, and an adrenal rush from a sensation akin to travelling at high speed on his bicycle.

(Push it!)

Cold, dark, exciting.

Dread clutched at his back with the desperation of a drowning man.

(Do it! Yeah, go for it!)

The it shifted.

Sparks.

Bumping.

Flying sensation through blackness.

Two viewpoints—neither making sense—converging.

He shook his head to clear it.

(What? . . .)

And realized he'd dropped the eggs, a dozen size sixes, all over the floor. Nausea rushed up from his bowels. He stepped over the egg massacre to the sink, retching. Once. Twice. Three times. Nothing came up; he hadn't eaten for hours. Retch number four leapt, hurting his insides, but that wasn't why he gasped. As he looked at the window, his eyes widened at his reflection.

Alex's reflection.

Not his.

Alex stared back at him, his deep-set eyes hooded like a cobra's. Jamie frowned at the optical illusion.

(No it isn't)

And then it was his face staring back at him.

Oh, God, I'm cracking up.

He felt the room spin. Then the darkness took him as he fainted.

"Sixteen."

"Inflation," Alex said, "or daylight robbery?"

Staff sat beside him on the bench, disinterest writ large across his ragged face.

"It's a steal at that price," replied Dawson. "Supply and demand. You know how many people have been busted this month? Isn't much about. But if you don't—"

"What d'you think?" Alex turned to Staff. Rivers grunted and lit a Marlboro. He knew too much about getting busted.

"Pay him."

Alex pulled out a fistful of crumpled notes. Dawson took the money as he stood.

"It's good stuff."

Alex took the proffered envelope, glancing around as he did so. It was almost dark, twilight's last gleaming hanging onto the horizon by its fingertips. A man walking a dog on the other side of the rec ground, and what Dawson said was true: too many busts. Best be careful.

"See you next week," Dawson said as he walked off toward his car, a green Morris Minor predating the Ark.

"Monday. History test." Alex couldn't resist the dig; a month into their first term in Sixth Form and Dawson's grades were slipping. The other teenager smirked, flashing him the finger.

"Wanker," Staff said, holding out his hand as he exhaled smoke. Alex pulled a book of Rizlas from his leather jacket.

"Who's going to Tully's?"

"Pricks from King Edwards. Tarts from the High School," Staff replied, taking the papers. "Who cares? I just want to see the look on his face when we turn up."

Alex chuckled.

"He'll probably be drunk out of his skull by the time we get there."

"Good." Staff belched. "Maybe he'll fall down the fuckin' stairs."

He finished skinning up the joint, passed it to Alex. The flame from his Zippo spluttered in the wind despite the shelter of his cupped hands. He inhaled deeply.

Staff had never liked Tully. No real reason, he just had a bloody-mindedness about some of the kids they'd been to school with—or in Alex's case, still went to school with—and Tully's boarding school accent and wisecracks were enough to mark him out as top turd in Staff's shit stakes. Usually his friend's prejudices were unfounded, a randomness Alex found entertaining. But if Alex were honest, there were a lot of people he didn't like either for no apparent reason, although there were many he hated because of the way they treated him.

He coughed as he passed the joint to Staff. "It's good." The dope washed through his arteries, making his head rush. He smiled contentedly. Smoking alone never quite cut it, but dragging with a mate put all the boring shit into perspective. He looked up the hill toward Ralph Taylor Lower School, its Victorian workhouse exterior standing firm against the darkness as the final strip of sunlight thinned on the horizon. In that headrush moment, the dope rolling through his mind, he felt time compress, contract, back flip on itself. Ralph Taylor Lower School, all gothic grimness, had been the crucible in which their friendship had been forged.

The first day he started at Ralph Taylor, an all-boys secondary school with twelve hundred pupils spread over two sites, Alex found Stafford Rivers—like most things—intimidating. It wasn't the violent way Staff kicked a football around the playground or his four-letter vocabulary, it was his ability to jump right into a scrap and beat the shit out of the other troublemaker that made Alex—all skinny, four-feet-ten inches of him—mentally sidestep. But within minutes of laying eyes on Rivers, all flowing control and assurance as he punted the Webley ball around the yard, Alex found he had other people to worry about. Really worry about.

Like Marc Hougan.

If there was a scale for rating preteen psychos, then Hougan scored an eight. At age eleven, the black-haired kid with mean eyes like a whipped Doberman was five-five and broad-shouldered with an attitude to match. Hougan was trouble with a capital T. Alex knew that story, having spent the best part of the previous six years trying to avoid the other kid's violent temper while they attended Newbridge Junior School.

But on this bright, sunny September day, Hougan's shadow suddenly cast a black cloud over his hopes for a better time. Alex's reputation at Newbridge hadn't been good either: afraid of certain teachers and wary of the other kids, most of whom didn't like him, he was a frequent truant. It was either face the terrors of Mrs. Bergen's math lessons or endure repeated scuffles with or torments from the kids who lived in the Weston housing estates. With at least one fight a fortnight to his credit, he was considered an outcast, making it easier for Hougan to pick on him. Mothers walking their children home avoided the sullen, unhappy, and ultimately misunderstood boy who at age six was trying to make sense of his father's death and the injustice of peer group rejection. All Alex had wanted was acceptance; all his long-suffering mother wanted was for him to be like his older brother Julian, eight years his senior and a picture of docile, studious piety, or his goody-two-shoes little brother Jamie, who never cried and was popular with teachers and kids alike. The week before Alex had started secondary school, she'd almost gone down on bended knee, begging him to wipe the slate clean, avoid trouble, and behave. Alex, sick of fighting, agreed, wanting to be popular like that little snot Jamie, but most of all wanting to please his mother. Yet Hougan, a curse on legs shaped by a brutal father, seemed to be a constant shadow at his heels.

Alex stood in the playground that morning watching Rivers and his mate Evans kicking the ball between them, thinking about Newbridge and how all that was in the past. Then Evans punted the ball to him. Surprised, he stopped it, sending it back with a swift sweep of his foot . . .

. . . only to find himself face down on the tarmac with grazed hands, a scraped knee, and torn trouser leg. He looked up, stunned.

"Hurst." Hougan spoke his name with a grimace, then spat close to his head. Evans and the others laughed. Except Rivers, who stared coldly at the two of them, his eyes narrowing slowly.

"Gimme the ball." Hougan stepped over Alex, whose hands were stinging from the fall, knee bleeding. "The ball."

"No," Rivers said softly. Hougan grinned sardonically, then charged him.

The fight lasted thirty seconds, the two boys pounding each other at full strength, fists, feet, and knees pummelling in a blur of movement before Mr. Palmer, the fey music teacher whose thinness belied his strength, appeared to separate them, whacking Hougan round the ear when he didn't stop. Rivers's nose was bloody but Hougan's top lip was split.

"Names," Palmer demanded.

"Stafford Rivers."

"Stafford Rivers, *sir*!"

Rivers refused to repeat his name.

"You?"

Hougan was silent.

"Name, boy."

"Marc Hougan," he replied, punctuating it with a bolus of bloody snot aimed at the teacher's feet.

"The infamous Hougan, eh? We've been warned about you." Palmer turned his attention to Hurst. "Get up lad."

Two minutes later, with seconds to go before the school day was officially due to start, Alex stood outside the headmaster's office, flanked by Hougan and Rivers. No one spoke or looked at the others. He knew then that nothing would change. It was the same as it had always been and looked likely to get a whole lot worse. If he was going to survive the next five years, he was going to need an ally. Standing in the gray, disinfectant-reeking corridor, his stomach churning with nerves, he decided Rivers would be that ally—regardless of what it took to get him on his side—unaware that the bond between them was already being woven by the Fates.

After a couple of thickly rolled spliffs, Staff was calm. He mangled an empty beer can as he sat in the torn armchair while Alex reclined on the bed, a bottle of Guinness in one hand, a joint in the other. Yeah, Ralph Taylor. What a long, strange trip it had been. Clint Eastwood as Dirty Harry looked down on him from the wall. *Go ahead punk, make my day.* More like make my night, he chuckled silently to himself. Staff was hidden in thought, his face carved in sand, his expression shifting as the wind of those thoughts altered the angles of his high cheek bones, his wide mouth. Alex flicked ash onto the cracked linoleum. The Floyd were playing again, the strains of "Dark Side of the Moon" this time. Yeah, some night. Staff hadn't spoken for nearly an hour.

"Money" started to play, and Alex began toying with his keys, examining them with stoned, languid fascination. The ring was a plastic holder containing two pictures. On one side there was a small photograph of the New York City skyline at night, the Empire State building looking incomplete without King Kong astride it; the other was a skull and crossbones under which the legend LIFE FAST, DIE YOUNG was inscribed. He wanted to live in New York one day, yearned to taste all it promised. Big cities in Britain seemed insignificant in comparison; even London lacked something when you held it up to the Big Apple he'd read so much about. But then anywhere was better than Bath, he guessed, feeling nothing but scorn for the West Country town in which he'd spent all his life; New York appeared as one huge adult Disneyland. Okay, so Bath had over two thousand years of history and culture, but that didn't mean a thing when you were seventeen, you had no money, and the future looked as promising as an old black-and-white photo you'd kept in your back pocket—faded and crumpled.

Staff startled him by standing suddenly, making for the door. He reappeared awhile later, tossing a black crash helmet to Alex, who spilled Guinness over the leg of his Levi's. Staff laughed. "We're leaving." Held up a set of keys in one hand, a red helmet in the other.

"On Brian's bike? You're bloody crazy. He'll kick the shit out of you when he finds out."

Staff laughed, tersely this time. "He'll never know. The old woman's pissed out of her head and won't hear us start The Bitch up. Let's go. Ninety down the carriageway'll blow out the cobwebs."

He was gone before Alex could object. Shit, why the hell not? It was 7:45 already, time to do something. If Staff wanted to risk a punch-up with his brother, fine, it wasn't his problem. Yeah, The Bitch, Brian Rivers's bike. A red Kawasaki Z1000—now you're talking. A thousand cc's of throbbing, rumbling four cylinder, four stroke. It would beat getting the bus to Tully's.

The yellow Capri was six years old and starting to rust around the wheel arches, but Harry Bledsoe didn't give a shit.

He wasn't happy though, as he looked at the engine one last time, wiping his oil-stained hands on a dirty rag, aware that Gibbons, the Hitler of Carpenter & Sons Fruit & Veg (Wholesale), was walking towards him. In fact, Harry wasn't happy full stop. His youngest kid was down with the measles, his wife, Kath, was hair trigger because it was that time of the month, and the Capri wasn't running properly.

He'd recently had the car in for a service, and the vehicle had been given a clean bill of health from the mechanic. A couple of new spark plugs and a replacement fan belt he could live with, but despite the mechanic's remark that the engine was in good nick considering the miles on the clock, the Capri hadn't started efficiently for the last week, producing a consumptive noise every time he turned the ignition and only jumping to life on the eighth or ninth attempt. To add insult to injury, Hopkins was off sick, and Harry was working double shifts because the mortgage rate was up again and he had a family of five to feed. He was tired and fucked off, and he wanted to go home but couldn't because it was 7:45 and he had another three hours to go.

26

Harry hated Mondays and loved Fridays—pub night, the only time Kath agreed he could go out and get plastered—but this one was a sack of shit the size of Big Ben.

He closed the bonnet of the car as Gibbons came up behind him. Harry had no idea what was wrong with the bloody thing. More money to spend.

"Get yer arse moving, Harry. The Bristol delivery should've gone out an hour ago."

"Yeah, I'm on my way." He tossed the rag to one side as he turned toward the fully loaded Bedford lorry. A trip to Bristol was the last thing he fancied, and it looked as if his plans for an early knockoff and a jar or two of Sam Smith's in The Queen's Head before closing were steadily disappearing up shit creek without a paddle.

"And don't forget the invoice this time."

"No, I won't, George," Bledsoe said as he opened the cab door, adding a silent *Go shag a sheep, you old wanker.*

Staff kick-started the Z1000 and The Bitch roared to life, all 1000 cc's of prime Jap engineering. Alex straddled the big bike, holding firmly onto the pillion bar. Staff turned. "Let's do it!" he shouted, revving the engine.

Staff slipped his visor down and the precisioned beast took off down Landsdown View. As they reached the bottom of the road, he pressed hard on the horn, the noise echoing off brick wall as they shot through the tunnel beneath the railway line, Staff slowing at the last moment as they reached the junction with the Lower Bristol Road, the brakes screeching in protest. The Herman Muller building was opposite, its lights still burning as the cleaners worked on the front offices.

They'd broken in for a lark a few weeks back after a late-night drinking spree and stole a couple of chairs from the board room, tossing them into the river Avon flowing behind the factory. Staff always knew what to do if the night was a dead loss. It had been a laugh, jimmying the men's room window, climbing in, and stumbling around in the dark until they found the offices. Staff had taken a shit on a secretary's chair and Alex'd pissed in a desk drawer, soaking a pile of personnel files. Yeah, that stunt had capped a boring night nicely. Now this one was shaping up as a riot, the Kawasaki rolling like a mechanized wet dream.

A stream of traffic passed, late commuters heading home for the weekend. As soon as the last car went, Staff put the bike in gear, accelerating with the style of a speedway rider. Within moments they were on a car's tail. The road curved to the right and visibility was limited. That didn't stop him from overtaking, dropping a gear, increasing the engine's roar as he continued to push the speedometer up, then slipping into fourth as they glided past the Hillman Avenger. Alex looked over at the alarmed driver, a fat businessman type, flashing fingers in a V as they took off. Yeah, it was going to be a good night. He could feel it all the way from his balls to the top of his head, his body vibrating in concert with the powerful bike. He looked over Staff's shoulder: the speedometer read seventy and they were in a fifty m.p.h. zone. Big fucking deal. Staff continued to accelerate, pushing the bike past the other cars. Up ahead the houses gave way to factories on the right and, on the left, the stone wall supporting the British Rail line connecting London in the east to Bristol in the west, the direction in which they were headed. Here the speed limit was sixty miles per hour; they were up to eighty. Ride that Bitch!

If he could have seen Staff's face, he would have seen his friend was smiling, a grim, mean smile charged with aggression. Staff took the bike up to ninety, tempted to give it full throttle, the cars behind them receding rapidly. There was no oncoming traffic as they reached the city limits. The street lights stopped, plunging them into a stretch of blackness, the railway line disappearing into a long tunnel, the factories replaced by the dark, silent, slow-moving expanse of the Avon on the right. The Bitch's engine purred with almost sexual satisfaction as it cut through the black, a thunderous ravaging red devil from hell.

Stoned on dope and speed, all head-rush perfection and oiled movement, Alex had no worries about Staff's ability to control the bike. He'd been riding motorcycles since he was thirteen, way below the legal age limit, but then legality didn't feature too highly in Staff's worldview: a little dope dealing here, a little breaking and entering there—he was small time in his crimes, but he believed if you wanted something, you should take it; if there was money to be made, make it whichever way you could; if there was a bike challenging enough to ride, then push it to the max, take it to the red line and beyond. Fuck rules and regulations. Alex felt his amigo lean into the wind and lowered himself as far as he could go. There was no past, no future (*God save the Sex Pistols!*), only *now*—and that was one huge, throbbing brain scream of speed and dark.

They approached the traffic lights at the point where the Upper and Lower Bristol Roads converged and stretched out in a mile-long expanse of straight dual carriageway. The lights were green and The Bitch blasted through at one hundred m.p.h.. Alex whooped inside his helmet. Yeah, this was it. Go for it. Fast, furious, totally exhilarating. All thoughts of Sixth Form, of essays, tutors, home, and boredom, were gone. There was only the sensation of speed.

And the dark.

The phone rang as Jamie was finally starting to relax after the panic of the dead faint.

He got up from the couch in the dimly lit living room, swayed slightly as a residual of the fainting vertigo flared in his head, and reached the receiver on the fifth ring.

The line was dead.

Balls. He hated that, not knowing who was trying to call, the tone mocking with its electrostatic hum. He sat beside the phone, shaking uncontrollably, his heart trip-hammering.

What's wrong with me?

He jumped as the phone rang again, picking up with a knee-jerk reaction in the middle of the second ring.

"Hello?"

Static. An echo of a voice. More static.

"I can't hear you."

It sounded like the voice said "Alex." Then the static faded, followed by a click.

Silence. Marred only by the ticking of the grandfather clock in the hallway. He looked at the peach floral wallpaper and felt sick.

The pattern took on a hypnotic aspect, flowers rotating, blending rhythmically.

The vision came.

It rolled over him with the relentlessness of a tsunami, a devastating sensation that rose up from his chest, pushing air from his lungs as his ribs cried out in agony as he felt them splinter. By the time it reached his head, his world was coming apart, the floral print fragmenting, leaves falling, petals scattering in a whirlwind of motion. . . .

and he was flying backward through cold, black air, arms backstroking wildly

(Oh God!)

legs pumping at nothing, he felt himself thrown into the black, up, upward, onward. All he could see was the dark and a smear of orange.

Then rolling

tumbling

with a bone-jarring crash and something inside him burst something else snapping spine shattering

(Oh my God!!)

skin ripping muscles tearing organs coming apart as he saw stars constellations galaxies nebulae unfolding in celestial majesty as his eyesight exploded.

(OH GOD! THE PAIN!!)

in a swirl of pink puce blood dark purple and then—

Nothing.

He heaved in a deep lungful of air

(I can't breathe!)

crying out like a baby taking its first taste of oxygen.

"No!"

Jamie's sense of balance went, and he collapsed back into the armchair still holding the phone, dragging it from the table, the bell jingling loudly as it hit the floor.

Rivers sounded The Bitch's horn as they reached the roundabout, a long, loud, blaring burst as he handled the bike with the tenderness of a lover on a first date, taking her around the traffic island twice before heading away from Keynsham and back toward the dull lights of Bath. Fourth gear and they were doing eighty. Fifth and the speedometer was nudging ninety-five.

The mile of carriageway was eaten up in seconds. Alex saw that the far set of lights were red as Staff dropped speed, decelerating rapidly.

Come on, change.

Seventy . . . sixty . . . fifty . . .

Come on!

The lights turned green.

Yeah, push it.

As if reading his thoughts, Staff twisted hard on the throttle, The Bitch whining in protest. They cut through the lights at seventy, veering to the left, taking the humpbacked bridge where the Upper Bristol Road crossed the Avon in a stomach-lifting jolt. The Bitch cleared the tarmac a foot and dropped into the right-hand curve in one smooth-as-silk switch. Before them lay Lower Weston: on the hill above, Newbridge. Way ahead was the city center and it looked like that was where Staff was taking them before heading up to Sion Hill and Tully's.

Alex's eyes narrowed unconsciously at the thought of the numbnutted dickhead. Phillippa had made the wrong choice there. Whatever Staff had in mind, it was going to be a party Tully would never forget.

By 8:50 PM Harry Bledsoe was pissed off. The drive from Bath had taken nearly an hour because of heavy traffic compounded by a three-car pileup outside Keynsham. But now he was in Kingswood and he would finally reach the Forbes warehouse in another ten minutes or so.

He wondered how little Mark was doing. The poor kid had looked like he was at death's door, the measles at its worst, when Harry'd left this morning. He'd give Kath a call as soon as he got to the yard to see how the four-year-old who looked just like his mother was doing. Marrying Kath had been the best move he'd ever made, and at that moment, as he sat in the truck at a set of lights in Kingswood, all he wanted was to be at home with his woman, seated in front of the TV with his kids asleep in bed, happy in the knowledge that little Mark was doing fine.

The bus behind him honked its horn and he put the truck in gear, moving slowly as the road was narrow, the traffic still heavy.

"I'll be home soon, darlin'," he said, smiling.

After an hour riding round the city, they pulled into Sion Lane around nine o'clock and were met with the sight of a police car outside Tully's house. Staff idled The Bitch's engine, hesitating, then killed it.

Loud music rolled out into the chilly night air as Alex lifted the helmet visor, surveying the street for signs of the Boys in Blue. Staff popped the bike's stand, removed his helmet, and turned to Alex with a disgruntled expression. He'd had too many run-ins with the pigs.

"I'll see what's up."

Alex dismounted, placing his skid lid on the seat. Staff grunted.

As Alex drew near the house, the music died, Gabriel's "Solsbury Hill" cut in mid-chorus, a faint sound of indignant voices following a beat of silence. He paused, then continued toward the detached house, his boot heels clocking along the pavement. When he was about two hundred yards from the house, a second police car drove up from the other end of the horseshoe-shaped street. He ducked into the bushes fronting the nearest house, watching as two cops got out and plodded flat-footed toward the other cops, who were now emerging from the garden with three teenagers behind them. One of the kids was Alan Birch, from King Edward's, a dealer who made Dawson look like the amateur he was in the dope stakes.

He looked back up the road. Staff was nowhere in sight.

The two cops took the guys Alex didn't recognize, and roughly frog-marched them to the car. Tully and a small group of kids, Phillippa among them, appeared at the garden gate and spoke with the senior cop, but he couldn't hear what was said. He hoped Staff couldn't see Phillippa. Words continued to be exchanged. Tully looked disturbed. The cop shook his head, placing a heavy hand on the short teenager's shoulder, gesturing toward the other car. Phillippa started to protest, a delicate blond bird who'd suddenly found her wings clipped. Tully turned, took her hand, said something, then walked off with the cop, the other teens standing with lost, confused expressions on their faces.

Alex jumped behind the privet hedge as the patrol cars pulled away and headed up the hill past the bike. Once they were at the top, he ventured another look toward the house, but Phillippa and her crowd were gone.

Staff was nowhere in sight as he ran back to The Bitch.

"Hey," he hissed.

Staff appeared from behind a high garden wall bordering a large modern house.

"Looks like—"

"Saw it." Staff's face was a mask of frustration. He flipped a cigarette into the gutter as he walked over to a green Metro parked nearby. He swung his right foot into the off-side rear end—once, twice—then switched to the other foot, pounding dents into the body work.

"Fuck."

He turned to the elm tree near the car, its branches reaching over the wall to down near the pavement. He leapt, grabbing a low branch, pulling down with his full weight. It broke with a dry snap, and he swung the limb in an arc at the car's windshield.

Again.

And again.

When the branch did little more than break off a wiper blade, he threw it to one side, resuming his kicking assault on the paneling.

A light went on inside the house.

"Come on."

Staff was on The Bitch before the words were out of his mouth, his foot kicking the start in one strong downward motion. The bike roared into life. He took off before Alex was securely in place, his friend nearly back flipping with the rapid acceleration.

He didn't stop at the top of the road, and Alex nearly lost it again, only managing to stay on by grabbing Staff's shoulders as they turned sharp right. Staff hit fourth as Cavendish Road dropped steeply beside the golf course, Alex holding on tight as The Bitch descended.

They drove to The Hat and Feather down on Walcott Street, Alex guessing where they were heading once they crossed Landsdown Road, nearly hitting a pedestrian as they rumbled down the incline to the end of the Paragon, its row of black monoxide-coated Georgian terrace exuding all the charm of fire-bombed Dresden.

Staff remained silent as he parked The Bitch outside the Hong Kong Garden restaurant, his blue eyes twinkling with barely contained anger as he removed his helmet. Alex tried to grin but Staff turned away, striding toward the battered double doors of the pub.

The Hat was a rundown spit and sawdust bar in an area the city fathers seemed to have forgotten. Only a minute's walk from the stylish shop-fronts of Broad Street, Walcott was a dark corner of poverty, drugs, and the occasional prostitute. The Hat was a shit hole, a meeting place for the lost, the outcast, the forgotten, those who didn't fit into Bath's orderly image of civil servants, secretaries, shop assistants, and the wealthy. On any given night, you'd find a couple of dealers, a rumble of bikers, groups of hippie throwbacks downing pints, wheeling and dealing, and talking dreams as worn as the bar stools cracking under the weight of professional boozers.

Staff pushed open the doors and disappeared. The Hat was their home away from home. Here they were accepted along with the other disenchanted youth sipping beer and listening to the jukebox. The Stranglers, the Pistols, Iggy, the Slits—this jukebox had 'em all. The pub wasn't a nihilistic haven, though; it served the nexus between generations, home to the last hippie tumbleweeds blown by the winds of '67, those who professed to have the answers, and the blank generation whose credo was *We don't care*. Alex liked it here and felt some of his frustrations ease as he entered to the dirty noise of the Stooges' "1969."

Staff weaved through the landmass of punters, making for the bar. The odour of Flower's Best Bitter, cheap lager, and spirits hung above the regulars like a cloud of halitosis. Staff ordered a pint of Skol and a Guinness while Alex manoeuvred into the far corner next to Smokin' Joe, an emaciated Hat regular, mindful not to bump against the group of skinheads next to the window. This bar was also the kind of place where the wrong move could earn you a smack in the mouth.

Staff joined him. Seeing his eyes still glowing with rage, Alex concentrated on the Guinness. Best not to speak until Staff was cool.

Rivers sighed after downing half his pint. "What now?"

Alex lit a cigarette. "See the late show."

"Come on! Piss on watching a bloody movie. There's other things."

"Don't know." It was true. He had no ideas at all other than getting stoned while watching slow-motion violence.

Staff grunted. "We got The Bitch. Think of somewhere to go."

"Bristol?"

"Nah."

"The Motorway?"

"No," Staff said again. "Cunt!"

"Come off it," Alex said, annoyed. "Give it a rest."

"Fuck you, she ain't your girlfriend."

"All right, just—"

"Look, I'm pissed off, right?"

"I know," Alex said after awhile, slapping him on the shoulder. "Forget Tully. He's down the Nick trying to convince the pigs he knew nothing about Birch's drugs, I bet."

Staff nodded, looking at the skinheads.

Alex put his drink down. "I gotta take a leak."

The Gents was at the rear on the opposite side. He started weaving through the crowd, navigating the bodies as deftly as he could, particularly past a cluster of mohawked punks drinking with a couple of members of the Bristol Angels. He stopped suddenly a few yards from the Gents' door. Standing right in front of him was a figure he recognized immediately, although he could only see the guy's back. That figure had haunted his dreams for too many years.

Hougan.

All six-feet-two of the hardcase was blocking him from the Gents, the black-haired troublemaker talking to a pair of underage girls.

Shit!

Alex froze. There was no way to get to the Gents without touching him, as the punters were packed tightly in this corner. Although he'd not had a run-in with his nemesis for nearly two years, more than a decade of trouble had instilled in him a Pavlovian response: Hougan meant trouble, Hougan meant pain. He unconsciously fingered his jawline, touching the two-inch scar under his chin, a present from Hougan on the Ralph Taylor rugby field. Apprehension grabbed his legs, and he lost the desire to piss.

"That was quick," Staff said as he returned. Alex shrugged. "Got an idea," Staff smiled meanly. "Let's drop by The Circle, see what's cooking. Maybe Alison'll be there." Alex shrugged again, picked up his pint. The idea didn't appeal to him, and as for Alison . . .

For two years they'd spent most Friday nights at The Circle, the St. Stephen's Christian Youth Club housed at the church hall, a Victorian nightmare of a building in the no-man's land of Walcot. They'd gone at the invitation of Adam Gibson, the reverend's son, and after a week or so, it became a fixture in their lives. When you were underage and had problems getting served in pubs, what could you do but make your own entertainment? The Circle had become that entertainment.

Once they'd exhausted the main hall's possibilities—skateboarding, football, swinging off the balcony—they'd discovered the dark corners of the building, places other games could be played. Like smoking weed in the empty caretaker's flat, throwing water balloons off the roof at people down below, and slipping fingers into the moist, hungry twats of choir girls under the cover of darkness in the cellar. For those with mischievous minds, The Circle was a jamboree of teenage temptations.

It was fun then, but now Alex felt he'd grown beyond The Circle's confines, had graduated to the real world of sex, drugs, and rock 'n' roll. Dropping by The Circle would be like digging up an old friend to sift through his bones in search of new ideas. But Staff put down his empty glass and made for the door before Alex could object.

He was a couple of hundred yards down Walcot Street by the time Alex finished his drink and fought his way through the punters, happy to put some space between himself and the spectre of Hougan. Since The Circle wasn't far away from the pub, Staff obviously wasn't going to bother with the bike. Alex ran after him.

The cup of tea sat untouched on the table as Jamie sat with his head in his hands.

Unlike the cup, his mind was empty. He had no idea how long he'd sat in the chair holding the phone like a lifeline thrown to a man in troubled waters, but he'd finally found the energy to make it to the kitchen where he'd brewed a pot of tea, thinking a good cuppa would revive him from his stupor. He made it, then lost interest.

Dread lay heavily in his stomach, an undigested sweetmeat. He felt lost.

Alex.

A vague image of his brother, frowning, tense, came to him in the white expanse of nothingness.

Something was wrong.

As he reached out to embrace the vision, to touch it, the image dissipated, danced intangibly into the distance.

It was gone.

He woke with a start when his arm slipped from the table, and he realized he'd dozed off. The clock on the mantle said 10:05; he'd been asleep for forty minutes. No, not asleep, somewhere between the two states of consciousness, like that guy in the Stephen King book, *The Dead Zone*. He'd been in the Dead Zone, a state of blankness, swimming on tides outside himself.

He'd felt this way once before when he was a little kid. He couldn't clearly remember, but as he reached out, a lost circuit reactivated, a circuit long dormant, burnt out by an overload of input.

Alex.

Alex was the key.

Alex had climbed on the roof of the garden shed, showing off. Jamie had been withdrawn all day; then, when Alex had struggled up through the branches of the tree, he'd known his brother was going to fall long before the corrugated metal gave way, throwing Alex into the flower bed below.

He'd known.

How?

He had no idea. Why hadn't he remembered what happened that day? He remembered the rest: Alex taken to hospital by a neighbour; their mother angry and upset—angry at Alex for climbing, upset at not having a car and being dependent on the neighbour; Alex with his leg in plaster for six weeks, Jamie envious because his brother didn't have to go to school.

Instead of relieving the apprehension, the unexpected recall increased his tension, the sweetmeat dread turning into anxious broken glass—sharp, stabbing—as his stomach churned.

The feeling, a gossamer strand of a priori knowledge, came to him again as a set of sensations: smells, textures, sounds—all alien yet terribly familiar.

Darkness.

Dust.

Cold stone.

Echoes. Voices in a cave.

A girl's voice. Giggly. Drunk.

(bored bored bored)

(bitch)

He tried to amplify the sensations.

(...n't like you...)

He tried to see.

(ibson...slut...)

But all he could perceive was frustration, traces of feelings, snatches of thought.

(...cking waste...time...Friday...)

The sensory input jumped and was replaced by overwhelming blackness, the rushing cold and pain.

(PAIN PAIN PAIN)

The world flying apart.

It was now 10:40, and he felt sick again. He started retching until his throat hurt, forcing him to swallow cold tea to ease the ache.

Something was wrong with Alex. Something worse was going to happen.

(What?)

But how could he find his brother before it

(What?)

was too late?

Alex unscrewed the bottle of cider, took a long swig, then passed it to Staff. Alison Gibson, Adam's sister, was giggling as she sat in the old wheelchair in the middle of the cellar cradling an almost empty half-pint bottle of Bacardi in her lap. He wrinkled his nose in disgust. The girl was nearly out of her skull.

"I'm bored," she said.

"Join the club," Staff replied.

Alex could just make out his face in the cellar's gloom, the only light coming from small windows along the far wall near the ceiling, orange light from the street lamps outside. It was barely enough to see by but dark enough for teenage secrets, of which Alison had many. Some he knew: She'd lost her virginity at thirteen, by sixteen she'd already had three affairs with married men (one a senior member of the church), and she regularly stole cosmetics from department stores. She'd told him most of this the morning he'd snuck into the vicarage to fuck her stupid right under Reverend

Gibson's nose. She'd also given him his first blow job on the roof of the church hall one summer night. They'd gone out for awhile after that—his mother had been delighted that he was dating the reverend's daughter—but he soon grew tired of her unfaithfulness. Alison was a slut, pure and simple. She couldn't get enough, and he'd wanted a steady, monogamous relationship, at least for awhile.

Staff drank deep from the bottle of Bulmers, then passed it back to him. Alison fingered the rum bottle. No one spoke for several beats, and he decided it was time to piss. Alex gave Staff the bottle, belching as he left the room for the toilet next door.

As he pissed off a full bladder, he felt light-headed, like he'd smoked another joint, and thought of rolling one when he rejoined Staff. But as he walked in, Alison's excited groans alerted him to the drunken passion before his eyes could adjust to the gloom. Coming nearer, he saw that Staff had the girl's red dress up around her waist, his right hand working inside her knickers as they French-kissed. Alison was trying to undo his belt. Alex picked up the cider, belching. Alison moaned.

"Don't be a stranger," she murmured as Staff stopped kissing her mouth, moving to her neck. Alex came closer. She reached out for him, found his cheek, touched him gently. "Kiss me," she said, then groaned again as Staff moved his fingers in and out of her twat. Alex reached her, their tongues entwining. Thoughts from the past—Alison blowing him in the back row of the cinema, spreading her legs for him on the vicarage floor—shot into focus, a blend of disgust and arousal clashing inside him.

He stepped behind her, and she tried to kiss his mouth but couldn't reach. He ran his tongue over her ear, feeling her shiver as he wrapped his arms around her, cupping her generous breasts in his hands as she leaned back against his chest. Staff removed her knickers, still working his fingers in and out of her body, harder, faster. Alison gasped.

"Slower."

Staff took no notice. His belt undone, she tried to get his cock out. "No, *slowly*," she said. He grunted.

Alex's hands were under her sweater, kneading the large breasts. He grasped hard. Alison squealed like a stuck pig.

"Don't—"

"Sssssshhh."

He saw Staff reach for the cider bottle. Then she cried out as he replaced his fingers with the glass neck. She started to struggle in Alex's arms, but his limbs were immobile. Months of working out with weights in the school gym had increased both his strength and his size; she couldn't break his grasp.

"No, don't—that *hurts!*"

Staff worked the bottle in.

Out.

In.

Out.

In.

She cried again, and Alex felt tears splash the backs of his hands. He felt disgust and frustration. And a glimmer of pleasure.

She was getting what she deserved, the prick-teasing bitch.

That was the booze and the dope talking, not his true self, he realized. His sanity flashed as a sick, secret part of him rose up from a hidden place.

Alison cried freely, mumbling "nononononononononono" over and over.

"The wheelchair," Staff said, removing the bottle.

Alex hesitated.

This is wrong.

But his dark side countered the thought, throwing up all the years he'd been snubbed by girls; the ones at Newbridge who constantly made fun of him; the ones in his early teenage years: a torrent of rejection and humiliation. Frances Clarke, daughter of the teacher who'd made his days at Newbridge such a misery, ratting on him for stealing a library book, her upper-class accent ringing in his ears.

Hurst took the book.

Frances and her stuck-up friend Melanie the fat pig laughing at him, telling him he'd never be anything, that he was worthless, no girl would—

"The wheelchair," Staff said forcefully.

Alex complied.

He felt like Alex the Droog from *A Clockwork Orange* about to do the old in-out-in-out.

He manhandled Alison over to the chair as Staff led the way.

"*NO!*"

"Shut the fuck up."

Alex stumbled to the front, holding her hands down as Staff moved behind her, Alison's arse pulled up over the back of the chair. Staff tugged his jeans down, his prick emerging, pointing like a divining rod in the gloom, searching blind for her hole.

Alex's anger stretched like an elastic band about to break—then snapped back with a pull of sanity.

This is . . . wrong.

His thoughts cleared. He wanted no part of this . . . brutality. He felt sick with fear as Staff picked up the Bacardi bottle.

"Staff, don't—"

"Hold her!"

Unable to see, alerted by their exchange, Alison struggled with new strength. Staff leaned over her, clamping a hand to her mouth, stifling her cries.

"Staff, no, this is—"

"What?"

"Wrong."

Staff paused. "You turning into a faggot?"

"No! It's—it's not right!"

"Fuck you."

Staff dropped the bottle, grasping Alison's hips, ready to penetrate her.

The fear became a new creature. Alex couldn't—wouldn't—help his friend. The creature was defiance, and he let go of her hands. She thrashed around, and Staff lost his balance. When he raised his arm to hit her, Alex leapt forward.

"Don't!"

He caught Staff's arm, pushing his friend back. They struggled for a brief moment, then Staff shrugged him off.

"Okay. Okay."

Alex reached for his arm.

"I said okay, damn you!"

Alison lay crumpled by the chair, sobbing hoarse, deep sobs, pulling her skirt around her legs.

Alex looked at Staff, the taller youth glaring at him, the meagre light from the windows illuminating lines of tension around his mouth.

"Okay," he said with unexpected softness, his arm going limp. "You're right."

Alex let go, unconvinced by the mood swing. Then Staff's face cracked like crazy paving, his mouth widening into a broad smile.

"You're right." He pulled up his jeans, pushing his erection inside with difficulty, the cock pointing like an accusatory finger.

"Let's go," he said.

Alison sobbed loudly.

Jamie was at the bottom of West Lea Road when the nausea hit him.

He staggered to a low wall for support as the sensation rushed up from the pit of his stomach to double him over. Nothing came up—there wasn't anything to come up.

(Alex . . . don't)

The sensation stopped as suddenly as it had started, but he waited until he was sure he could walk straight.

He had to find Alex.

Alex was in danger.

(Where?)

(. . . wrong . . .)

Jamie didn't have a clue. All he'd known was he had to get out of the house.

With the slow gait of a somnambulist, he continued walking, heading for Newbridge Hill as if gravitational forces were pulling him toward the river. It was irrational to be walking away from the road that would take him to Rivers's house, the only place he thought he might find Alex, but nothing seemed rational. Instinct took his hand and he quickened his pace.

Elfman placed his hand on Bledsoe's arm.

"Thanks for waiting, Harry."

"Sure." Bledsoe took the invoice from the warehouse foreman.

It was 11:07, and somewhere nearby a police siren cut through the Bristol night. He wanted to be at home, a beer in hand, his feet warming in front of the gas fire, not standing around sixteen miles from Bath. But at least the work was done. Home beckoned.

"See you next week," Elfman said.

He smelled beer on the foreman's breath and thought, at least you got one in tonight. Still, there was a bottle of Pils waiting in the fridge, and Kath always had a plate of sandwiches ready for his return.

Bledsoe swung himself up into the cab, starting the engine as Elfman waved.

Broad Street was deserted as they headed for the Paragon, calm now after their confrontation. Staff hadn't spoken for half an hour, seemingly ashamed of his behaviour. Alex had made sure Alison was coherent enough to understand his threat before they left The Circle.

If you say anything I'll make sure your father gets the photos.

Fucking as many guys as she could get her hands on was not enough for Alison. She had to keep a visual record, photographing them post-orgasm with a Polaroid. But even this hadn't satisfied her. Tired of her organ gallery, she'd started using the self-timer to record liaisons with herself as the star of the show. But like a secret journal, written with the perverse hope that someone will read it, such a confessional only became valid when shared with another. She'd made a mistake when she showed Alex her works of art, though. It had been the nail scratch that drew blood; he stopped going out with her the following week, though not before he'd stolen

44

several prize pictures to show around at school—including one clandestine shot of Mr. Dixon, the church warden, masturbating on the couch in the vicarage.

Satisfied she'd say nothing, they left, an uneasy silence between the three of them. When they exited the hall, Staff started off in the direction of the abbey and city center, attempting to walk off his rage, frustration, and guilt, coming to his senses as the haze of dope and alcohol dissolved.

Alex knew him well enough to realize that Staff was no rapist. He felt sympathy for his amigo, walking with his head down, shoulders rounded as if under a tremendous weight. They were bonded by a hopeless boredom and the unspoken knowledge that the future held little in store for them. Especially Staff. An alcoholic mother, a distant father. Worthless qualifications. Now he had no job, little money, and no girlfriend. Although Alex was studying for his "A" Levels so he could go to university, he had no desire to go to another small town to study for another three years. Then what? A career? As what—an accountant? A civil servant? Yeah, with a three-bedroom house, a heavy mortgage, a wife and three kids. Great. He'd wake up one morning to find he was fifty, an overweight businessman like all the rest. Staff would be living in a council house with his wife, kids, and a criminal record. That's if you live that long, he thought. Staff made him think of "My Generation"—hope I die before I get old. Prison, death, or a council house. Was there any difference between them?

When they reached the top of Broad Street, Staff turned.

"Thanks. I was out of order."

"Forget it." Alex lit a cigarette.

They came to the alleyway that cut through The Paragon, its steep steps reminding him of the ones in *The Exorcist* on which the priest dies struggling with the demon and his crisis of faith.

Alex had no faith in anything. His life was one long, straight road, neither yellow brick nor paved with gold, just a brainnumbing expanse of flat black tarmac measured out in birth, school, work, death. Bath was ancient, would stand for hundreds of years. But he would be long gone, either dead in his fifties of a heart attack or dead of boredom long before then. Thackeray may have written "As for Bath, all history went and bathed and drank there," but Alex felt he was drowning under its cultural weight, a culture in which he had no place. Defoe was right when he described the city as a place conducive to committing the worst of all murders—killing time.

There is no God, no point, Alex thought as they descended the steps. He frowned as Staff stopped on the pavement.

"What's—"

Staff gave him a terse wave. "Catch this."

Five hundred yards away, almost hidden by the shadows cast by the abandoned bakery, two figures scuffled in and out of the light from the street lamps like drunken dancers.

"This could be interesting," Staff said.

He moved along, watching closely.

Alex held his ground. The two opponents were mismatched—one tall, broad, powerful, the other around five-three, of light build, and paying for it. The tall bloke was pushing the smaller, toying with him, keeping him at bay with his longer reach. The small guy tried to kick out, provoking a punch in return, which slammed him against the bakery.

Alex drew a breath through clenched teeth.

Hougan.

"Staff"" he said.

He turned, nodding. "Got it."

Alex felt anger rise from the depths of his gut like heartburn. The same old song and dance: a song of fists, a dance of pain. Hougan had the smaller guy—it was always a smaller guy, he thought—in the palm of his hand, trapped, angry, caution thrown to the wind. It was always the same, ride someone's case till they responded, cause enough hurt for the other to lose control, then move in for the kill. Hougan was slamming the small guy against the door, the sound of the guy's head hitting wood loud enough for him to hear.

Painful memories came with each blow:

Hougan punching him unexpectedly in the face at Newbridge.

Hougan ambushing him one rain-splashed day as he walked home.

Hougan suspended for smashing an older kid's head on the playground.

Hougan tripping him on the rugby pitch, kicking him in the face, making out it was an accident.

Alex taken to the hospital: ten stitches and a shot for his shattered front teeth.

Hougan swung a roundhouse into the bloke's head. There was a whack as fist connected with face, the smaller guy rebounding off the wall as blood poured from his pulped nose; a punch to the guts and the opponent went down fast.

Alex looked at Staff, his expression hard. "Let's do the bastard."

Staff nodded.

Hougan stood over the slumped body, ready to lash out his foot. The other youth, barely conscious, raised an ineffectual hand. Hougan pulled his foot back with deliberate slowness, savouring every wrinkle of fear on the bloke's face, unaware of Alex and Staff approaching from the other side of the road. Seeing that he was about to kick the guy's head, they rushed him.

Hougan turned as Staff ploughed into him, taking them both down as his right fist connected with Hougan's sternum. Hougan tripped over the downed youth's legs, pulling Staff with him but not able to twist away as Staff's full weight landed on his body. Staff punched his stomach, but Hougan retaliated with his left fist, catching Staff on the side of the head. Staff saw stars, pain racing down his neck. Hougan growled with the fury of an enraged bear, heaving Staff off as Alex came in.

Alex hesitated. A mistake. Hougan scissored his legs, taking Alex beneath the knees, sending him over to land heavily on his left shoulder, his skid lid flying. He cried out. Staff, despite the bells ringing in his head, backhanded Hougan across the face. Hougan grunted. Alex shouted "fuck," kicking with his right foot at Hougan's balls. He missed, his foot scraping hip bone. Staff stumbled to his feet and kicked. His foot hit Hougan's chest, snapping the youth back, slamming his head to the pavement.

"He's mine!" Alex screamed, diving as he brought his right fist down like a piston, spreading Hougan's nose across his face.

The pain in his left arm was intense, but not as intense as the raging anger exploding his reason. The frightened, wounded animal inside him emerged with teeth bared, claws drawn, as years of fear and hurt rushed out in a flood of adrenaline.

He punched again.

Again.

And again.

Everything blurred into a red haze, and he didn't feel or hear Hougan's jaw break or his teeth shatter. Nor did he hear Staff shouting at him to stop.

He brought his fist down a fifth time, catching Hougan on his left cheek and sending his head over at an unnatural angle, the neck snapping. Deep inside Alex, in that sick, secret place, a voice began to laugh with insane hysteria. He screamed "you fucking bastard you fucking bastard" as Staff slapped him hard, displacing him from the saddle of Hougan's chest.

Alex leapt to his feet, his mind caught on some mad wavelength, waving his fist.

"You want some of this? Come on fucker!"

Staff, his head throbbing, looked at Alex as if for the first time.

Alex went to kick Hougan and Staff grabbed him.

"He's dead!"

He slapped Alex a second time. Alex froze a beat, then shook his head.

"What?"

"He's dead. You broke his fuckin' neck. Jesus. Alex, he's fuckin' dead."

He looked down at Hougan, whose face looked like several pounds of dog meat.

"God . . . God, oh Jesus God . . . nononono God no, Jesus."

He started to rock back and forth, his voice dropping.

Staff looked up the street. A car approached from the Beaufort

Hotel end.

"Come on," Staff said, "help me."

He started dragging the body into the dark alleyway beside the bakery. Alex was still rocking, his arms cradling his chest.

"Do it!"

Alex stumbled.

"Shit." Staff pulled Hougan's body out of the light.

The car was closer.

"Alex!"

Alex moved slowly.

"The other one!"

Alex looked blank.

Staff went to the beaten youth. "Come on, you stupid fuck!"

The car was almost on them.

Staff grabbed the semiconscious bloke, heaving him from the doorway. Alex understood now, panic replacing shock. He reached down, taking the youth's legs, and helped his friend haul the dazed youth into the darkness as the car passed.

The youth groaned again.

"What do we—"

"Get the hell out," Staff snapped, taking Alex by the arm as he stooped to pick up their helmets. The car hadn't stopped.

Alex hesitated as Staff gave him the red one. He looked at the alley with the expression of a confused child.

"Move."

He took the helmet.

Jamie was down on the Upper Bristol Road near the river when his left arm started tingling, pins and needles running from shoulder to waist. He stopped.

The road was deeply dark here; the only light was that cast by the high orange lamps on the other side of the river where the Lower Bristol Road turned into carriageway. A gravelike stillness hung over the open fields and boatyard, yet he felt the air dance electrically. He sat on the wall massaging his limb.

(out of here)

He'd been following an internal compass with the blind faith of a sightless pilgrim, his mind tabula rasa, free of conscious direction. Now the compass spun wildly, a vertiginous spiral of confusion.

(move)

The thought was faint, his limbs leaden. He knew his journey was almost over. Whichever uncharted road he was traveling, his destination was on the other side of the river, and he had no control over whatever events were in motion. He was a sailor adrift on a psychic sea in a rudderless boat, at present suspended on a tidal change. Then the compass stopped spinning, and he continued.

Staff tolled The Bitch down Queen Square, carefully observing the speed limit. To Alex, it seemed they were moving at a snail's pace.

Hougan was dead.

He felt nothing.

No remorse, panic, no residue of the nausea he'd felt as they walked to the bike, when his stomach had suddenly performed a forward roll, expelling Guinness and cider over the pavement in a hot rush.

Empty.

His head was unnaturally light and clear.

He'd killed him.

Alex laughed silently as Staff headed down toward the Lower Bristol Road.

The clock in the cab said 11:35 as Harry took a wide curve. From his high seat, he could see the mile-long carriageway lit up like a neon strip across the uneven hedgerows and dark farmland.

The lights were green as he came out of the curve and he accelerated, willing them to stay that way.

He yawned.

Damn it, he'd drive the truck home. If he took it back to the depot, he wouldn't get home till midnight—if the bloody Capri would take him there. The last thing he needed right now was to spend time under the bonnet trying to get it going if it wouldn't start.

Home.

Beer and sandwiches.

Screw it, he was going to take the Lower Bristol Road. That way he'd be in front of the fire within ten minutes.

Alex lifted his visor and tapped Staff on the back. He was still taking it slow and the pace was irritating Alex.

"Head for Bristol," he shouted.

Staff nodded.

Staff's home held little appeal to Alex, and his own mother's house seemed light years away.

You can't go home again.

He'd left the safe, boring confines of middle-class suburbia, in mind if not in body. He was no longer Alex Hurst, he was Alex the Droog. He'd tasted the rare delicacy of the old ultra violence and was reborn. Nothing could touch him. Hougan was gone and so were the old fears. He sensed a change in Staff, too. They'd been into the fire and emerged unscathed.

He put his fist in front of Staff's face, making a revving motion. He nodded with enthusiasm.

Full throttle.

The bond between them, two spirits mismatched by social class yet emotionally joined, a pair of empathetic siamese twins, was stronger now, unbreakable.

Staff took The Bitch up to seventy-five and Alex smiled.

Nothing mattered. Only speed, men, and machine molded into a ménage à trois of rumbling, accelerating motion.

The houses gave way to factories, and soon the factories would give way to the long, black stretch before the carriageway.

He felt elated. What was the line from that James Cagney movie?

"Top of the world."

Yeah. Top of the world, Ma.

Alex laughed.

Jamie's consciousness fractured as he set foot on the humpbacked bridge.

One moment he was looking ahead, the next he was paradoxically gazing down on himself from a great height, a small figure almost eaten up by the dark, and glancing up over the brow of the short bridge toward the traffic lights. His split vision lasted a second, an eternity, then he felt himself dropping out of the sky, descending at an incredible speed, his own body rushing toward him. He heard a rustle of huge leathery wings rippling through the night sky, ancient, unworldly wings not touched by time.

He cried out as something swept into his body, a high-pitched whine shrieking through his ears for an instant.

Silence. Total. Still. Heavy with a strange promise.

Dread and anxiety departed, the stillness a sensation heretofore unimaginable, teasing every nerve ending, every molecule.

It was about to end.

Harry rubbed a hand over his tired eyes as he ploughed down the carriageway at eighty-five.

Sleepiness was creeping up his shoulders. He yawned.

Half a mile to the second set of lights, then the Lower Bristol Road. The lights were red. He braked, hoping they would change.

Jamie saw the Bedford truck coming down the carriageway as he heard the loud rumble of a motorbike behind him, a ways off but growing louder with every second.

The lights went green, and the truck accelerated.

The motorbike's rumble increased.

Harry saw the bike approaching at what seemed Warp Factor Five. One second its headlamp was a small yellow cyclopean orb; the next, much larger.

The crazy bastard must be doing a hundred, he thought, stifling a yawn.

The light suddenly wobbled. A trace of sparks flew up like crazed fireflies. The lamp angled toward the truck.

Before he could cry out, Harry was thrown against his seatbelt, his head whiplashing as the bike impacted into the truck's engine.

Harry screamed.

Jamie's eyes widened. The night exploded with the deafening sounds of 350 pounds of bike melting into the front of one and a half tons of truck.

The Bitch was doing 113 as it hit, the truck 89—a total impact velocity of 202 m.p.h..

High speed switched to slow motion, and he saw every body-pulping detail with unnatural clarity.

The pillion rider lifted up over the head of the driver and came apart in a spray of red, like an overripe tomato hurled against a wall. Strands of muscle, fragments of limb spreading outward, the body's impact smashed the windscreen. The bike crumpled in on itself as the engine grill seemed to eat it whole, smiling a big bad wolf grin as man and machine merged into muscle and metal, innards and engine.

The truck continued for ninety feet at a skewed angle, riding up the pavement to Jamie's left, heading for the wall as metal scraped on tarmac, gouging furrows in the earth's dark flesh before coming to a stop only a few feet from the stone, sparks vapour-trailing its movement.

Silence suddenly descended with the finality of a theatre curtain bringing the last act to a close.

September 19, 1980.

There had been a severe frost the night before, and the flowers on the graves were dying.

Jamie pulled his coat belt tight around his waist, blowing on his hands and wishing he'd brought his gloves. The cemetery was deserted, although it was midday. Even the birds in the trees were quiet; the only noise was the faint rumble of trucks on Rush Hill.

"Well, Alex, how does it feel?"

His words floated on the autumn air, and he felt self-conscious. If this were a scene in a Brian De Palma movie, he thought, Alex would come bursting forth from the grave in front of him.

But that was impossible.

When the police and ambulance men arrived at the scene, there had been no body: Alex had ceased to exist, his mortal remains spread over a wide area by the force of the crash. If not for the fact Stafford Rivers had been recognizable—albeit impacted into the engine block with such force that it took the medics three hours to cut out his mangled corpse—it would have taken the police days to identify the pillion passenger. Alex had become a pathologist's nightmare, a minute jigsaw of humanity. Nothing fitted together. The largest part of his body was a section of rib cage and spinal column, but what could it be attached to? There were no limbs. Only fragments of bone, tatters of skin, traces of muscle, a handful of teeth, and pieces of cranium. His brother had been vaporized. There hadn't been enough to bury, and what little was left filled only two small plastic bags. Alex wouldn't become worm food, even the morsels that remained; he'd been cremated, all fifteen pounds of him. But their mother insisted on a gravestone, his testament, to be laid beside the plot inhabited by their father.

Jamie was surprised by his reaction to Alex's death. He'd felt nothing then and felt nothing now, staring at the grey concrete slab with his brother's name on it. Perhaps in years to come he might— at least that's what his doctor said. But he doubted it. Though he'd loved his brother in the unspoken manner of male siblings, he'd experienced a great relief after the funeral chaos had subsided. He'd expected the house to be gloomy after the ceremony; instead it appeared as if the three-bedroom semi had been rebuilt.

He, Jamie Hurst, had been reborn.

Alex, he realized, had cast a shadow over their lives, and with his passing, the storm clouds broke up, floating away as a new sun shone forth. The shadow, however, still cloaked their mother. Jamie didn't think it would ever leave. She'd become too used to wearing black to change her wardrobe. A year to the day and she was still on tranquilizers, despite Julian returning to live with them, having quit his job on a North Sea oil rig. Jamie, on the other hand, had gone from strength to strength. He'd passed his exams with flying colours and was on the way to a place at Oxford. He'd sold his first short story to a prestigious literary magazine in January and was halfway through the first draft of a novel, two hundred pages written in a white heat this summer.

Life made new sense now. He understood how Saul must have felt on the road to Damascus: he'd been blind, and now he could see, though not with the eyes of a seventeen-year-old. No, he saw the world through the eyes of an ancient touched by arcane knowledge. Once he'd felt eclipsed by the darkness his brother drew around himself; now he felt bathed in light, baptized by a grace unimaginable before the accident, untouched by the slings and arrows of adolescence.

Alex had lived his dark dream—live fast, die young—and now it was Jamie's turn. Where his brother had failed—or succeeded, depending on your viewpoint—he would succeed on his own terms.

Only one doubt assailed him, a question perhaps best left unanswered.

What had happened that night, and why?

When the bike had hit the truck, he'd stood for an eon—in reality less than a minute—then walked away, not experiencing any feeling akin to those he knew he should feel at the instance of violent death: shock, horror, loss. Of course, there was no way he could have known it was Alex. In fact, he had not known—that terrible, liberating knowledge came later. Yet Jamie *had known* on some deeper level, a primitive, reptilian level of consciousness.

He'd walked away unaware that there was a blind man trapped in the cab screaming silently in mute agony, his vocal chords severed by the shattered windscreen, and as Jamie crossed the river, he felt some part of him—innocence, perhaps—depart on eldritch wings, heard leathery membrane flap and rustle up into the black sky. The only sensation wrapped around his heart was an indescribable peace. When he reached home, still in a somnambulist state, he'd gone straight to bed, falling into a dreamless sleep, the quiet repose of a baby untouched by earthly fears and the burden of adult consciousness. He awoke the following morning to the sound of the doorbell and, seconds later, his mother crying.

And so Jamie's world had changed.

Alex had lived a lie, a falsehood woven by those who were imprisoned by their own frightened isolation. So long as the lawn was neatly mowed, the floral print curtains hung correctly, and the checks didn't bounce, there was no teenage suicide, no incest, alcoholism, rape, drug abuse, famine or war—except in the newspapers. The middle class were too smart and too stupid to let those ills touch them. But Jamie would explore the lie, try on its masks through the role-playing of fiction, seek the truth, however ugly. And if there was a price to pay, when the time came, he would freely give the ferryman his coinage and cross the river one last time, secure in the understanding that he'd traveled roads known only by a select few: the dreamers, the mad, the restless.

He sneezed. He was coming down with his usual winter cold and the September chill didn't encourage lingering in the open.

"Good-bye, Alex." Jamie's voice was loud against the cemetery's tranquility.

As he turned, he noticed a crow watching him from high up in the branches of an old oak. The bird cawed, rustling its feathers.

His last respects paid in full, Jamie walked up the steep incline toward Rush Hill and school. When he was but a dot on the landscape, the crow took flight, arcing up into the clear sky, its wings a black apostrophe on the vast, impersonal cerulean expanse.

PAVLOV'S WRISTWATCH

As soon as the tube train entered the tunnel, Hatchard felt uncomfortable.

The sudden rush of rotten air made his ears pop, and as he swallowed to clear them, he felt the crowded compartment close in. Sweat began to pool under his arms making his blue polyester shirt stick to his skin. He tried to breathe shallowly to conserve oxygen, but this did little to reduce the smells attacking his nose.

A garlic pong clouded the carriage, coming from a portly Asian man to his right. He hoped the man would get off soon; he hated the smell of garlic. The smell swirled around him, clashing with the sickly sweet smell of perfume coming from the woman on his left. Fortunately, as the train pulled into Highgate Station, the woman, her face a mask of Max Factor, stood up to squeeze her way towards the door. As she went, a youth in a tattered denim jacket slipped into the vacant seat. He was wearing a Walkman, noise overflowing from the headset that looked to Hatchard like an Aliceband with tiny earmuffs. He began to bite his already ragged nails, gnawing at the quicks.

With a jolt, the train lurched as it quickly departed from the station, throwing him against the portly man.

"I'm sorry," he mumbled, but the man ignored him.

The youth placed a new tape in the machine, tapping his foot to the staccato beat hissing from the headset.

Tick . . . tick . . . tick . . . tick, tick, tick . . .

Hatchard's throat went dry. The clock-like noise, steady, relentless, unnerved him. He tried to push the thought from his mind, but it was no good, it had already taken root. Try as he might to imagine something nice (a dish of ice cream, yes, a big dish of raspberry ripple crowned with a maraschino cherry and wafer fan), the face of the Crocodile bled through the melting confectionery. It was taunting him. It couldn't come for him here, not with so many people around. You couldn't be taken by a Crocodile in such a place, could you?

How could it?

Could it?

But the Crocodile was the Crocodile. It knew more than he. There was so much he didn't know or understand. He suddenly felt very cold.

Tick, tick, tick ... tick, tick, tick ...

He squashed his eyelids to shut out the world and began to mumble his prayer.

"I am a free man. I do not believe in clocks. Clocks are BAD. I am free of time. My time isn't up yet because it doesn't exist. I'm free. Crocodile, you cannot touch me."

Against the black screen of his squeezed eyes, the Crocodile leered its greedy grin, opening its mouth, the echo of the clock that beat in its sepulchral belly teasing him.

Tick, tick, tick ... tick, tick, tick ...

He continued to scrunch his eyes until they hurt as he repeated the prayer, more forcefully this time. Still the clock sound continued to chip away at his nerves.

The train arrived at Archway. Some people got off. Many more boarded. Why didn't the youth leave? Oh, please make him stop! He opened his eyes in panic. Didn't the other passengers realize what the youth was doing—calling the Crocodile, playing its game? No. They were fools. Blind. Unaware of the huge shape lurking behind them, dogging their every step, pretending nothing mattered except getting to work. As he looked around he saw no one was taking any notice of him. They were unaware of the seriousness of their situation, the idiots. That, of course, was what the Crocodile wanted. Not him, not just Stephen Hatchard—it wanted them all. And the youth was calling it with his tapping. Now he knew the awful truth. Somewhere ahead of the train the Crocodile lay in the tunnel, its body grown huge on the dead flesh of others. Then he thought the train could be inside the Crocodile, the tunnel its throat, its destination the cavernous belly.

No, how could it?

His imagination was running away, trying to take him with it, trying to take him to the Crocodile. But he wouldn't go! He was a FREE MAN.

As the train pulled into Tufnell Park, there came a beeping sound and the portly man tugged up the sleeve of his raincoat to consult a digital watch.

This was too much! He stood up, jostling a man reading *The Times*, pushing against the newspaper.

"Watch it," the man said.

Hatchard whimpered as he squirmed his way towards the doors. "Stupid git," someone else moaned as he pushed frantically forward to reach the platform before the door closed.

"Manners," said a woman as he shoved her in desperation.

"Excuse me, excuse me," he mumbled, remembering manners maketh man, even in the face of death.

There! He'd made it. He was out!

His breath came in short gasps which attracted the appalled attention of a young woman rummaging in her handbag as he leapt out in front of her. He smiled sheepishly, but she backed away, disturbed by his unkempt appearance. He began to trot towards the stairs. It had been a silly, no, *dangerous* idea to take the tube into central London. He should have known better and taken the bus. Relieved by his escape, he grinned a Cheshire cat grin to himself as he reached the flight of steps.

Rain started to fall steadily as he trudged up Ballard's Lane towards home, prompting him to quicken his pace. The sky had been low and heavily overcast all morning, pregnant with a promised downpour that had finally come to term, falling like the tears of God, washing away the encrusted scabs of litter choking the gutters. He slipped his father's books inside his army surplus coat, pulled the frayed collar around his ears, and lowered his head against the water.

father would be cross if there was the faintest damp mark on the books, so he stopped under a depleted tree, its leaves taken by the unusually strong autumn winds they'd had of late, repositioning the brown paper bag containing the books beneath his worn Harris tweed jacket. It was a ways still to the old Victorian house, and rain was now descending in icy sheets. Better he catch a cold than return home with wet books.

The traffic lights were green at the junction with Sunningdale Road. Cars sped past, travelling too fast for the weather conditions, and as he stood by the curb, one hit a puddle sending a small wave over his trousers. He groaned. The lights seemed to stay green for longer than usual, two emerald eyes staring at him. At this rate, the books would get wet if he took his usual route. Since he was a free man, he decided to go another way, hoping to speed his journey. He turned left into Long Lane, trotting now, trying to avoid the cracks between the paving stones. After a while he was drenched but could see the rooftops of Squires Lane and HOME. He was a CLEVER BOY. If mummy were still alive, she would have told him so.

Though she had been dead for many moons (the only way he could gauge forward movement was via the lunar cycles, because they were natural, like the passing of the seasons, and his father felt that was the way things should be), he still missed her. When she had been pleased with him, he was rewarded with a dish of ice cream or a plate of Jaffa cakes. Now, whenever he ate them, he thought of her. But on those times she thought him a BAD BOY, he'd been sent to his room. He'd never questioned his punishment. mummy was always right. "You are FREE but you have to learn," she used to say. That had been mummy's responsibility, to teach him the things he needed to know. Of course it was, she'd been a teacher before she got A-GRO-PH-OB-I-A and was confined to the house. Yes, he missed her, even though he was now an adult, could take care of himself, and more importantly could eat ice cream whenever he wished.

Rounding the corner he realized he was by the cinema. This was fortunate as the Finchley Odeon had a large awning jutting from its front. He crossed the road to stop beneath it, looking intently at the bright colours of the film posters.

The Odeon was a large old cinema that, in his childhood, had had one huge screen. mummy used to take him there whenever there was something she thought suitable, which wasn't often. But moons ago it had been turned into one with three screens. Standing outside the grey, worn building, he tried to recall the last time he'd visited the picture house, but he couldn't remember. He mainly watched films on television.

One screen had a film called *Platoon*. The poster showed a man on his knees, arms out in a V, his head back as if crying out to the heavens asking the rain to stop. It looked like a war film. He liked war films but mummy had disapproved. They were violent and evil, she said. War was BAD. Maybe he'd come and see it if the rain stopped and father fell asleep early. The second screen had a scary-looking film called *Hellraiser*, and he shuddered as he looked at a poster showing a piece of flesh pulled back on a hook. He didn't like scary films. They frightened him, and the world was so big it was already scary enough. He moved to look at the third screen—and froze.

No! Not again!

It . . . it . . . was too much. First the terrifying experience on the tube, and now this. The Crocodile was playing with him, taunting him like a cat with a mouse. There on the poster was the beast itself, leering its evil, knowing smile, the eyes narrowed to slits as it licked its lips as it menaced the Pirate. The shock of the image made him lose his grip on the books beneath his coat. They fell to the pavement with a heavy slap, making him start from his transfixed state. Stooping to lift them from the ground, he did not take his eyes from the poster. Was it a trick of the light as his angle of vision altered, or did the Crocodile wink at him? Of course it was no optical illusion, the reptile was filled with cunning. It winked again, saying silently *you are mine*. He couldn't stand there any longer; every part of him felt touched by cold, wet fingers. He turned to run, gasping as he collided with a tall, grey-haired man. He squealed piglet-like and bounded across the road, narrowly missing a red Vauxhall Chevette, the tall man watching, a concerned expression on his face.

As he reached the other side, he dared look back. The tall man was still watching him, then turned to the movie poster. The angle of light on the plastic covering obscured the Crocodile's image, cutting the poster in two. It was gone. All he could see as he disappeared around the corner was the film's title:

Peter Pan.

He shivered in the porch, fumbling for his keys. He found them and opened the door. Slamming it against the cold and wet, he sneezed.

"Stephen?" his father called from upstairs, the sound that of fingernails on a chalkboard. He moved slowly up the tall, shadowy flight of stairs, the top cloaked in darkness. "Yes, father."

The elderly man was propped up in bed, his frail frame cradled by three pillows. As usual the reading light was on, throwing an orange slash across the blanket on which lay a pile of books.

"Did you get them?" father asked in a hushed tone.

He nodded, offering the soggy bag.

"Ach! Look at you!" the old man said. "My books! Go dry them, then yourself. The books first!"

"I'm s-s-sorry, father, I'm—"

"Go dry them!"

He turned and headed for the bathroom. "And bring me a glass of water," the old man added, his request punctuated by a coughing fit.

After he wiped the books and brought father the water, Stephen changed into clean clothes in his room, leaving the wet trousers in a tangled heap on the bare boards alongside piles of dirty laundry and a strewn selection of magazines: *Newsweek, The Plain Truth, Harpers, The Face, Country Living, Cosmopolitan.* He'd found them neatly tied with string next to the dustbin at number fifty seven a few days before, rescuing them before the dustmen took them away. Magazines held his attention better than books because of the photos. Even if he didn't understand the articles (*The Plain Truth* was clear enough though; that one said the world was coming to an end, and he knew it was the Crocodile's doing), the pictures provided him with endless interesting discoveries. Like something called the G Spot, a man who looked like a pretty girl but was called Boy George, and the President of America was an old actor who once appeared in a film with a monkey called Bonzo.

He sneezed again as he looked at them. It was still raining so there was little chance of a trip to the cinema. Not that he could go there with the Crocodile waiting so close. Once he was in the dark, he knew it would get him.

Aware he was hungry, he sneezed again and started for the stairs.

Although it was HOME, the gloomy hallway was ripe with hidden menace. He hated passing the collection of skulls on top of the bookshelves, their vacant eyesockets black, mysterious. But he liked looking at mummy's books, old volumes by people called Hardy, Dickens, Trollope, Christie, and the children's stories by E. Nesbit she used to read him. *Five Children and It* was his favourite. Then there was father's books. Nonfiction. Volumes of Skinner, Pavlov, Watson, Hull, Freud, and Ellis, and many, many others—SERIOUS WORKS father called them. He'd tried to read them once but couldn't understand the words: all he knew was that they were PSYCHO-LOGY books because that's what father was—a PSYCHO-LOGIST—or had been until his accident.

Stephen trod carefully down the stairs. Some creaked, and the sound scared him. He might fall. He went to the kitchen once he safely reached the bottom.

All the refrigerator had to offer was some soup from the day before and a piece of cheese. He'd have to go shopping but didn't like the idea of getting wet again. But there was ice cream in the freezer section. He smiled, then sneezed again. He sat at the table, digging in. Neapolitan. Not as good as raspberry ripple.

He looked out the window. Rain was pelting down now, the sky low, very dark.

(Like the night mummy died.)

The rain was pounding the flowers on her grave and he frowned. He would have to get more as he hated the sight of the earthen mound without their pretty petals giving the ground a splash of colour. mummy had loved flowers so much. father said it was a waste. Still, he tended the grave with loving care, just the way mummy would have done.

Drip . . . drip . . . drip . . .

He shuddered. The tap was leaking, making hollow sounds in the sink.

Drip . . . drip . . . drip . . .

Watch noise again.

He rushed over to turn it off. The handle was stiff, wouldn't turn any further, and he grumbled to himself.

Drip . . . drip . . . drip . . .

No! He hated the sound. Ticking. Time had no place in the house. father said so and he was always right; that's why there were no clocks.

(I AM A FREE MAN!)

The wind rattled the window pane. Outside, a gust lifted the rain-lashed roses from the sodden earth, spreading yellow petals over the overgrown lawn.

Drip . . . drip . . . drip . . .

He couldn't listen to the sound, he'd have t—

"Stephen!" father suddenly shrieked from upstairs, making him jump, making him drop the bowl of ice cream. It shattered into four pieces on the cracked red linoleum.

"Stephen!"

He ran from the kitchen.

Drip . . . drip . . . drip . . .

Up the stairs.

Creak . . . creak . . . creak . . .

His father's face was red with rage.

"Look!" the old man cried, his long beard jerking, spittle flying from his lips as he held up one of the books, a rare copy of Fodor and Katz's *The Structure of Language*.

"Look, you simpleton!"

The edges were damaged, probably as a result of dropping the books. But there was more. Worse. The inside of the back cover was marked by a stain, still damp.

"I'm . . . m . . . m . . . s-s-s-s-orry, f-father" Stephen mumbled, trying to control his stutter.

"Come here!"

He shuffled towards the bed, knew what was coming.

Father reached for the birch rod he kept beside the bed.

Stephen hesitated.

"Here."

No. Not the rod. Please, not the rod again!

"Stephen! You—you cringing son of a whore."

He stepped to the bed and extended his left hand.

The rod came down. Hard.

The first blow stung.

The second made his hand feel like it did the time he burned it on the cooker.

The third made him cry out.

"Shut up!"

father went to hit him again, and he pulled back.

"Whoreson!"

The old man suddenly pushed himself away from the pillows, his speed belying his aged frailty. The blow caught Stephen across the face. He squealed, feeling his left eye flinch with the pain.

Then father began to gasp. Deep, agonizing gasps as his asthmatic lungs tried to pull in air. He clutched desperately at his pyjama top, dropping the rod on the bed, trying to reach the respirator on the bedside table. Books, the empty glass, and the respirator went flying.

"Help . . . me!" father gasped.

Stephen stood still, his hand burning, his face throbbing, eye smarting from the blow.

"Help . . . me . . ." A whisper this time.

He moved, scampering for the respirator, thrusting it into father's hands. The old man pressed the button, the oxygen hissing into his mouth as he collapsed back onto the pillows.

Stephen stood there, afraid to move, to speak, tears running down his cheeks.

The Crocodile! It was the Crocodile's fault! It had scared him, made him drop the books.

father wheezed for a while, but his breathing eventually steadied. The old man looked at him with contempt.

"Look . . . look what you caused, boy. You want me to die?" Stephen shook his head—no. "You fool. I was cursed the day you crawled from your mother's womb." father paused. "I wanted a son, a son who could continue my work. What did I get? An imbecile. Don't look at me with those pitiful eyes—your mother's eyes. Not mine! Just like her—weak." He wheezed. "The sight of you makes me sick."

father turned away.

Stephen stood there terrified, his stomach churning with hurt and fear.

"Go."

Stephen turned, shuffling, heading for his room. Outside, a huge gust of wind pushed against the house, and as he went down the long dark hallway he could hear the trees tapping against the bathroom window. He'd gone but a few feet when father called his name again. He went back to the bedroom.

"My books," the old man said.

Stephen picked up the volumes lying on the floor, copies of *Behaviorism*, *Beyond Freedom and Dignity*, and Chomsky's *Language and the Mind*, placing them neatly on the bed.

"Good boy," father said softly.

Another gust beat against the house, the branches of the elm outside father's room tap, tap, tapping forcefully against the window like the fingers of an old man seeking sanctuary from the storm. father ignored the noise, settling back into his pillows, closing his eyes.

Stephen went to his room. Stepping over the pile of magazines, he threw himself on the bed, sobbing as he crawled beneath the dirty blankets, pulled them around him as he tucked himself into a ball.

Eventually he slept.

He awoke in the dark to a steady roar of rain on the roof, rhythmic sprays against the window. His face hurt. His hand hurt. His stomach groaned with hunger. After listening to the rain until he felt totally lost like the little boy he'd read about who'd survived the sinking ship only to spend five nights adrift on the ocean, he crawled from the bed deciding to eat some soup.

Drip . . . drip . . . drip . . .

The tap in the kitchen continued to taunt him, but he decided he was going to eat the soup hot instead of cold and lit the gas stove. The wind continued to lash the rain against the windows, drowning out the dripping noise.

"mummy," he said. "I wish you were here."

Tears, silent this time, fell as he stirred the soup. His left hand was red and swollen, and his eyelid, bruised, nearly covered his eye, reminding him of the Pirate.

(Crocodile)

Dread lay on his shoulders, rounded despite his twenty years, like a heavy overcoat.

"mummy."

Drip . . . drip . . . drip . . .

It was no good, the tap was too much. He poured the barely warm soup into a dirty bowl and went to the lounge where he wouldn't be able to hear it.

The television was an old black-and-white Ferguson set he'd also discovered in the street on one of his seek-and-ye-shall-find missions. mummy and father never allowed one in the house when she was alive, but with father bedridden, he didn't know Stephen had one. He switched it on, turning the volume up so there was no chance of hearing the tap.

BBC 1 was showing the news.

Boring.

ITV had a quiz show.

Maybe.

But BBC 2 was showing a wildlife programme. He smiled faintly. He liked wildlife programmes. mummy said they were WHOLESOME. Like those Disney films she took him to.

(Crocodile)

He gritted his teeth.

(go away)

David Attenborough was in Egypt walking across sand, pyramids jutting up into the sky behind him like upside-down ice cream cones.

Lightning lit the sky through the lounge windows. The picture jumped. Seconds later thunder crashed. He whimpered.

A storm.

Like the one the day he'd buried mummy.

David Attenborough was talking about scorpions and the television showed one on the sand attacking a bird, its tail flicking out—once, twice—the bird jerking, then flopping on the ground.

A flash. The picture went fuzzy.

He spooned up the last of the soup, set the bowl on the worn green carpet and hugged himself, shivering.

(mummy)

(why is mummy cold?)

He would never forget the day the Crocodile came for her. It had been a few days after she'd taken him to see *Peter Pan*.

Like this morning, the day had started sunny, though warmer because spring was coming. father had been more withdrawn then usual, poring over his books while propped up in bed, and barely acknowledged their presence when they brought him lunch.

The afternoon passed quietly. He built a Lego house, coloured in one of his colouring books, read a Bugs Bunny comic. Later he fell asleep, curled up on the couch. The BAD DREAMS came again.

It started after seeing *Peter Pan*. In the dream he was walking. Never running, always walking, his legs stiff. The dream world was a dark, empty ground like the old land beside the petrol station at the East Finchley end of Long Lane. Something was coming. Something was out there in the dark. When he looked, he couldn't see it. But he knew it was there. The dream—mummy said they were NIGHTMARES—would end when he reached a sudden brick wall without end. He would cry on waking.

This time he awoke to the sound of his mummy screaming.

He thought he was still dreaming, but the persistence of the sound pulled him from the womb of sleep, aware father was shouting—angry, unpleasant words. Even if their meaning was unclear, the tone of voice was not. Then it changed. mummy stopped screaming and father, he realized, was shouting for help. He ran to the bedroom.

She lay on the floor, her neck a lump of purple bruises, her green eyes bulging. father was on the floor, too, as if a giant had picked up the bed, tossing him to the floor like a thin wooden doll, his withered legs poking from his pyjamas, the stumps of his ankles pointing to mummy's body, two fingers without nails.

Stephen cried out, bending over her twisted body. What was wrong?

(mummy)

father started shouting again, demanding to be put back in bed. Stephen ignored him. mummy. What's wrong with mummy?

He held her hand. It was limp. Help me, father shouted, adding, she's dead.

(ded)

How?

It took her, father said. The Crocodile came for her. Came to take her away. I stopped it. But the shock killed her.

Stephen cried. Hoarse, desperate sobs that made his chest hurt as he cradled her body in his lap, father glaring at him.

Later, after he had placed father back in bed and carried mummy downstairs to lay her on the couch, he smashed all the plates and glasses in the kitchen, fear and sorrow giving way to a TEMPER TANTRUM, only this time mummy didn't send him to his room because she was DED—and that meant he didn't have a mummy anymore.

father, surprisingly, didn't complain about the noise from the kitchen. Later, when Stephen was calmer, he told him to bury her in the garden by nightfall. Then it started raining suddenly as black clouds covered the sun, and he froze as he looked out the window because

(Crocodile)

one cloud looked like a giant, one cloud looked like a troll, but the other one the other one looked like looked like

(Crocodile)

the Crocodile.

It rained.

And rained, turning the garden into a sea of mud.

Darkness fell.

He couldn't sleep. He sat in the armchair looking at mummy lying on the sofa as rain drummed on the roof, rolling down the windows like a flood of tears.

When he went to move her, mummy had turned a grey colour and beneath the smell of lavender water

(do you like the smell of mummy's perfume, Stephen?)

she smelled like the old carpet he had once found in the street, soggy and rotten.

He buried her and then the truth sank in: she was gone.

The Crocodile had taken her.

As he finished packing the topsoil down, it started to rain again, but lightly, not with the scary force of the previous night's storm.

Tonight, so many moons since then, the storm sounded like it was directly over the house as a crash of thunder made the windows shake. Then the television and the lights went out. He whimpered and started reciting the PRAYER.

"I am a FREE MAN. I do not believe in clocks. Clocks are BAD.

(the watch)

I am free of time

(that was a SECRET)

My time isn't up because it doesn't exist.

(his SECRET)

I am free. Crocodile you cannot touch me."

Lightning flashed, illuminating the corners of the room. Shapes moved. SECRET things. Creatures he couldn't see it in the dark. But they could see him, oh yes, old things. Rotting things. Ded things. CROCODILE things.

"You cannot touch me!"

(could it?)

Lightning.

The things in the corner moved again.

Thunder crash.

"Go away!"

The lights came on. He shouted with surprise, jerking on the couch. Then the television picture stuttered to life and David Attenborough was standing beside a big river.

"—but perhaps most regal of Egyptian wildlife is the crocodile," he was saying, the picture changing to film of logs in the water. Only they weren't logs they were—crocodiles!!

Stephen shrieked and ran to the television set, twisting the on/ off knob so hard it came off in his hand. He ran back to the couch and pulled himself into a ball, arms tightly clasped around his legs.

It was here!

He held himself so tightly his arms ached and his legs were seized by cramps. His eye throbbed, his hand was stiff, and his nose was running. The beast was here. It was in the house. It had been playing with him, taunting him and now—

Lightning.

The lights flickered, then died.

Thunder crashed.

No! No! No! Nonononononononononon . . .

A slow roar came from outside the front of the house, long and low like the noise the dinosaurs made in the cartoons. The sound of glass shattering came from upstairs. father cried out, a terrible screaming wail that cut off—

Then . . .

Then nothing.

He pulled his arms around his head, crying, whimpering.

mummymummymummymyummymymmy—

A shout. Weak. Dying.

Then just the sound of the rain.

It had come. It was here.

The Crocodile.

Lightning. Fainter this time.

He peered through his fingers. His left eye was almost closed now and he couldn't see properly. But the things were still there, were closer, moving out of the corners, closing in on him.

"father!"

He bolted from the couch

(father!)

collided with the coffee table, knocked it over, nearly fell himself. He ran for the stairs, tripped, fell, landed heavily on his left hand and cried out.

"father!"

Thunder rumbled.

He reached the top of the stairs, turning towards father's room. Shadows had turned into black curtains that seemed to hang from the walls to cover the floor. The hallway had grown longer, too. Now it seemed to stretch before him like a narrow passageway, its size not right, the open doorway leading to father's room, a small shape standing out, dark, but lighter than the walls.

"father?"

Nothing, only the soft roaring voice of the rain.

One step. Two steps. Three steps. He started down the hallway. *It's not real, it's not real, it's not real.* It's just the hallway. A hallway with bookshelves and books and

(skulls)

(ded things)

Just a hallway

(rotting things)

just the hallway, and at the end father would be sitting in bed waiting for the lights to come on.

"father?" Almost a whisper.

Seven steps. Eight steps. Nine steps.

He had to see. He had to reach father.

Twelve steps. Thirteen steps.

"I am a FREE MAN. Crocodile, you cannot touch me."

He stepped into the doorway.

Lightning flashed, blinding him.

When his eyes adjusted, he screamed. A long, hysterical screeching painful scream as he turned to run for his bedroom.

The Crocodile's shape was halfway through the window, its massive head and shoulders on the bed, *on father*, as it ate him up.

He ran, knocking against the bookshelves, crashing into the opposite wall as he raced for the door, hitting it so hard with his full weight he nearly threw it off its hinges. He slammed it behind him, skidding on the magazines under foot, his breath coming in frantic huffing-puffing-blow-your-house-down gasps as he pulled the chest of drawers away from the wall with his good hand, dragging it against the door, sliding down to the floor with his back against the hard knobs.

The darkness was DARK.

Light. He must have light!

(torch)

His torch! Where was it?

He turned, pulling out the bottom drawer, pulling screwed-up shirts, twisted pairs of trousers.

The torch. His hand touched it, his thumb rubbing the button like a magic spot.

Light.

He sighed. Light was GOOD.

And—

And he couldn't hear the Crocodile. But it was out there. It knew where he was, and once it had finished with father, it would come for him. He felt safer now he had the light. Maybe he could blind it and escape. No, no, that was no good. The Crocodile would get him. What could he do?

(watch)

He sneezed.

(??thewatch??)

The watch!

(SECRET)

Yes, *his* SECRET. The watch he had found on one of his seek-and-ye-shall-find walks around the neighbourhood. The little old watch with the cracked glass, a watch called TIMEX lying among the folds of a torn dress in the bins outside number 213. He'd kept it, brought it home, although clocks/watches were forbidden in the house.

(?why the watch?)

The watch. It was his SECRET. A secret like the other secret things he'd found: the magazine filled with pictures of men and women with no clothes on, the broken radio called HITACHI, the empty chocolate tin, the playing cards with naked ladies on them . . . .

Blood pounded in his ears, and his nose was running steadily now, but he ignored the snot flowing over his lips as he rummaged in the drawer for the chocolate tin. He found it but couldn't open the lid because his fingers were slippery with sweat.

Open! Open!

The lid popped off.

There were the naked lady playing cards—and there was TIMEX. It was cold in his hand, yet reassuring in its simple, dangerous form. He put the torch down so he could wind it, wind it so the Crocodile would hear it. The stiff fingers of his left hand held TIMEX carefully as he fumbled with the tiny knob sticking from its side. His sweaty fingers turned the knob, slipped, turned harder. Once, twice, three time, four time.

Nothing.

TIMEX was ded.

He shook it.

Shook it again.

Then—

Tick, tick, tick . . .

The house was silent. It was out there though, oh yes, it was out there.

"I am a FREE MAN."

He opened his mouth, placing TIMEX on his tongue.

Why the watch?

Because . . . because if you wanted to gain the power of your enemy you ate its heart to make you invincible and the Crocodile's heart was the clock that ticked ticked ticked inside it.

(nationalgeographic)

The tribe called CA-NNIBALS ate the hearts of their enemies to take their strength. He knew. He'd read it in that magazine with the naked black women—*National Geographic*—yes, that was it.

CA-NNIBALS ate their enemies and became as strong as them.

CA-NNIBALS didn't eat CA-NNIBALS.

TIMEX was cold and didn't taste very nice. He hesitated, then swallowed.

And gagged.

TIMEX was in his throat. He tried to swallow again. It wouldn't move! He tried again.

Tick, tick, tick . . .

And started coughing.

Tick, tick, tick . . .

He couldn't breathe!

Tick, tick, tick . . .

He clawed at his throat. It felt like he had swallowed a rock. He gasped, fingernails gouging his skin. Gasping, gasping.

Tick, tick, tick . . .

No! No! It had tricked him. The Crocodile knew about TIMEX, had fooled him.

He felt faint as he tried to stand, still grasping his throat, retching, gasping. He stepped back putting his foot on the slick pages of a magazine, and fell over.

Tick, tick, tick . . .

He could hear it, hear the Crocodile coming.

Tick, tick, tick . . .

It was outside the door. He wheezed, trying desperately to breathe, fingers digging into his skin now. He had to—

Tick, tick, tick . . .

hehadto—

The Crocodile.

CITIES OF NIGHT

Tick, tick, tick . . .
The Crocodile.
Tick, tick, tick . . .
The Crocodi—
Tick, tick, ti—

CHURCHES
OF DESIRE

What the twentieth century needed was eroticism;
what it got was pornography.
—Henry Miller

Meredith shivered in his brown leather jacket as he stood before the porno cinema. The wind was rising, the streets devoid of life, yet his body shook not from the chill factor but from a deep, sudden sense of dread. After hours walking the Eternal City's empty thoroughfares in search of a fellow soul with whom he could share a moment of sexual warmth, his journey ended here.

It was once said all roads lead to Rome; all the Roman roads he had traveled in his nocturnal hunt for release seemed to lead here. And as he stood before the building, profound desperation pulsed through his tired, alcohol-soaked body. Just looking at the place made him feel sick.

The facade of the Passion Pussycat cinema was an affront to good taste. Green and purple neon mixed to create an emetic spill of light which washed over the marquee to luridly shower the sidewalk. Its curved front was segmented by electric signs depicting nubile Sixties-style go-go dancers with cat ears and tiny tails. There was no indication of what was screening inside.

A newspaper scuttled against his legs, making him jump, then performed a dervish dance to the gutter. He ran his hands over the week's growth of stubble coating his face to massage his tired eyes. He guessed the program would consist of typical Scandinavian, German, and American hetero hardcore—par for the course and boring. But whatever was playing there, perhaps at least there might be some buggery to keep him entertained, although he hoped if there were German movies unspooling, the footage would not be as extreme as one he'd caught in a Parisian theatre.

The loop had started mundanely with a domestic scenario involving a couple, the man going to take a bath. The scene soon turned into a laughable water sports sequence when the woman rinsed his hair with her urine after he shampooed it, but this was succeeded by an anal scene with a surgical device that had been clinical in its presentation, almost abstract in its relentless close-up and, even to Meredith's jaded sensibilities, offensive.

He stood hesitantly like a schoolboy on a first date, the promise of a sexual encounter almost unreal after the endless hours he had obsessed over the subject. Yet it was more than nervousness; a primal instinct made his balls contract painfully to the point of almost groaning. But there was no turning back. Not now. Not after the day's hollow promises had faded as breath to the wind. All Rome had to offer were vague hopes of financial gain and a cold, dirty room at the *pensione*. With that thought in mind, he walked up the steps to the door and opened it.

. . . and the world of concrete and glass, stone and slate, garbage and dog shit disappeared, broken by a surging synaptic fracture . . . and what lay before him was in one instant a glimpse of total destruction, unrelenting holocaust, a subliminal flash frame instantly replaced by the stronger all encompassing vision of a Void—black, unforgiving.

Meredith turned from the doorway to vomit his dinner of spaghetti carbonara and several glasses of mediocre frascati on the grime-encrusted steps. He stumbled with a second heave, grabbing the incongruously fake Doric columns of the façade for support, easing himself into a sitting position a few feet away from the puddle of bile. He looked up the street in an attempt to clear his rolling vision. In the distance were two faint figures, one tall and painfully thin, the other short and squat. With the final wave of surreal nausea he wouldn't have been surprised if they turned out to be the Walrus and the Carpenter. A coughing fit disrupted his eye line, his mind rolling vertiginously, and a distant voice questioned how he had come to this, reached such a state of dissolution.

He knew the answer.

As the telephone rang for the seventh time, a sense of hopelessness descended on Meredith like a carrion bird swooping to a corpse in an arid landscape.

Come on! Answer the damn phone!

The tension in his stomach tightened another notch. Since arriving in Rome two days ago, he'd been feeling a sense of trepidation so strong he could almost smell it, an aroma that churned his gut and diminished his appetite. Worrying he'd developed a stomach ulcer, he clutched the call box receiver so tightly his arm trembled, jarring loose a length of ash from his cigarette. His mouth was dry, and he badly wanted to take a pull from the bottle of Johnny Walker in his bag.

The ringtone buzzed for the eleventh time and he hung up, running a hand through his thick black hair, pushing back the stray strands from his forehead, then threw the cigarette to the floor. On the opposite side of via Paisello, trees moved with the early evening breeze. It was 5:45 PM. He'd try Masullo one more time. After he took a quick pull from the bottle.

Where the hell was the producer, or his secretary for that matter? There wasn't any reason she should be ignoring the phone; he'd called each day at the same time in a frustrating attempt to get Masullo to finalize a time for the proposed interview, already rescheduled four times in the past week. With the way things were going, it looked like *Film Comment* wasn't going to get the definitive story of Italian exploitation movies. This was Masullo's chance to gain some mainstream respectability, which, for a producer of over thirty cheap horror movies and softcore skin flicks, was hard to come by, and Meredith couldn't understand why he was being given the run-around. Still, the producer of such bad-taste gems as

Emanuel and the Satanists, The Sex Crimes of Dr. Crespi, and pseudo-documentaries like *Savage Africa*, complete with scenes of clitoral circumcision, probably didn't care about anything other than money. Meredith could relate.

A sharp knock on the glass of the booth cracked him from his reverie. A large woman in a sickly green raincoat was rapid-firing unintelligible Italian through the glass that kept the chill of the Roman night at bay. Her face was a sour rictus, the corners downturned over cheeks the color of dough like a bloated, tragedy mask, and the coat fabric taut over her huge breasts.

Meredith vacated the booth as the woman pushed past him into the cubicle.

"Fuck you," he said with a smile. *On second thought, don't.*

The woman was truly gross. A dried shitty substance stained the back of her coat and legs, and her black hair hung in greasy rat's tails.

As far as he could make out, all Italian women belonged to one of two groups: over twenty-five and overweight, like the whores at the hotel, or under that age and curvaceous. He'd seen one Dachau-thin woman in, he surmised, her late thirties, a walking skeleton who served in the café near the station. But she had to be the least attractive woman he had ever laid eyes on, a woman who seemed thinner each time he saw her. Still, the opposite sex wasn't on his list of priorities.

He lit another cigarette while the woman dialled. The brown stain disgusted him. Rome was potentially the dirtiest city he had ever visited, the buildings heavily blackened from the cancer of carbon monoxide. And as soon as he stepped off the airport bus he'd trodden in a sizable turd—human, not animal. *Great.*

Dirty. Smelly. Winos in the gutters near the *pensione*. Rubbish spilling from the bins by the Villa Borghese. Shit in the Tiber. Meredith had had enough.

He had, however, much more to worry about than shit and magazine articles. More to the point were screenplays and movie deals. If Masullo would agree to read one or two of Meredith's novels, he felt certain they could get a deal going. *Film Comment* would have to make do with what he sent them. At least he'd interviewed Dario Argento, Joe D'Amato, and Ruggero Deodato. But he had a lot riding on the idea of selling Masullo the rights to at least *Blood Stunt*, if not *A Killing For Christmas*. Throwaway thrillers deserved to be made into movies by hack producers, and Meredith was under no illusions about art; all he wanted was money. And soon. If he could get Masullo hooked, he could be out of debt for the first time in seven years.

A grunting noise made him look up. The green blob vacated the phone booth, bustling past with a flourish of body odour. Meredith belched in response as he fished in his pocket for a *getone* and re-entered the cubicle.

The phone buzzed against his right ear.

One . . . two . . . three . . . four . . .

Jesus! Answer the bloody thing!

. . . six . . . seven . . .

A click.

"Pronto?" said a woman's voice.

"Zebrafilm?"

"Yes."

"This is Bruce Meredith. I'm calling again about the interview of Signore Masullo."

"I have bad news, Signore Meredith. Signore Masullo asks me to apologize for not being able to see you this evening as was suggested. He has to go to Milan for a meeting. But he can see you at 10:30 AM on Monday."

"What? I have to return to London this weekend. Is there any chan—"

"In that case, Signore Meredith," the voice interjected, "I'm sorry, Signore Masullo has been very busy. Perhaps you will be in Rome again soon?"

Meredith threw down his cigarette. "No, that's out of the question. The magazine deadline is in two weeks. Would it be possible to see him this weekend—say Saturday?"

Please say yes!

"No, Signore Meredith. That's not possible. Thank you."

The line went dead.

Bitch!

Monday! Damn Masullo. Damn Rome. Damn the whole shitty country.

He stepped from the booth and stood a while, worrying his bottom lip before fumbling in his shoulder bag for the bottle. He took a large pull, the Scotch hitting instantly, burning his gut in a fiery rush. Without further thought, he began to walk.

A light breeze rustled the trees which whispered their secrets in return. What could he do? He couldn't really afford to come here in the first place and had only managed to do so by conning his sister out of five hundred quid under the pretence of repairing his car, conveniently neglecting to tell her he'd sold it. He couldn't cancel the return flight as he didn't have enough to purchase another ticket. If he'd thought the situation through before coming, he could have anticipated delays, made provisions for an alternative course of action, but as usual he had done everything in a rush. It was too much to think about, the decision requiring a ruthlessly objective look at his position, so he did the usual—procrastinated for several minutes while he paced up and down, neither thinking nor acting, and lit another cigarette. He looked vacantly at the trees, the pavement, the walls. He would decide tomorrow. He needed to rest, relax. And that meant one thing—sex. A night of fucking would burn out the cloud of depression that was already filling his system like ink in water. If he could get laid, he'd awaken refreshed in the morning, be able to take his situation in hand. Sex always provided peace of mind.

He turned into via Piciano, moving slowly along the northeastern edge of Villa Borghese. Each step he took, however, increased his steadily deepening depression. His mind performed cartwheels. Images from the past appeared in a montage of disillusionment: Vanessa stating she'd need the money back by early November as it was for Christmas; Michael crying after the violent argument;

Alison, his agent, informing him he had to cut back on the sex scenes, especially the rape of the pregnant woman in *Dead Dogs and Englishmen*, because every publisher she showed it to found the novel gratuitous; Wilmott, his bank manager, turning down his request for a loan; Michael leaving, bags hurriedly packed, tension charging the smoky air of the flat.

"You selfish, self-pitying bastard!" His lover threw the words at him as he gathered his belongings in the hallway. "I'll be back for the rest of my stuff tomorrow, and I'd appreciate it if you won't be here. I don't ever want to see you again!"

Meredith was silent, a contrite expression on his face, a bottle of Scotch still in his hand. Michael was so angry they'd come to blows over the damn thing. Embarrassed, he tried to hide it behind his back but Michael saw him.

"Put the bloody bottle down! Stop pissing your life away."

"Sorry," he mumbled.

Michael fiddled with the straps of his baggage as Meredith watched him, not sure what to say or do.

"I'm sorry," he said again.

No response.

Michael looked up, tears in his eyes.

"You're always sorry afterwards. But words aren't enough. When you drink you're like a little kid—*and that's all the bloody time!*"

Meredith stared at the carpet.

"This is it. *Over. Dead.* You killed it."

With that, Michael was gone, the door slamming like a gunshot in the heavy air.

Although he'd felt a tremendous sense of relief after the last of Michael's possessions had been removed, the first few nights without him to hold had been an empty, cold time. But there were always other bodies to be found, and since the split his sex life had been a calm sea dotted with occasional faces floating like driftwood through a perpetual twilight. It was easier that way. Still the immediate problem was how to find someone in this godforsaken place. The local cruising scene, if one existed, was nowhere to be found, and the only form of night-time sexuality he'd seen was transvestism, which held no appeal. The only possible place he could think of was the Spanish Steps.

While passing them the previous night, he had been surprised by the number of people spread out on the impressive monument and the relaxed atmosphere. Couples entwined passionately, all but copulating, locked into their own romantic universes. Cigarette smoke drifted on the breeze, mingling with the sweeter aroma of hash as a guitarist had strummed old songs. The Steps were a short walk away and would be a good starting point. Failing that, the main railway station would almost certainly provide what he was looking for.

He'd gone but a few yards and had turned into via Veneto when he came across the first gaggle of transvestites he'd seen that night. One, a blonde wearing an awful wig, tried to waylay him, but he continued without stopping, scowling. When he reached Piazza Barberini, he paused to scan the headlines of English newspapers on sale at the cramped news cabin. Try as he might to focus on the front pages of *The Sun* and *The Star*, his attention was drawn to the tawdry colors of the hardcore magazines on sale.

Teenage Lolitas promised all girls under sixteen with text in English, German, and Italian. Who, he mused, cared about text? He'd always smiled at the French slang for such publications—books to be read with one hand. But what he found most interesting was the plethora of *fumetti*—pocket-sized, crude, explicit comics filled with a staple diet of black magic, murder, sadomasochism, rape, and mutilation. There were dozens of titles ranging from entrail-eating zombie stories to tales of futuristic sex and violence and more mundane narratives of adultery and wife swapping. Nothing was left to the imagination, atrocities bursting forth on each page like rotten foliage. He'd found one in his room at the *pensione*. After skimming thirty pages of dialogue he couldn't translate, his eyes had widened at a sudden explosion of brutal sex and degradation— close-ups of fellatio, sodomy, and a young man having his skull smashed open after orgasm by the husband of the woman he'd just serviced. Somehow, he felt these popular comics told him more about the Italian cultural psyche than he wished to know, a worldview consisting of naked lust and commonplace violence. But after all, this was the country that had made throwing people to wild animals the main form of entertainment. He laughed aloud as a black vision eclipsed all else; so this is what it all comes down to— two thousand years of civilization and it's the same as it ever was. This is where it ends.

A sober-suited business man examining *S&M Sextacula* peered intently at Meredith over his horn-rimmed glasses, and Meredith walked away with the bitter laugh still staining his lips.

As if submitting to the dark reality was his only means of finding hope, he felt a strange sense of correctness in his situation, and he suddenly saw it for the killing joke it was—a long, hollow laugh in the face of nothingness.

He continued to chuckle to himself until he came to the junction, his attention shifting to the pleasing smells coming from a restaurant on the corner. His stomach growled in appreciation. He entered without further thought, drawing the aromas from the kitchen deep into his blackened lungs.

Like the previous night, the Spanish Steps were littered with people. Small groups and couples. The lone guitarist, now surrounded by a small crowd; here and there, young boys on their own or in twos and threes; couples, limbs entwined like vines, smoking, kissing, caressing. At the bottom he turned left under the pretence of looking at the Keats house, allowing his gaze to wander in the hope of making eye contact.

Directly in front of him, two teenagers spoke softly, the taller of the two nodding towards a pair of giggling girls seated a few feet above them. To Meredith's left, near the seat of the Steps, sat a solitary handsome youth dressed in brogues, tapered trousers, and a red pullover. The writer walked towards him.

"*Buona sera,*" Meredith said as he sat beside him. The boy—no older than seventeen he judged—nodded.

"Do you speak English?" The boy nodded. "Perhaps you can help me," he continued slowly. "This is my first time in Rome. Can you recommend a good nightclub?" The boy did not turn to face him for several seconds, then looked in his direction, staring past Meredith. Above them the guitarist started murdering "Ticket To Ride."

"There are some." He spoke softly, trying to enunciate correctly.

"Anything to suit a man my age," Meredith said. The boy looked at him then. Meredith stared back at the boy longer than was polite. He lit a cigarette.

"There is a place. Not a nightclub."

Meredith waited for him to continue, but the boy was not forthcoming.

"Would you show me where? Is it far?"

The boy remained silent, then: "Pardon I have to meet my girl," he said crisply, standing. "I have to go."

The boy began to trot towards the fountain at the base of the Steps. A slender blonde girl was heading in his direction. She smiled, waved, opened her arms. The boy ran to her. They embraced. Meredith watched them sway away arm in arm.

"Bitch," he muttered under his breath. The boy was nice looking and had a good mouth. "I bet you're going to suck his little dick until it's as dry as a twig," he added before a coughing spasm cut off his bitter words. He ground out the cigarette.

It was nine o'clock.

The entrance hall of Stazione Termini was largely deserted as Meredith entered the doors opposite the huge clock that hung above the electronic information board. It was nine twenty-seven the mute display informed him. His feet had started to hurt. It looked like coming here was a bad decision. There was no one around except a gypsy woman with a small child in her arms and a comatose wino sprawled beside the photo booth near track seven. The woman saw him and started in his direction.

As he turned to go, the woman grabbed hold of his left arm, pulling frantically at his jacket. Like other cities the world over, Rome had its underclass. New York had its legion of homeless,

London a rag-tag army of alcoholics and meths drinkers, and Paris was a chain gang to its migrant workforce of Moroccans. Rome, however, was infested like a flea-ridden junk yard dog with gypsies such as this wretch clutching at his clothes, beseeching him for money in whatever dialect she spoke.

He jerked away. She continued to claw at him undeterred.

"Get off!"

She paused for a beat, then continued her litany of despair, and his temper erupted.

"*Fuck off!*" He pushed her away. She stumbled, nearly dropping the child.

With a screech she flew at him, pounding his back with her free arm, her tone now abusive. The child started to cry loudly. Meredith strode towards the nearest exit, but the gypsy was persistent, and the blows continued to rain down on his back.

He stopped suddenly, stepped to the right and turned, swiping her hand away, glaring at her, his eyes inflamed with rage.

"I said, *get the fuck off me*, you diseased cunt!"

Like a slap, his words silenced the woman for an instant; then she started to coo as she placed her arms protectively around the child, a calm expression of total hatred directed at him. The filthy brat was silenced by its mother's soft sounds. She turned, moving away at a measured pace. He watched her go, unnerved by the sudden outburst. Then the gypsy stopped, turning to face him. He took a step back as if pushed by the force of her expression, an expression which went beyond loathing, beyond hate. But there was something else he could not read. A glimmer of fear was apparent and . . . revulsion? She began to babble, then spat two words at him.

"*Il morto.*"

Even with his limited command of Italian, he understood.

Dead man.

She spat at her feet then ran towards the nearest exit, the words hanging in the air.

Dead man.

The frozen moment was broken by a coughing fit that swept up from his gut to constrict his throat, his heart juddering in response, legs rubbery as gravity increased its pull, making him stumble to the nearest wall for support, the hundred yards elongating as his sense of space expanded, rolled, a wave of nausea hitting his system in a huge spasm. He closed his eyes to halt the roller coaster motion and took a deep breath, counting slowly to ten. He opened them, coughed and tried to focus, blinking rapidly.

Go. Get out of Rome, his instincts screamed, *return to London*. To familiar territory. But he would be lonely there too. Lonely. Lost. As he always had been.

No. No, he would find a kindred spirit to ease the emptiness with, someone with whom he could forget his troubles, albeit temporarily. There was one other place he could try—the porno cinema near the *pensione*. There he was certain he would find what he was looking for; there among the other lost souls would be a fellow spirit in search of release, fulfillment.

He forced himself to smile, smile and regain his former optimism. His consciousness pirouetted with the slapstick grace of a clown. It worked. A ray of optimistic sunlight penetrated the storm clouds of depression that approached, breaking the darkness up into jagged shards as he pulled the bottle from his bag, and his internal horizon lightened further as he took a deep pull, coughing as the scotch caught at the back of his throat. He needed to sit down. The café where the Dachau woman served was opposite, its light an island in the darkness pushing against the glass wall of the exit. He lurched away on shaky legs. He had to keep it together. One step at a time. He negotiated the revolving door and made it over the tram tracks to the café without falling flat on his face.

The bar that dominated the room was long and thin like the woman who served behind it. She stood looking down at the wood, a ghost of a time not so long past, her thinness painful to observe. *The Dachau woman*. What had caused her to resemble a victim of the Final Solution? She was white as a sheet, her cheeks deprived of the faintest hint of pink, her eyes the color of bruised mushrooms. If she heard him enter, she did not acknowledge his presence. Neither did the three locals huddled around a TV set in the far corner, their attention consumed by *Magnum P.I.*

The woman—surely she was thinner than the previous day, but no, that wasn't possible—continued to look at the counter as Meredith ordered an espresso in his halting command of the language. As she turned to the coffee machine, he noticed the spinal defect which pushed her head forward, explaining her limited movements. She handed him a steaming cup of black liquid with a trembling hand as he slapped down his money and shuffled to the nearest seat, turning his back so he wouldn't have to look at her funereal visage.

Meredith continued to tremble on the steps of the cinema, his stomach raw from its expulsion. The figures were closer now, and he could see it was the Dachau Woman and the fattest of the bar's occupants. The man was absently rubbing his crotch as he escorted the emaciated woman, though as they drew nearer, Meredith realized the man was not holding her arm but caressing her ass. The thought of those two in a sweaty sexual embrace did nothing for his nausea. Yet it had been the atmosphere in the bar—or rather the invasion of the whores—which had finalized his resolve to come here. He looked up. The couple stopped by a dimly lit doorway and entered.

Doors. Opening and closing.

They seemed to punctuate every aspect of his life.

A sudden cold draught and explosion of noise from behind pulled Meredith from his thoughts as two of the whores who plied their trade outside the *pensione* entered the café. They cheerfully stepped to the counter, laughing and joking in a torrent of sound and broad gestures. One lifted her ample bosom to the other and broke into a loud cackle, the other echoing her movements, then joining her friend's laughter with a deep chuckle.

Each night these women had fractured his sleep with their nonstop chatter and bargaining outside his window. He'd dubbed them The Three Weird Sisters: Miss Piggy, The Vacuum Cleaner—because her mouth, a perfect puckered circle reminded him of the line "nothing sucks like an Electrolux" from a blatantly sexual advertisement for a domestic appliance—and Mother Mary. They stood on the corner by the *pensione* for over twelve hours at a stretch, gossiping, joking, smoking, spitting, and scratching their fat assess.

The first night he had not been able to sleep before 3:00 AM with the noise coming from the street—initially the wailed hymns of drunks stumbling from the bar down the street, then from the endless chattering of the whores. Periodically a car had drawn up, and he'd heard doors opening, then slamming shut, each vehicle pulling away fast only to return a while later as the cycle of copulation continued throughout the night.

Miss Piggy made a masturbatory motion to the Vacuum Cleaner who laughed again, then whispered to her companion who giggled in reply, pointing at Meredith. The Vacuum Cleaner blew him a kiss then returned to her conversation. The Dachau Woman was pouring two shots of rum without request, obviously a ritual for the whores, who toasted each other, swallowed in one, threw their money down, and departed as they had arrived—loudly.

Although his feet still ached, his legs were regaining their strength and he felt restless, the appearance of the whores once again bringing thoughts of sex to the fore. He started to luxuriate in a sense of inevitability and, as if lured by an invisible Ariadne's Thread of lust cast by the streetwalkers, stood from the table and departed the lifeless café.

So here he was at the cinema: tired, queasy, and shaken. But the thought of returning to the grim confines of the *pensione* stirred his resolve. He'd check the place out. What he'd felt a few moments ago was the culmination of days of heavy drinking and a poor diet. No wonder his stomach had rebelled.

He stood.

And entered.

A dry, dusty smell hit his nose, the smell of a place not inhabited by men but rodents. The interior was red, tidy, and functional though, not an abandoned place. The only decoration was two wilting potted palms standing sentinel on either side of the doors he assumed led to the screening room beyond. Inside the ticket booth sat an overweight middle-aged man with black hair slicked back in an attempt to cover his large bald patch. His complexion was sallow, waxen under the spotlights illuminating the booth. Meredith placed a 20,000 lira note on the counter. The cashier continued to concentrate on his cuticles. By one pillar to the right lounged a swarthy, sneering youth, his body language sexually aggressive, his jeans taut over muscular thighs as he reclined, his rough trade gaze passing through Meredith's flesh as if he could see into his soul. He knew then he had come to the right place.

Click.

He turned to face the cashier. A ticket protruded from the metal counter like a small pink tongue. He took it and his change, stepping to the left of the booth to enter the inner sanctum.

For an instant, blindness caressed his eyes—total, eternal. Then, some distance in front, a scrambled rainbow of light jumped, and he made out a fuzzy rectangle of video-generated imagery accompanied by a soundtrack of muted voices. He stood against the rear wall, mentally counting to ten as his eyes grew accustomed to the darkness. The light from the enlarged video image cast meagre illumination on the aisles before him. A nigrescent sea of seats dotted with heads bobbing in the blackness like buoys came into focus. Here and there tiny beacons of cigarettes, clusters and constellations of red points, produced trails of smoke that hovered like ground fog above the body of men that composed the congregation in this church of desire. The majority of heads were separated by empty seats, the fractured symmetry of which was disrupted by occasional groups of twos and threes. But these couplings were in the minority. This was the refuge of the lonely, the lost, not a place for comradeship, yet paradoxically a vessel for communion with the flesh.

Meredith strategically took a seat in the back row to survey the audience. Onscreen a girl with hair the color of rotting wheat swallowed a skinny, erect penis.

Reverential silence blanketed the cinema—viewers seemingly entranced by the litany of lust groaning from the screen. Meredith lit a cigarette.

The girl continues to deep throat the long, thin phallus. Suddenly it twitches spastically, and a dribble of sperm leaks from the girl's lips as she continues to eat it, then two jets of semen shoot from her nose.

The image jumped, faltered, faded. There was no discernable movement in the audience and the house lights remained off. Onscreen a rectangle of dots and wave patterns writhed, reminding him of the opening to *The Outer Limits*, but no Control Voice sounded from the speakers, no new picture took the previous one's place for what seemed like minutes. Finally, a smeared visual flicked onto the screen. Music with too much treble tinkled along in accompaniment.

On the left side of the auditorium, a figure rose to use the exit, the movement prompting Meredith to try to make contact with a fellow lost soul. Sticking to the row he was in, he picked his way along to the other end where a man of similar age sat. Meredith selected the seat next to him, opening his legs so his right knee brushed the other's left thigh. Yet the man remained immobile, even when Meredith let his hand fall to his crotch as he watched out of the corners of his eyes. The man continued to stare dispassionately at the screen.

A white Rolls Royce cruises on an Alpine road. Inside sits a Big Man sipping champagne, a woman on either side of him. One, a short blonde with her hair up in a bun, giggles as she drinks and caresses her naked breasts.

Meredith turned to his neighbour, smiled, and hoped for eye contact, but the man ignored him.

Lost in your own little fantasy, aren't you? Probably about the blonde and what you'd like to do to her. What a waste.

The girl pours champagne over her breasts. The other woman, a brunette, leans over the Man to lick at the liquid, the blonde's nipples erecting.

Meredith stood, walked back along the row of seats to cross the aisle. Three rows in front sat another man. Balding, overweight.

No, too old.

The Big Man, the blonde and the brunette, he dressed in a red robe, enter a large room. The blonde and the brunette are naked. In the center, a group of nine people surround a young woman laid out on a table, silk cushions beneath her. She has a cock in her mouth. Another thrusts in and out of her cunt. The crowd masturbate, caress each other in slow abandon until they perceive the presence of the Man. The orgy pauses. The crowd clears and the woman on the table turns over to present her backside to the Big Man who opens his robe, his huge erect cock ready to enter her. She starts to fellate the phallus of a skinny youth as the man sodomizes her. The group then couples in abandon.

Meredith paused to watch the film, smiling to himself before letting his eyes wander.

To his right, in the middle block, lounged a boy in his early twenties. Meredith honed in on him.

Onscreen the woman groans as the skinny youth ejaculates on her face. The Big Man does likewise, his semen covering her back in a spurting torrent. The group responds in a frenzy, the other men baptizing the woman with a monsoon of ejaculate.

He sat next to the boy, spread his legs to brush his thighs. The boy turned. Meredith looked him in the eyes while fumbling for his lighter.

"Pardon," he said.

The boy nodded slowly then provided a light.

In the sulphurous flash of the flame Meredith knew the boy was the one. A perfect complexion—olive-skinned, a light corona of stubble adhering to the fine, neoclassical lines of the face, the hair jet black, magnificently sculpted over the scalp. His eyes, Meredith saw in the instant of the flame, were brown, an unusual shade between gold and bronze. His lips were full, rich, ruby. Ripe for kissing; created to suck cock.

Meredith felt the heat in his groin explode through his system, causing him to look away, shocked by the fallout from the chemical charge passing between them. The boy continued to hold his gaze.

Onscreen the image skipped as a new film replaced the previous loop, and Meredith was glad of the distraction.

A close-up of a mouth, open wide.

The camera pulls back to reveal a man, naked except for a leather harness, strapped to a chair. A tall dominatrix, her black hair matching her cat suit, nails his scrotum to a piece of wood. In the background, two older men bugger a child.

A boy or a girl? Meredith could not be sure.

Next to the pederasts is a woman, her feet and hands chained to a wall, her body systematically invaded with sexual devices wielded by a woman of indeterminate age.

A title slowly superimposes over the torture tableau: By His Cock, Crucified.

Meredith chuckled at the pretension, then dared to look back at the boy who was still gazing intently at him, a trace of a smile on those inviting lips.

Onscreen, the masochist screamed.

The boy stood, squeezed Meredith's knee, moved towards the exit.

He was halfway across the auditorium before Meredith started to follow. He dropped the cigarette, nearly tripping with eagerness. The boy went through the left exit door.

Meredith discovered it led to a short, narrow corridor which then opened up into another foyer area. To the right was a bar with a few patrons, but Meredith barely gave their frozen faces a second thought as the boy was heading in the opposite direction. Meredith moved quickly. He could not lose him.

Curving to the left, the corridor paralleled the auditorium. Both walls and carpet were deep red. Small orange spotlights cast pools of tangerine on the floor. Every fifteen feet a palm that had seen better days resided in a red pot.

The boy stopped and turned, smiling with satisfaction as he spied the pursuing writer.

Meredith stopped dead. Something was not right. The adrenalin spiked in his already amped up system. Warning signs flashed.

No.

Dread gripped him, desire and fear in conflict.

He stumbled as he turned, heading back in the direction he'd come.

Meredith ran, the sense of danger increasing with every step. As he rounded the curve and approached the bar area, his heart faltered, a steel band tightening around his chest. He collided with the wall, clutching at his torso.

Oh God, I'm having a heart attack!

No! NO!!!

Then he was filled with a vision of the boy's eyes. Inviting, placid, offering peace. He gasped.

The image persisted as his breath came in tight wheezes. Then he sensed a presence behind him, felt a hand on his shoulder transferring a sense of emotion unlike any other. He turned, falling into the boy's arms. He looked into that angelic face. The boy smiled faintly. Their tongues automatically entwined, and he stroked the boy's crotch which felt full and heavy. After a moment the boy pulled away, yet it was not a rebuff. He smiled, squeezing Meredith's groin in return, began to unbutton his jeans, turned to face the wall.

Finally, he was in.

Moving gently, Meredith pulled the boy toward him, devoting his attention to the hymn of his thrusts. From the auditorium came a distant sound of applause mixed with screams.

The boy's heat excited him further, and he knew he couldn't last long. Tension in his groin rose like water filling a lock, and the threshold breached far quicker than expected. Then, behind the bodily heat came a numbing coldness, a chill so sharp it cut into his cerebral cortex, suddenly disrupting the wave pattern of lust instinct; time and sense of place expanded, contracted; the chill expanded into eternity. Meredith opened his eyes, panic cementing his chest.

Before him was the Void. Total, unforgiving, relentless. To

ejaculate into such a place struck him with primal terror, the horror of the Void absolute. Surely, to give an offering to such a place would not be enough; he would be consumed without trace. If he had sought the darkness before, he had done so in error. Now he wanted no part of it.

Then it was gone.

Meredith withdrew as his cock jerked spastically, spitting his seed onto the humus lining the palm's pot. He grunted. The boy stood still. For an instant the image of the Void returned, then was gone as quickly as it had arisen. He felt suddenly sick, as if a cold ethereal hand grasped his scrotum, passing through the skin to penetrate his bowels. The boy turned to face him.

The smile was still on those ruby lips, but the light that had resided in his eyes was gone.

Meredith, dazed, was pushed firmly to his knees; the boy's erection appeared in front of his sweat-washed eyes. He opened his mouth. The offering stretched him to the limit. Meredith squeezed his lids shut as the boy pushed into his throat, suddenly slapping Meredith as the writer tried not to choke.

"Look at me," the boy said, his voice only a fraction above a whisper. "This is my body; this is my blood. Drink in remembrance of me."

He withdrew, spraying the writer.

The world went white.

Meredith lay there for an uncertain time. Were minutes seconds or the other way around? He had no idea, no sense of proportion. Eventually he wiped the semen from his face, pulled himself upright and moved towards the bar area, the sensation of a frozen hand performing a five finger exercise in his guts. Sweat crowned his brow.

Three people sat at the bar. The woman behind the counter ignored him as she carefully wiped a glass. She was familiar. Where had he seen her? Her hair was the color of rotting wheat, but he couldn't find the jigsaw piece to complete the picture. Two men were in front, one seated on a high stool. The man turned to Meredith as he stumbled past at a snail-like pace. The man, too, was familiar, causing further confusion in Meredith's dislocated consciousness. As he inched by, he noticed the man's fly was open, his penis hanging off the stool rim, puncture points in the phallus suggesting stigmata.

Where had he seen him?

(Screams)

Nails through flesh . . .

Thinking clearly required too much effort. Despite throwing up before entering the cinema, he still felt drunk; the alcohol remaining in his system had him cornered, was ready to lay him out in the third round.

He shuffled into the street. The two thousand yards to the *pensione* took an eternity to cover.

Of course, the Three Weird Sisters were outside the impoverished Spanish style hotel, its edges crumbling with age, the walls tattooed with a patina of carbon. Miss Piggy laughed at him as he careened by with the precision of a seasoned drunk. He tried to snarl "fuck you," but his words came out "*fug tu!*" his speech slurring with every increasingly swaying step. He'd never felt so tired.

As he came through the entrance of the *pensione*, the concierge looked up for an instant then resumed watching the TV set behind the counter. The Englishman's condition was nothing new; the old man had seen it many times—impoverished tourists who couldn't hold their wine. Nothing mattered to him anymore and hadn't since the passing of his wife; yet he flinched when the guest kicked open the door to his room, realizing the fool had collapsed onto the creaking bed and wasn't going to close it. He forced himself from the comfort of his armchair to trot down the hallway, pulling the door closed without looking in on the prone figure of *il morto*. He'd watched the process take place before. Once had been enough, and if it took place behind closed doors, even if they were his own, he could convince himself it didn't exist. The world was changing in strange ways and denial was his only defence. But the sex zombies, the emotionally dead, posed no threat to him. They stuck to their own kind, their bodies rotting as they performed their dance of empty desire. The old concierge grunted to himself, fully aware of his own mortality; he was not long for this world and wanted to live out his last few days as peacefully as possible. Let them inherit the earth.

Several minutes later he heard the bed creak through the thin wall. It would be the last noise to come from the room for some time.

Inside, despite the unbearable weight of exhaustion pushing down upon him, Meredith managed to raise himself from the mattress to discard his clothes and crawl between the dirty sheets.

It had begun.

The road lay before him bright in the sexual flush of a newly aroused sun—a future of limited possibilities, restricted variations of the sex act, for their bodies were not strong. A barren future, predictable, life-negating, not life-affirming, sterile in its simplicity. Yet what faced Meredith did not appal. He welcomed it with open arms and mouth, and it in return welcomed him. Not with arms but with a multitude of genitalia and orifices—big ones, small ones, every taste, color, texture. A pornucopia of organs transformed from the frustrated parameters of the human state to that of a new flesh. Flesh, nerve endings, and blood that now coursed with a life and death of their own—a transmutational entity so powerful the host would atrophy within months.

In truth, the transformation had begun long ago. A summation of desires misaligned, of emotions discarded, left to fracture in the cold expanse of a life misdirected.

Meredith lay between the dream and the desire, comfortable between the sheets of change. Somewhere in his cortex memories skipped like daguerreotypes; flickered, jerked, then faded—fragmented scenes from his childhood, soft-edged with an innocence long lost, revolving one last time. He frowned, then smiled serenely in his sleep of the damned as the dream took shape, wiping the screen of the old, tired images, replacing them with visions of the future. The future inside his body.

Time would be short, but what a time. The fact there would be no laughter, no light, no love didn't matter anymore. If indeed they had once truly mattered, they seemed now nothing more than trivial concerns, of little consequence to the wider scheme of death within life. That was all behind him. It was easier this way, lack of choice soothing in its streamlined shape. And in the dream a line from a song crept unbidden to provide a momentary soundtrack: *Don't dream it, be it.*

He slept on, safe in the knowledge his sisters outside were spreading the gospel to the heathens. All over the world, it would be the same:

One Church, one Body, one Belief.

The Church would welcome fresh converts that night, and there would be new films to watch, new stories to tell, Meredith's amongst them. In the name of the Father and the Son, the congregation would sing silent praises to the Gods of Flesh and Fluids.

Meredith, after years of searching, finally slept like a newborn baby, his shallow breath rising and falling in a psalm to the rhythm of a deathly desire.

—*Rome, 1985; London, 1986. Revised, Atlanta, 2010*
For Dario, Fiore and little Asia (who ran away from me).

MEMORIES OF LYDIA, LEAVING

Carpenter drains the tenth glass of the evening dry, grimacing as the generous shot of George Dickel scorches his throat.

—*Three years*—

Three long, lonely years. Years consumed by memories, the recollections as clear yet intangible as the faintest whiff of sour mash. Thirty-six months of sadness. Years when days would suddenly cloud with the thunderheads of feelings past meeting the empty horizon of the present, the persistent pain in his heart temporarily alleviated by a torrent of tears.

Once, not long after she had died, he'd broken down in the street.

A mailman had stopped to ask what was wrong, but the display of concern had only made his condition worse, even if it proved not everyone in New York was a soulless bastard.

—*Three years*—

Occasional glimpses in the bathroom mirror

—*She used to sit in there when she wanted to be alone*—

show the lines on his face growing clearer, accelerated by the drinking and smoking, especially on the annual seven-day binges, the third of which he is halfway through, getting steadily shit-faced.

Three years carrying his love of a dead woman around like a ketchup stain on a shirt, not having the strength to do the laundry and try a fresh start.

—*Three fuckin' years*—

Lydia had been, for a short time, his everything. Confidante, soul-mate, critic, ardent supporter, lover, nymph, Muse. The Little Woman with the Big Heart. His Heloise, his Isolde, his Guinevere.

—*Romantic fool*—

His Lydia. His *dead* Lydia. Dark-haired beauty with an olive complexion, five-two of passion, energy, almost frightening intellect, and a sense of humour Arsenio or Letterman would envy.

—My love killed her, not the razor blade she ran across her wrists—

He pours another shot of Dickel and stubs out a cigarette, immediately lighting another one. The sulphurous bulb of the match gutters in the gloom as he inhales, its acrid aroma temporarily cutting out the smell of the burning scented candles illuminating the room.

—Just the way she liked it—

The first time they'd met she'd beat him to the punch, flicking a Bic as he tugged the matches from his pocket. There was no wind that night, the flame thrusting up towards the tip of the Marlboro, the move as cool as Bogart lighting Bacall's in "To Have or Have Not," as he and Lydia stood outside the bookstore on East 19th Street. He asked her to join him for a cappuccino. She agreed, and they sat outside Dojo on St. Mark's Place watching the street life drift by like human tumbleweed as he got wired on caffeine and she listened to his thoughts on the Escher exhibition at The Psychedelic Solution. She thought the artist's woodcut entitled Relativity unexciting; he politely argued its merits, lit her cigarette—she smoked Winston Lights—before she could flick the Bic, ordered more cappuccino. She had a Perrier and lime. They smoked and drank until 1:30 AM, neither seemingly wishing to return to their respective apartments, he finally breaking the conversation with a courteous excuse so she didn't feel he was trying to pick her up. Phone numbers were exchanged; a further meeting suggested. He saw her to a taxi, then walked to his studio apartment on East Seventh Street.

The memory is as clear, as fresh as the wind that suddenly descended that fall night.

She steps gracefully into the taxi, her long black hair spraying out like the demure gesture of a Japanese maiden opening a paper fan. A delicate smile spreads across her lips, the dark brown eyes catching the fallout from the overhead lamps, refracting the yellow-white in a warm, sensual glow. A fog of taxi exhaust slides around her legs like a loyal dog as she climbs in, closes the door, and, with a small wave, is gone.

His life has been running down like an old clock since the day she died. He knows it but doesn't care. There is no point anymore.

—Tonight it ends—

The glass is dry, the bottle of Dickel almost empty.

He pads barefoot to the refrigerator, plucking a Heineken from the six-pack he'd bought a couple of hours ago. It isn't Dickel, but beer is booze. He slouches back to the desk, gazing with the eyes of a love-sick school boy at his favorite photo of Lydia.

He'd taken the picture on their short visit to Niagara Falls in the spring after that fateful fall. Along with his painting, his photography gave him pleasure nothing else came close to. Except Lydia. She had freed his soul from the labyrinth of loneliness. Their intimacy was more than sex; they were soul mates.

After making love to her the first time, every relationship he'd had seemed indistinct, like a watercolour left exposed to the elements, its pigments running into each other.

Before Lydia, art had been his only passion. Painting led him to another place; the truth behind the lie. But part of him—the nagging voice of self-doubt—questioned his talent. If he had the soul of an artist, why was he a bank teller? Why didn't he throw in his job?

—Because I'm afraid; I've always been afraid—

His soul screams out for expression but the Nine-to-Five Man inside laughs at the pile of unfinished oil paintings stacked in the corner of the room.

—Call yourself an artist? You'll never be a Monet or a Van Gogh. Let alone a Keith Haring.—

But tonight he would bring his work to its logical conclusion. No more continuing to labour at the EuroAmerican Bank on Park Avenue South, a junior teller processing other people's pay checks by day, trying to paint in the evenings, attempting to capture the essence of the world around him, drinking himself into oblivion to numb the pain because all he can see is emptiness and death.

If all life leads to is death, then let it end now. The photograph:

Lydia is dressed in a blue sou'wester with hood, her hair, that luxurious cascade of black, neatly tucked away. Behind her the water thunders down in a heavy drape, precipitation filling the air like the gossamer clouds of a dream. A head and shoulders shot, her pert breasts jut against the plastic, a promise of the flesh beneath the synthetic cover; temptation at the bottom of the frame.

Tears sting his eyes, and the image drifts out of focus. Most people carry their memories as photos in their wallets, his is tattooed on his heart, each indentation a razor cut. His chest tightens, constricted by emotional cement as deep sobs rise in his throat.

—I killed her with my love—

The green of the Heineken bottle mirrors the lime of the umbrella she carries in the photo, the umbrella that stands in the corner beside the door. He smiles bitterly through the tears at the thought: there are more memories of her leaving than arriving, as if their relationship was nothing more than a dress rehearsal for her final departure.

Lydia dons the coat, picking up the umbrella as she moves to the door.

"I'll probably have to work late," she says as she reaches for the bolt. "Don't wait up."

Weary from the day's office politics and the crowds of people cashing checks, he drifts off into a deep sleep before she returns, dreaming of vampiric women floating down Broadway, waking with a shout as she slips into bed.

"Shhh," she coos, holding him in her arms. "It's okay, I'm here."

All their daily rhymes balanced apart from their sleeping habits, he an early bird, she preferring to rise as late as possible before running off to work.

Their love blossomed like an orchid in the hours of darkness. The first month they were together he spent an increasing amount of time in her apartment as they wrapped themselves in a cocoon of tenderness, talking, holding each other until the early hours, she telling him of her past in Chicago and he telling her about his childhood in Pennsylvania, two kindred spirits creating a mutual space, a fortress against the abrasive assault of Manhattan's manic rhythms. Those nights played havoc with his sleep patterns, but he was punch-drunk from the unexpected intimacy and excited by the way Lydia welcomed him with open arms into her world, her sacred place,

"This is strange for me," she says one night as they luxuriate in the tranquility of post-coitus, limbs entwined, two semi-colons curled together on the couch. *"I didn't want one . . . a relationship . . . those I've had . . . they went sour. . . ."* She pauses in some private reverie. *"After the last one, I went off men. But you're not like the rest."*

And so it seemed.

He rediscovered aspects of himself he'd buried since early adolescence. Lydia brought out a playfulness in him, and in return, he made her laugh, filled her with joy, ignited a fire in her eyes. She was the one who said, "I love you," first—his Lydia, his older woman who looked like a little girl, her perfectly proportioned, petite form that of a girlchild just reaching womanhood. He responded in kind, his feelings unhampered by the caution he'd felt in previous relationships. For the first time in his life, he felt loved and loved truly in return.

The wave of tears subsides. Empty, he pushes the beer bottle to one side and goes to the kitchenette to fetch another. He catches sight of his reflection in the cracked mirror over the sink. He looks like shit.

—It's what you deserve—

Sipping the beer, he returns to the lounge. It is almost exactly as it was when she lived there. The wallpaper is the same dark red, the black carpet still stained with spilled candle wax knocked over in the throes of passion, the book shelves dusty. He has kept most of her belongings: her books, records and tapes, knickknacks, even some of her clothes. It is morbid, he knows; probably unhealthy—or so a shrink might say. But they keep her memory vibrantly alive, He looks at the portrait of her above the TV set he never watches. She was happy the day he painted it; yet there is, he notices now, a sadness lurking behind her Mona Lisa smile. She'd said no one had been able to capture her looks or her heart the way he did, that he was the only one who could see and understand the pain she'd experienced as a child, abused by her stepfather from the age of eight until he was killed in a bar fight when she was fourteen, repeatedly raped and beaten by the boyfriend she had when she left home at seventeen. Was it any wonder she mistrusted men, that she'd been unable to maintain relationships?

—Even ours—

Although they spent most of the first three months they were together indulging in mutual pleasures—watching movies, going to galleries, cooking for each other, taking long walks in Central Park—there were times when she would leave for several days, often at short notice, to visit friends in Boston. He never went with her, partially because she never invited him, but mainly because he respected her freedom, and besides, it gave him the chance to see his parents in Pennsylvania.

She appears from the kitchenette as he returns from work. She is smartly dressed in a long flowing skirt, silk blouse, and red shoes. He knows she is leaving and tries to hide his disappointment.

"I've got to see Jeanette. Her boyfriend dumped her; she's in a bad way. There's a train to Boston at 7:35."

"We're going to the Met to see "La Boheme" tomorrow night, remember?"

She looks embarrassed. She has forgotten he'd promised to take her after she told him it was her favourite opera.

Lydia turns away under the pretence of picking up her pocketbook, not able to look him in the eye. She's hurt his feelings but cannot find the right words to reassure him.

"Lydia?"

She looks up quickly, a distant expression on her face.

"I'll be back, I guess. Look, I've got to go or I'll miss my train,"

"Okay. Let me walk you to the subway,"

'There's no need, really,"

But he goes with her anyway. The conversation consists of small talk. She says she'll meet him outside the Met at 7:00 PM. They kiss farewell, and she seems to drift down the steps into the subway at Lexington and 86th as if the world around her does not exist.

Returning to their apartment on East Eighty-Third Street—he gave up the lease on his so they could be together—doubt nags at the back of his mind. Look at the picture; it appears normal. Look at it again, and it has changed.

Lydia is gone.

Night falls. Despite bone-weary tiredness, he cannot sleep so goes out to buy beer from the Deli across the street. He drinks until unconsciousness claims him.

He should have seen the signs but was dazzled by love. Any man in his right mind should have realized the relationship had changed, yet his heart was in his head. She loved him. It was selfish of him to expect her to be there all the time; they were settling into a new rhythm of life, and during the period of balancing, he had to modify his expectations. But it was self-deception; he didn't want to face the fact her manner was changing, that the moment of true intimacy had passed. She was withdrawing into herself, slowly pulling away, and the more he reached out, the more she pulled back. Oh, sure, on the surface everything appeared the same, but after you lived with someone for a while, you began to subconsciously pick up on details in the other person's behaviour, to see the gap between what was said and what was done. Instead of dealing with the signs, he'd ignored them, and clung to his idealism like a shipwrecked sailor clinging to a life raft. In doing so, he failed to see that she, too, was shipwrecked, adrift on the sea of her own instability, that his desire for intimacy pushed her towards the rocks of desperation.

He sits at the desk, shaking. Why is he doing this to himself? She was unstable—

there was no way he could be held responsible for her death. After all, she'd made three suicide attempts before meeting him and had never told him. He only found out when he met her mother and brother at the funeral, only then learned she'd spent six months in an institution undergoing psychiatric evaluation following the third attempt. But he did feel responsible, and still does. He'd failed to see the signs, failed to respond to her needs by clinging to his own, and in doing so, he'd pushed her over the edge.

He picks up the bottle of Dickel and takes a big pull, leaving only a drop. Barely a mouthful. It doesn't matter. The beer and sour mash are working their dark, obliviating magic. The room spins suddenly, a nauseous tilt-a-whirl, and he can hardly sit up straight, self-pity and self-disgust sloshing around inside him like oil and water; self-pity because he is alone—as he has always been—and self-disgust because he lacks the strength to overcome his weaknesses, his neediness.

It is the sixth month of their relationship. The passion has cooled, the lovemaking no longer as exciting, as all-consuming as it once was. Long periods of silence replace conversation, and Lydia is spending an increasing amount of time at the gallery she works at on Green Street. He senses she is avoiding him, trying to ignore the promise of what they've shared. She doesn't have to work the hours she puts in, so now they are living a lie: the apartment they share is not a home; it has become a prison.

They are in bed. He dreams they are there asleep, waking as she gets up. She's going to the bathroom, he thinks. But she does not return. He gets up to search the dream apartment.

She's not there,

The door to the hall is open. He goes outside, vulnerable, naked, The hall is not that of the apartment building; it looks like a hotel. Disoriented, he turns to go back, but the door has shut. He has no choice but to find her.

He walks the hallway, his hands covering his genitals. All the doors are locked. Then he hears voices coming from the room at the end.

Greg Vale, an old high school friend, appears with a girl on each arm. Their laughter stops as they see him. One of the girls stifles a giggle.

"Have you seen Lydia?" he asks.

"Yeah, she's left you." Greg looks sad as he speaks.

Then he and the girls wander away, absorbed in their intimacy. Carpenter walks back down the hall. Now he cannot find the door to the apartment.

He wakes with a start, his heart beating triple-time. Lydia lies beside him on her back, the serenity of sleep casting her face as a mask of innocence.

But he knows.

She has left him. Her spirit is gone.

The following night, she slashes her wrists.

The memory of that Wednesday is so clear it seems like only last week.

The day started out filled with promise, a sudden Spring after a barren Winter, and for the first time in months he felt unrestrained enthusiasm. The mail had arrived early. There was the usual pile of junk mail, a letter for Lydia from Boston, and a card from the Pictures of Lilly Gallery down on Spring Street. Another show, he thought as he turned it over. Sandreen, the manageress, was an old friend, a punky lesbian with purple hair whom he'd met while doing a night course in Modern Art at S.V.A. She was always sending him invites to openings even though he'd stopped going, depressed by other people's successes and the mediocrity of their work.

He had to read the card three times before the truth hit home:

Hey, Jim, don't be a stranger . . . Bobbi wants to talk business . . . Jim Carpenter, come on down! It's show time!—YES, YOUR SHOW!!! We want to give you a spot!

Luv, Sandy.

Three kisses and a purple lipstick smear.

It was too much to hope for . . . and yet. Bobbi, Sandy's lover, had always expressed an interest in his work. Were they serious? He'd give them a call once he got to work. No, he'd call them now, even if it was 7:30 AM. They often stayed up all night partying; maybe they were awake.

Lydia was still asleep as he crept back into the apartment. He took the phone into the bathroom and dialled. On the third ring, Sandy answered, and it was true!

They wanted him and his work.

Okay, so it was to be part of a show called "Upper East Side: Visions Above 60th," and he was going to be one of five artists exhibiting, but so what? A dream was about to become reality.

Unable to resist, he woke Lydia to tell her the good news. Once she came to full consciousness, she smiled a deep, loving smile, the kind which he hadn't seen in several weeks. She hugged him, said they should celebrate. He suggested dinner at Franco's. It was agreed. He kissed her again, wishing he could go back to bed to make love, the nightmare forgotten, but he was going to be late for work so he reluctantly departed, leaving her letter on the table.

The day dragged, the bank's interior a jailhouse of lifeless angles, soulless lighting, antiseptic steel and glass. Still, nothing could contain the joy pulsing through his veins, the sense of achievement.

During his lunch break, he took a walk up Third Avenue to gaze at the jutting spire of the Chrysler Building, his favourite monument on the city skyline. Its Art Deco architecture always instilled in him a sense of wonder, its gargoyles sleek and otherworldly, even if they were made from hubcaps. He stopped at a pay phone and called Lydia.

She didn't sound too happy, and there was an air of hostility in her voice he couldn't fathom. He asked if everything was okay. She replied she couldn't talk with people in the office. Bad news? No, just something I've got to talk to you about. Concerned, he pressed for information.

"Look, I'll tell you tonight." She hung up on him.

He walked back to work in a state of confusion, but she called him five minutes after he returned to apologize, said her boss was bugging her and she'd started her period early. Said she loved him, said it was nothing serious, that she'd see him at the restaurant at 7:00 PM. He felt better and thought no more about it.

7:15 PM and he sat at the bar nursing a Manhattan. Yeah, it was a cliché, but tonight it felt like it was his town. Lydia was usually half-an-hour late so her not being there was no big deal. She'd probably gone home to change, deciding to dress up for the occasion. But by 7:55 PM, worry and hunger began gnawing at his insides. The maître d' said he couldn't hold the table longer than another fifteen minutes so he phoned the apartment. All he got was the answering machine.

At 8:10 PM he told the maître d', a short, officious man with slicked black hair, to cancel the reservation. He called again. Just the machine.

His back muscles were tense with apprehension as he ran out onto Fifth Avenue to hail a cab, anxiety digging sharp nails into his abdomen as the car crawled up Third through heavy traffic, All thoughts of the show, of the new pictures he'd been thinking of doing were erased by Lydia's absence.

He looks at the unfinished paintings gathering dust in the corner of the room, His show? Hah. Visions Above 60th—all he saw that night was a vision of Hell.

As he reaches for the door, he knows something is terribly wrong, The thought is not conscious; it comes from some dark, instinctual level below reason, and as he touches the frame, static pricks his fingertips as if in warning. As he enters the apartment, the emotionally charged air rolls over him like a tsunami, sweeping away control.

"Lydia?" His voice trembles as he speaks.

There is no answer.

He goes to the kitchenette. Signs of violence: broken glass coats the floor, crunching underfoot, the sounds grating on his flayed nerves; in the sink are a pile of burnt photographs, the ashes wet leaves of nitrate paper. He picks one up, the only one not fully burnt.

It is of Lydia and someone else, but the other figure is unidentifiable, the image charred to a soggy black.

An empty Smirnoff bottle lies beside the garbage can, its neck smashed off.

He races to the bedroom.

Empty.

The sheets are ripped apart. Purple pieces of cotton litter the floor like confetti. Lydia's favourite dress, a midnight-blue cocktail number in crushed velvet, is twisted in a heap on the chair.

The bathroom.

He tries the door. It's locked.

"Lydia!"

The door will not budge. He slams his shoulder against it in a futile effort to snap the lock. They make it look so easy on TV. On the fourth attempt, the frame gives a little, but his muscles agonize against the wood.

He returns to the kitchenette, panic scrabbling inside his chest, as he searches under the sink for a screwdriver. Finding it, he runs back to the door.

It takes tremendous strength to pry it into the frame, his bruised shoulder complaining as he tries to leverage the lock.

"Lydia! Lydia!

She doesn't respond, and his urgent panic fuels the strength he needs.

The frame gives with a short crack, the door swinging wide, propelling him into Lydia's private hell.

She is almost completely submerged under the red water, a horror movie heroine in a scene recalling Rossetti's "Lady of the Lake" as written by Poe, a bloody razor blade lying quietly on the tub's rim.

He screams as he rushes to her, plunging his arms into the warm red not caring about his best suit or Brooks Brothers' shirt.

He is soaked as he hauls her limp body from the tub. She's unconscious, barely breathing, and as he pulls her clear of the dark water her arms flop, revealing the deep gashes in her wrists, faint lines of blood still trickling from the self-inflicted wounds.

He pulls her clear, her legs dragging over the porcelain, trying to reach for a towel in which to wrap her. A heavy rag doll, her weight is too much to bear and he slips, Lydia, his dying Lydia falling on top of him, a final breath escaping from her lips. He doesn't notice in his panic and pulls the large pink towel around her, reaching for two hand towels which he ties around her wrists before racing to the phone. He dials 911 and sobs for paramedics.

But before they arrive, he realizes she is dead.

They find him in the bathroom cradling her lifeless body against him, hysterical sobs echoing off the tiled walls.

He picks up the photo of Lydia standing on the bow of *The Maid of the Mist* and begins to sob again. It was this night three years ago he last held her in his arms, the lifeless shell of the person he'd loved more than any other, and now the black weight of remorse pulls him down into the pit of total depression.

It is time to end the pain.

He pulls the desk drawer open and removes the .38 Special he'd taken from his father's gun collection last week. Three years of carrying around memories of the woman he'd loved, retreating steadily into a haze of alcohol are too much to bear. That and the terrible realization his art is meaningless.

He puts the gun to his head, His finger squeezes against the trigger. And . . .

Nothing.

He can't do it.

He is weak, and the thought tears him apart.

Too weak to deal with life, too weak to end it.

"You fucking coward," he whispers, placing the gun's barrel in his mouth, cocking the hammer with his right thumb.

His finger caresses the trigger.

—*squeeze*—

He tastes death—cold, hard, metallic.

Just one little squeeze, and that's it. Over. Done. His hand shakes.

—*do it!*—

He yanks the gun from his mouth.

"I can't!" he cries. "I'm too fucking weak." Deep sobs of utter despair rip through him as he puts the gun down on the desk, sliding from the chair to crumple in a heap on the floor. Within seconds he passes out.

He wakes on the couch sensing someone in the room.

The candles have burned themselves out with the exception of the fat red one on the bookshelf. Confused, his eyes try to penetrate the gloom.

The kitchenette—someone is in the kitchenette.

He stumbles off the couch, his head throbbing, heart trip-hammering in his chest.

"Who's there?"

He freezes as he reaches the doorway.

Lydia stands in front of the sink. She wears her favourite blue dress as she sorts through a pile of photographs, a Bic lighter on the counter.

"Lydia?"

She ignores him as she continues to look through the photos, pausing on one particular shot.

"Darling?"

He moves closer.

I'm dreaming. This isn't happening.

He halts at the threshold of the door as if he is staring through a window.

Lydia starts to shake, her small shoulders slumping as she begins to cry. Screwing up the photo in her left hand.

"You bastard," she hisses, reaching for a glass beside a vodka bottle. She gulps down the liquor, then hurls the glass against the wall. The smash echoes loudly in his ears.

"I hate you!" she spits at the photo, holding it up as she picks up the lighter.

He moves closer to see what she sees.

There is a man he doesn't recognize in the picture. A large, older man with his arm around Lydia, both of them smiling at the camera.

She flicks the Bic, directing the flame to the photograph. The paper catches immediately, a tongue of fire licking its way up the image. She holds the photo until the flame sears her fingers. She picks up another picture and repeats the ritual.

He watches as she holds up each photo, her face set in bitter determination as she feeds them to the flames. The stranger is in every one: holding Lydia, kissing Lydia, laughing with Lydia.

She burns out the stranger from the last picture and turns in Carpenter's direction, gazes right through him, and walks into the lounge. She sits on the couch, the letter with the Boston postmark in her hand, shaking again, seemingly more from anger than sadness. She reads the letter then crushes it in her delicate fist, throwing it into the waste basket beside the TV.

He stands helpless, confused. He moves to touch her, reaches out to tell her it's okay—he's here; he feels her pain, can taste her sorrow. If he holds her, shares the pain, it will be okay. Together, they can drive the darkness away, fill the room with light. Isn't that what Love is? The power to change, the ability to transform?

He bends forward.

"Lydia," he says softly as he extends his left hand.

As he touches her shoulder, she fades for an instant, flickering like an image on a damaged videotape.

She suddenly stands and moves towards the waste basket. She leans down, plucking the offending ball of paper from the trash, uncrumpling the screwed up pages. She flattens them out as best she can, then folds them in half. She pauses, struggling with her tears, and goes to the book case in the furthest corner of the room. She selects a volume, and slips the letter inside. Tom Robbins' "Even Cowgirls Get The Blues"—one of her favourites—then sits back on the couch, stifling her sobs.

The room darkens.

He wakes on the couch, aware he needs to use the bathroom. He sways drunkenly as he unzips his fly and fumbles for the light switch. Light explodes in his face.

Lydia lies in the bathtub. Tears rolls down her cheeks, a razor blade poised over her left wrist.

"Goodbye, Roger," she says softly.

The blade cuts deep.

He wakes on the couch, roused from sleep by the light touch of lips on his.

Lydia, naked, wet, pale, oh so pale, stands over him.

"I'm sorry."

He reaches out for her but she fades into the darkness.

"Release me," she whispers.

He wakes face down on the carpet, his brain throbbing with a jackhammer hangover.

"What the—" he slurs before belching, a bolus of vomit cresting his throat. He pukes on the carpet and groans.

—dreams—

Strange dreams.

But he never dreams when he's drunk; at least he never remembers if he does. That's the beauty of booze; it brings oblivion.

—Lydia—

She was here. And something else . . .

—the letter—

Stubbing the toes on his right foot, he swings himself in the direction of the bookcase. His vision rolls as he tries to find the Robbins book, gagging as he fights against hurling a second time.

There. Tugging it free from the embrace of a Ludlum and a Jong, he weaves back to the couch.

He opens the book.

And the letter flutters free.

It takes him a while to focus on the neat, ornate handwriting. "My Dear, Dear Lydia,

"I don't know how to begin this, filled as I am with both sadness and joy . . ."

The following three lines are crossed out. "Perhaps Truth is the only way.

"After all these months, Carol and I have decided to resume living together. And in time, we hope that we will be able to work things out. . . ."

He skim-reads the next couple of paragraphs.

"But please do not feel what you and I have shared this past year has been in vain, or the frivolous desire of a middle-aged man. Our love has meant more than words can express. . . ."

He doesn't need to read the rest. Jeanette. Boston. It was all shit.

He staggers up off the couch towards the desk, his mind silently screaming at the terrible truth—that Lydia had lied to him, that he has lied to himself.

It is time to end the Big Lie.

He picks up the gun. Opens his mouth.

If truth is knowledge, and knowledge is power, then let that power give him strength.

He squeezes the trigger.

BLACKPOOL ROCK

Fame, Darren Franks mused as he poured a large shot of Johnny Walker Red, was a fickle mistress at the best of times. But there came a point when one morning you realized the woman you'd been sleeping with was a phony. It was like picking up some babe in a bar, balling her ass off, only to wake up and see her for what she really was—an aging hooker who'd given her favours to so many others that no amount of make-up could disguise the decay.

"Here's to the great lie," he said, toasting his reflection in the dressing room mirror.

Elvis toasted him back.

Elvis Darren Aaron Franks Presley.

Darren scratched at his left sideburn. Damn, his skin allergy was starting to act up. Come tomorrow he'd have a rash like a teen with primo acne.

"Did you ever have these problems?"

Elvis squinted back at him.

"No, of course not. You were The King. Me, I'm just The Great Pretender."

He emptied the glass and rubbed his chest. Goddamn indigestion. He should have bought a big bottle of Mylanta before leaving for this tiny, uncivilized country. His guts had been churning since the Tuesday flight out of Atlanta, and the food here didn't help. Bland or greasy—take your choice. When he'd asked Davies, who ran the club, for Mylanta he might as well have been speaking Creole. Yeah, well, that's where fame got you—a weeklong gig at a cheesy cabaret joint in the English Northwest.

For One Week Only! All The Way From The U.S. of A! Top Elvis Impersonator Darren Franks!

He hummed a few lines of "What A Wonderful World," grimacing as the whiskey continued to burn his insides. Yessiree Bob, what a wonderful, wonderful world it was. At least the trip had gotten him away from Carrie and the kids.

A knock at the door diverted his attention from the mirror.

"Yeah, who is it?"

Another knock.

"Yeah?!"

The unwanted visitor rapped three times.

"Shit," Darren muttered, rising from the worn leather chair. Maybe it was the writer who was traveling up from London to do a piece on him for the . . . what was it? *The Sunday Express*. Some lowbrow news rag. A reporter called Hurst. Guy was supposed to be here hours ago.

Darren opened the door.

A leather gloved hand grabbed him around the throat, forcing him back into the room. Strong fingers crushed his windpipe, strangling the cry of surprise trying to crawl out his gaping mouth. Then a hand holding a white cloth clamped over his face.

Within seconds, Darren was unconscious.

You could always rely on British Rail to let you down. The 16:10 from Euston had departed ninety minutes late, which meant they missed their scheduled connection in Preston and had waited another two hours for a train to Blackpool. It was now nearly midnight, and Jamie Hurst was pissed off.

Why couldn't they have driven like civilized people? He looked at the reason sitting beside him in the back of the cab and let the thought go. He was too tired, too hungry to be angry. Irritable, yes, which was why he'd hardly said a word for the past hour, letting Beth murder the silence with her endless chatter. But being short with her wasn't going to get him anywhere.

"So was this where the IRA tried to blow up Thatcher a few years ago?"

"No, that was Brighton. Bastion of Tory conventions."

Although Beth was attractive, her endless chatter and ill-formed knowledge irritated him. That, and the perfume she always wore.

The cab pulled up sharply.

"Grand Hotel," said the driver.

Jamie looked out the window at the facade of the Victorian building looming over them. Like all the other buildings he'd seen on their drive across town, the Grand whispered memories of better days. Times long gone in this forsaken corner of Thatcher's Britain.

He paid the driver, tipping him well. Might as well divert some Southern expense account money into the pockets of the Northern poor.

"Thanks very much, Guv," the cabbie said, touching the brim of his cloth cap.

The cabbie's gesture was so Dickensian he didn't know whether to laugh or throw up. The cabbie probably thinks I'm just some spoiled Southern arsehole.

You cynical bastard, Jamie silently reprimanded himself. Just because you don't like being up North doesn't give you the right to think like a prick.

Jamie pulled their bags from the cab's boot. Beth was still going on and on about something.

"Hmm?"

"How about a quiet dinner for two. Maybe by candlelight?"

Oh, God, she was trying the seduction routine again. Jesus, American women seemed to think about nothing other than having a few inches of Englishman inside them. Beth's constant hint-dropping reminded him of his first trip to New York. After three women had tried to bed him in two days, Jamie had come to two conclusions—one, most American women were obsessed with sex, and two, it wasn't his body they wanted, it was his accent.

"I've got a swine of a headache," he replied honestly. "Let's just check into our rooms and get some rest. I should call the Lucky Strike and try to touch base with Franks. Judging by his ego he'll probably throw a fit because we didn't make tonight's show."

"Okay, then how about—" Beth replied, obviously disappointed, but her question was cut off by the revolving doors.

*

Was he dreaming? Darren didn't know. His head was filled with mist.

"He'll be here tomorrow," said a male voice.

He couldn't hear the other person.

"I promise. He's looking forward to it."

Something else was said, but consciousness slipped gears and neutral took over.

And with it, the merciful static of unconsciousness.

Jamie dumped his bags in the closet and collapsed on the bed.

Malcolm, you swine, I could hit you for this!

He grimaced as he ran a hand over his face, the softness of the bed embracing his back. But the truth was he couldn't give Malcolm shit for saddling him with Beth—or setting up the assignment, the first of a series. If Malcolm was fucking Beth, then the slightest criticism was going to alienate his editor. And even if good old Malcolm Jones wasn't slipping Beth Golden the pork sword, any kind of criticism was going to place him in his editor's bad books—a situation he could ill afford at the moment.

You are between book contracts and have a mortgage, old son, so don't forget that a series of articles for *The Sunday Express* are going to go a long way to keep the wolf from the door.

At least Beth hadn't forced the issue when he'd headed for his room. Another situation like the one at The Crown and Two Chairmen, when she'd been smashed and clingy, would have tried his patience. Maybe she was getting the hint.

He struggled up from the bed and dialled room service. After he ordered a beer and a ham and cheese sandwich, he opened his shoulder bag and pulled out his diary.

Jamie seated himself at the small desk next to the TV set, pen poised over virgin page, trying to ignore the emetic green wallpaper with the gold rococo design.

So here I am in gloomy Blackpool with a randy American photographer. The wallpaper is an affront to good taste, the bed too soft, and I have a bad case of British Rail bottom from spending hours on a wretched Inter-City ride to the working class Las Vegas of the Northwest.

Anyone who thinks writing for a living is glamorous needs a lobotomy!

Paul Theroux probably summed this place up best in his English travel book, The Kingdom: *"Blackpool was perfectly reflected in the swollen guts and unhealthy fat of its beer-guzzling visitors. . . ." Those words have stuck with me since I first read them, so accurately reflecting my impressions when I first passed through back in '82.*

Ah, well . . . I guess there's no point complaining. An assignment's an assignment.

He put the pen down, focusing on the cheap wooden surface to avoid the nausea-inducing wallpaper.

What bothered him wasn't the assignment per se. Writing a profile on an Elvis impersonator wasn't difficult. The truth was Jamie just didn't like the North. The atmosphere of despair born of the Conservative Government's industrial strip-mining, of unemployment, of poverty, made him uncomfortable. And let's face it, he thought, the locals had every reason to despise Southerners. As Thatcher was so fond of reminding the Great British Public, *we live in the Post-Industrial Age and the job market is changing.* It had changed all right. In ten years, the Bitch had seen to that; it was no longer North and South, but a geography of Have and Have Not.

More than the location he found himself in was the fact he'd been having one of *those feelings* since he'd boarded the train in London. The prescient sense of dread increased as he awaited the arrival of room service: the kind of sensation—a sixth sense glowing dully at the back of his brain like an early warning radar—that he'd been cursed with since the day his brother had died violently in a freak motorbike accident ten years ago.

Alex Hurst had lived fast and died young, a wild rider on the Dark Highway. What disturbed Jamie hadn't been the suddenness of Alex's death but rather the fact he'd known something was going to happen. The way he'd been drawn to the crash site at the moment of impact, puking his guts out with fear before the incident, watching his brother's hideous death with cold cinema verité detachment.

That dreadful instinctual a priori knowledge had plagued him on several occasions since then. *He'd known* his Mother was going to have a stroke hours before it happened, even though he was over a hundred miles away. *He'd known* Jessica, his first serious girlfriend, was going to commit suicide. She'd been unstable—you didn't have to be Sherlock Holmes to deduce that. But he'd never consciously realized how close to the Abyss she had wandered during those heady days at Oxford. That reality—and not being able to prevent it—had hit him hardest of all. Sometimes a tsunami of guilt wiped him out when he thought of his Mother. Guilt that came not from grief but from not feeling *anything*. Deeper than the remorse he'd wallowed in for a period after Alex's death. For someone so sensitive to his environment, the sad fact was a part of his emotional cortex seemed as dead as the significant others in his life whose sad fates played out in advance in his mind.

"Enough moping," he muttered, picked up the telephone, and dialled the number of The Lucky Strike Cabaret.

George Robles cracked open the door to the spare room to see how the American was doing.

Elvis—or the closest version this side of Heaven—lay unconscious on the single bed, hands and feet tied securely. Robles paused in case he was faking it. After watching the prone body for a couple of minutes, he realized he couldn't detect the sound of the man's breathing.

No, he couldn't be dead! Not yet, not before . . .

Robles went to the bed, kneeling beside Darren Franks. He sighed with relief. The American was breathing so shallowly his chest barely moved. Good. He'd gone to too much trouble, risked everything for this chance to bring happiness to Michelle. With his luck, the American could have had a respiratory disorder or an allergic reaction to the chloroform.

George Robles knew all about bad luck. It had shadowed him his entire life. If luck were a lady, then she was a spiteful, stuck-up bitch who had turned her face away from him since he was a child. He also knew about pain, fear, and bitterness. And resentment at the unjust world, its mindless crimes, and twisted jokes.

Like the curse placed on Michelle, his once-beautiful daughter, who'd suffered for most of her seventeen years and would be lucky if she saw another two.

Well, she wouldn't. He'd already decided that. She had suffered enough and deserved the blessing of the King—and then merciful freedom from the prison of her pain.

Robles walked slowly, softly from the spare room, afraid the American would wake and he'd have to explain.

That would come later.

After the persuasion.

The digital bedside clock showed 1:34 AM.

Jamie rolled onto his side trying not to let frustration fuel his insomnia. The headache throbbed passionately behind his closed eyes, the ham and cheese sandwich a lump of lead in his stomach. But between the thesis of incipient migraine, antithesis of indigestion, lay the synthesis of the premonition which teased and tormented his tired psyche.

(white)

He groaned involuntarily, massaging his wrists.

(sore)

(ropeburn)

He felt sick. Not because of the indigestible lump of hotel food laying in his gut but the overpowering medical smell that permeated his nostrils.

(. . . ere tomorrow)

"Go away," he muttered under the covers. "Leave me alone."

Whatever signals he was picking up, he didn't want to know the source or the reason.

(white walls, hard bed)

(sore)

The medical smell again.

"Fuck."

Jamie stumbled from the bed towards the bathroom, bile crawling from his stomach. He hated being sick, and the worst part of the psychic sensual overload was the puking. He made it to the porcelain bowl in time. Just. Lumps of ham and cheese evacuated his mouth in a bilious rush, his sternum heaving painfully. A second ejection. A third, the malty taste of the beer with which he'd washed down the sandwich underscoring the stomach acid. A dry heave punctuated the vomiting fit, a static band of white noise humming in his ears. Thank God he hadn't eaten Shepherd's Pie or something heavier.

Seconds rolled sluggishly into languid minutes as Jamie hunched over the cold toilet bowl in case his stomach jumped again. Then, shaking, he stood, stumbled to the wash basin, and ran the cold water. He splashed his face, rinsed his mouth, groaning.

Knocking.

What? Someone knocking at his door.

Again. Louder.

Without thinking he went to the door and opened it.

"I couldn't sleep."

Beth stood there with a sheepish smile on her face and a diaphanous blue silk dressing gown almost covering her naked, alabaster skin and firm, prominent breasts. A nipple peeked out at him from behind the fabric.

"Oooh," she added, noticing his nakedness, her eyes dropping to his flaccid penis.

Jamie grabbed the sash of the gown, pulled her inside, slamming the door.

"What's up?" he grumbled.

"I couldn't sleep."

Brandy on her breath.

"So?"

"So . . . I thought . . ."

The dark of the doorway swallowed him. He didn't feel embarrassed by his nakedness. But he suddenly felt cold, vulnerable, lost. The white noise buzzed in his head, fractured by faint blips of psychic radar.

(sore)

    (uck is thi)

"Are you all right?"

"No. Go back to bed."

He swayed, stumbled, held the wall for support.

"Are you sick?"

"*No* . . . it's nothing."

He swayed again.

Jamie flinched as Beth's soft, warm hand found his face.

"Poor baby."

Too weak to resist, he pushed her gently into the room.

"Get into bed."

He placed a hand on her bum. The skin was hot beneath the cool silk. "Go on."

A smile on her lips, Beth let the robe slip from her shoulders as Jamie retreated momentarily to run water in the bathroom.

Darren Franks blinked against the brightness of the naked light bulb hanging from the ceiling's center.

What was this fucking shit? Kidnapped. That much was fucking obvious. By who? Fucking Elvis fans? Yeah, well, anything was possible. There were enough fucking mush-heads out there who loved Elvis so much they didn't want to believe he was dead. It was cultural obsession bordering on religious psychosis—and part of the reason he earned the amount of green he did.

But this sucked the big, fat hairy one to the root.

He'd pretended to be unconscious when the creep had entered the room. He'd been so nervous, in fact, he'd almost forgotten to breathe. Real smart. The fucking asshole thought he'd croaked. Stuck his greasy head right next to Darren's mouth. Smell of the fuckwad's hair lotion almost made him toss his cookies. Bastard fucking piece of shit, just wait 'til you untie my hands, I'll fucking choke every last ounce of shit from your skinny body.

Fuckfuckfuckfuckfuck. Darren struggled against the ropes,

wincing. His skin was raw.

Why didn't matter. *Who*, he didn't give a shit about. All he wanted was to break loose and take a king-sized dump before he shit his Calvin Kleins and brown-stained his best Elvis-in-Vegas white pantsuit.

Yeah, it sucked.

uckfuckfuckfuck . . . fuckfuckfuck . . .

The stream of profanity pulled Jamie's consciousness down from the cresting wave of orgasm into a psychic undertow that made his back spasm. Beth perceived it as onrushing ejaculation, thrusting her hips towards him.

"Yes, yes!"

Jamie's sphincter muscle contracted, puckered unexpectedly, stopping him mid-hump.

Oh, no.

His bowels felt ready to let go.

"Oh, yes, baby. Give it to me."

Jamie felt his rectum move.

But nothing happened . . . only he could feel it . . . and the humiliation . . .

(aww no)

Beth stopped thrusting her hips, said something he couldn't hear through the sensory feedback.

His penis softened.

(ashamed . . . ohfuck . . .)

Jamie nearly collapsed on Beth, cushioning his suddenly supine form on knees and elbows, moulding to her shape like Plasticine, his head burrowing into the pillow beside hers.   *Apples.*   Her hair smelled of apples. Fresh, clean. *Timotei shampoo*, he thought, images from a TV commercial dispelling the helplessness, the isolation, emptiness.

"What's the matter?" Beth whispered. "Don't feel bad. It happens sometimes."

"Hold me," Jamie said. "Don't let me go."

He nuzzled her ear with his nose, drinking in her smell, her essence, the scent of apple shampoo cocooning him from the dark despair hovering over his back.

Beth hugged him. Tight.

"I know you're awake. Stop faking," said the voice in the doorway. "We punish fakers."

The voice was thick with Northern brogue.

Darren opened his eyes, turned his head towards his captor.

The man in the doorway was skinny, around five-foot-ten, weedy-looking, long arms. He wore a wrinkled green nylon shirt, faded brown polyester trousers, plaid carpet slippers. His eyes were deep-set, red-rimmed as if he hadn't slept in a while. A black forest of stubble covered his cheeks. He hesitated as Darren looked him in the eyes. The man dropped his gaze, looking at the worn rug on the floor.

"I've shit myself. I've already been punished. Please untie me so I can clean myself," Darren asked, trying to moderate his tone to sound as reasonable and nonthreatening as possible.

The man sniffed. "Yes, I can smell. Good. Maybe you'll learn humility."

Darren's anger flared. He bit his tongue to control it. Don't let the bastard see he's got the better of you.

"Look, I don't know what all this is about, but you're making a big mistake. If you think you can get ransom for me, sorry, you got the wrong guy. Willie Nelson, maybe."

"I know who you are," the man replied coldly. "That's why you're here. Ransom? No, that's not what this is about."

"Then what is it?"

The man came closer, and Darren could catch a faraway glint of something unhealthy in his captor's man's eyes—a dark mote of madness.

"You're going to help me. And if you cooperate, then I'll let you live."

Darren went numb.

"What . . . what do you want?" His throat was dry, and his voice threatened to crack.

"You're going to make love to my daughter."

After they made love a second time, successfully, gently, Jamie told Beth what was wrong. All of it. As they lay together, limbs entwined, the warmth of her soft skin keeping the sensation of isolation at bay, the words spilled from his mouth. At first a trickle, like a mountain stream struggling free from winter ice, then a torrent as the words rushed into a river of confession. She listened attentively, occasionally asking a question when he wandered from a particular point, lost in memory, blinded with guilt. Years of keeping his secrets locked away in the closet of silence had exacted a toll on his ability to be intimate. Jamie had kept the world at arms' length, had tried to find truths in the mirror of fiction. More often than not, all he'd found were more questions, bigger lies. But as he talked, the burden lessened, and for the first time in as long as he could remember, a measure of inner peace calmed him, tuning out the psychic static.

Beth asked him about Alex. She wanted to know how different they were, as if Alex's dark reflection could shed some light on the man she was attracted to and whose bed she was at last sharing. He told her. And about Jessica. Beth held him tighter.

"What does this have to do with Franks?" she asked later, as the digital clock clicked to 5:44 AM.

"I don't know. I called The Lucky Strike. He'd gone for the night. I called his hotel. Wasn't there either. I left a message. Maybe it has nothing to do with him."

"But you said as soon as we got on the train you started to get the feeling, and it increased as we neared Blackpool. It would be logical—"

"There's nothing logical about my gift," he interjected, tensing.

"Gift. Huh," he grunted. "*Curse*."

Jamie pushed himself away from Beth slightly.

"What do you want from me? Why are you attracted to me?" he asked, his voice earnest.

She chuckled softly. "It's not your accent. It's . . ." She paused, trying to find the right words.

"When I first met you, I saw a young, attractive guy. Talented, witty, and yes with one helluva sexy accent. But sad. Gentle . . ." She broke off, sighed. "I don't know, just . . . don't murder my feelings by putting them under a microscope."

Neither spoke for a while, then Beth reached out for him again. "Come here."

Finally, they slept.

Jamie dreamed of a white room, of rope, and a girl who looked like Jessica.

Robles sat at the end of Michelle's bed, watching her sleep peacefully in the moonlight spilling through the curtain-less window. There was no need for them on the second level—no prying eyes to protect against and his now-teenage daughter had been born blind. And paraplegic.

Robles took a deep draught from the can of bitter he nursed in his right hand, tears of frustration welling in his eyes.

What kind of a life was this for a young woman, imprisoned in a useless body, lost in perpetual darkness? Aside from music, he was her only friend. He hadn't let her suffer the taunts of children or the indignities of a cruel world. No, he had raised her himself, educated her, and tried his best to give what little happiness her sad situation would afford.

And for the first time in his life, George Robles was loved.

Come tomorrow, he'd return that love. The King would wine and dine his Michelle, tell her she was beautiful, make love to her. And later, when she slept, her loving father would take away her pain, and Michelle would find peace at last.

Despite her thin, almost skeletal body, she looked beautiful to Robles. So beautiful he wished he could slip into bed beside her and hold his lovely daughter, who never complained about anything he did for her. But that was . . . unhealthy. He couldn't do that.

Some mummies did though. Oh, he knew that all right. It made him feel sick.

Robles drank his beer to take away the taste of the bad memory.

As Darren came to, vague thoughts of Carrie and the kids drifted like phantoms through his drugged mind. Then he opened his eyes and remembered where he was.

That bastard had chloroformed him again. Why?

Then he realized he was naked from the waist down and understood.

The crazy son of a bitch had removed his soiled pants and underwear, cleaned his shit-encrusted ass, and tied him up again. Relief clashed with anger, humiliation with disgust. That creep had touched his cock, his balls, his asshole. *What else did he do while you were unconscious*, his mind screamed, *suck your dick?*

Darren struggled against the rope. His wrists were raw but anger overrode pain.

"Fucking son of a bitch! Let me out of here! Someone untie me!" he bellowed.

Maybe there was someone else in the house. Maybe someone who didn't know what this crazy fucker was up to.

Darren bellowed again as loud as he could, twisting his shoulders, tugging at the ropes.

Within seconds, the door opened. The man entered, his face flushed, a leather belt in his right hand.

Darren clammed up as the man sprang to the bed, the belt coming down fast in a vicious arc. It whipped across his chest. It hurt like a mutherfucker. Again, again. He cried out.

"Shut up!" the man hissed. "Shut up!"

"You goddamn son of a bitch!"

"Shut up!"

The man raised the belt, aimed it at Darren's face. "Don't make me hurt you," he said, suddenly trembling. "I . . . I don't want to hurt you. Please, just cooperate with me, and I'll let you go."

His expression was earnest, his eyes red as if he'd been crying, Darren thought, and now he was shaking.

"Okay. Okay! Don't hit me," Darren said as calmly as possible. His chest stung beneath his newly laundered white jacket and silk shirt. The belt buckle had pounded his ribs, and he could feel the onset of bruises the size of pickled eggs.

Try to reason with him. Don't provoke him.

"What did you do to me?"

Confusion showed on the man's face. "What . . . what do you mean? I . . . I cleaned you up. It wasn't very nice."

"Why didn't you let me do it myself?"

"I couldn't risk letting you free."

Darren was silent, trying to think what to say.

"I . . . I didn't touch you, if that's what you're thinking. I'm not a p-per-pervert."

Right, you fucking loon. You kidnap me, tie me up, strip me and wash my balls—and you say you want me to make love to your daughter. You may not be a pervert but normal you ain't either.

Darren forced a smile. "Thanks."

The man dropped the belt. Tears welled in his eyes. His narrow shoulders sagged.

"Just tell me what you want. I'll cooperate," Darren said softly, straining to ignore his own feelings of humiliation and vulnerability.

The man sat. "All I want is for you to make my daughter happy."

"Okay." Darren paused. Get him talking. Humour him. Get him to trust you. "Why don't you introduce yourself, and tell me all about it."

"My name's Robles. George Robles."

Jamie awoke surprisingly refreshed despite lack of sleep. He felt invigorated, weightless, as if he were walking an inch above the ground. He hadn't made love to a woman in nearly two years. But sex with Beth wasn't what made him feel this way. Rather it was the understanding she'd expressed, the compassion and tenderness. She didn't just want to fuck him after all—she wanted *him*. He'd spent too long hiding himself from others and had forgotten how fine it felt to be wanted. And, he had to admit, the sex was good, too.

He picked up a slice of cold toast from the remnants of their room service breakfast. Beth was singing in the shower. He smiled to himself, sat on the bed, and opened the book Beth had shown him while they'd eaten.

I Am Elvis. A Guide To Elvis Impersonators.

He hadn't realized the Elvis cult was so widespread on this level. The book featured sixty three performers devoted to keeping The King's memory alive and contained photos, biographies, agency addresses, even astrological signs. Some of the Elvis clones had gone so far as to have plastic surgery to further their likeness to Colonel Parker's former meal ticket. A number of others stretched incredulity even further. The Lady Elvis. The Black Elvis. Dimitri Katzka, a large Greek expatriate with a thick beard, didn't resemble Elvis one bit, and, the biography stated, wrote short stories and books about psychotherapy. And, of course, El-Vez, The Mexican Elvis.

Jamie chuckled at that one. He'd heard his records and he wasn't half bad.

And there was Darren Franks posing moodily for the camera, dressed in a black velvet pantsuit, holding his microphone like it was a woman's hand.

Birthdate: February 23rd, 1956. Starsign: Pisces. Height: 6 ft. Weight: 210 pounds. Favourite Elvis songs: "Heartbreak Hotel," "Suspicious Minds," "An American Trilogy."

"An Elvis fan since the age of seven, Darren Franks began performing as The King of Rock and Roll during his high school days in Stone Mountain, Georgia, but nearly quit the business when Elvis died," read the biography.

"I was working as the manager of a Texaco station on Lawrenceville Highway, and I went numb with grief when my cashier told me the news on that terrible day in August, 1977. I tried to drive home, but I was so overcome with emotion I had to pull the car over, and I just sat there and cried for an hour," he remembered.

"But like Elvis, Darren decided the show must go on.

"My first thought was, 'I can't do this no more, it wouldn't be right.' I had a show booked that night, and I didn't think people would want to see me when they knew we'd been robbed of the greatest entertainer who ever lived. But as I sat beside the road with tears in my eyes, I had a vision of The King, and I knew he'd want me to carry on. The audience did, too. There wasn't a dry eye in the house that night, and I knew the Lord had blessed me with the gift of being able to bring happiness to other folk—just like Elvis."

Jamie laughed, nearly choking on his toast. Did Franks really believe he was chosen by God to impersonate a guy who died on a toilet seat? The press clippings he'd researched were nowhere near as entertaining as the profile in the book.

"Before I go on stage, I say a prayer to Elvis asking for his blessing, and to thank him for the joy he allows me to bring to people in his name," was Franks' closing quote. Jamie rolled his eyes.

"You're happy."

He glanced up at Beth standing beside the bathroom door, a towel wrapped in a turban around her head and nothing else.

"Have you read this?"

"Sure. I'm surprised you didn't know about it."

"Malcolm isn't very reliable when it comes to providing research pointers."

Beth sat next to him. They flipped through the book, laughing together as he read aloud about a four-year-old Elvis impersonator.

"I tried Franks' hotel again," he said, suddenly breaking off their reverie. "Still no answer."

"The Lucky Strike?"

"No, I called there, too. The manager's not in yet." He shrugged. "It's early. I've left messages for Franks to call here before noon. Said we'd be over at The Strike by 1 PM."

Beth smiled, reached out to wipe a toast crumb from Jamie's lower lip. He kissed her fingers.

They made love until noon.

Darren listened to Robles recount the story of the death of his wife, about Michelle's afflictions, and the general tragedy of his life. It was enough to send anyone off the tracks, and Robles' train had obviously derailed a long time ago.

"I couldn't bring myself to tell her Elvis was dead. She'd lost so much already. When she listens to his voice, she's at peace; she . . . she forgets her pain. She says he's an angel. Only an angel can sing like that."

Robles paused, lost in memory. "I can't stand to see her get worse and worse," he said suddenly. "It's not fair. The continual pain, the drugs. She has no life, no future. Who's going to take care of her when I'm gone? They'll put her in a home. And they'll mistreat her, just like they did my mother."

Robles continued to ramble. Most of what he said made sense. But it was too weird, too twisted. The more he said, the more uncomfortable Darren became.

There's something he's not telling me, his instinct whispered, like a jigsaw puzzle with key pieces missing. Do you honestly think he's going to let you go? Maybe, if all he wanted was for Darren to make love to the girl. He didn't want to ask what Robles had planned after that.

"George."

Robles continued talking about tragedy, how life was cruel—that God, if he existed, was a sadist.

"*George*," Darren said. "I need to piss. And I'm hungry and thirsty."

Robles looked up from the carpet. "I'm sorry." His tone sounded genuine. "I'll get you water and a pot."

"I'd like to piss in the john, freshen up. And . . ." Darren looked down at his wrists. ". . . I'd appreciate it if you untied me. I'm bleeding, and my wrists are sore."

"I . . . I can't do that. You might run away. I'll bring you a pot, water, make you a sandwich. But I can't untie you."

Darren clenched his jaw trying to control his anger. Untie me, you fuck, and I'll strangle the shit out of you—no, control it, make him believe you mean it.

"Please. I'm uncomfortable."

Robles stood up. "No."

He headed to the door, then turned back. "Don't shout again. I'll hurt you if you do. We can't let Michelle know you're here. Not until it's time."

The cab turned onto the Golden Mile near the Blackpool Tower and Beth strained to get a better look at the 500-foot tall Eiffel-like structure.

"That's it?" she said in disbelief. "I thought it was bigger."

"This is England. Everything's smaller," Jamie replied.

"When do they have the illuminations?"

"August through October. It's quite an event. Keeps the holiday-makers happy. It's the locals' version of Disneyland," he added cynically, referring to the annual extravaganza of illuminated figures which turned the resort into a huge Christmas decoration.

"Eight million people," said the cabbie.

"Excuse me?' Beth replied.

"The illuminations," said the cabbie. "That's how many people came to see 'em last year. Right spectacular it is, too. Me kids love it. Nothing like that down south. Great place, Blackpool."

Beth tried to hide a smirk. Jamie looked out the window, embarrassed the cabbie had heard his disparaging remarks.

"Here's The Strike." The cabbie nodded his head in the direction of a poor man's casino, its front a mosaic of neon tubing and flashing lights flickering ineffectually in the weak rays of the May sunlight.

The inside of the cabaret-cum-disco-cum-casino was just as tacky as the exterior, a discordant mix of lurid, flashing orange light bulbs and full-length mirrors.

As Jamie stepped through the double doors the interior dissolved.

He was standing in a sparsely furnished room with white walls, a single bed in one corner. He smelled piss.

(someonegetmeoutofhere)

(ant untie you)

(cooperate)

Then the image, the voices, vanished.

"You okay?"

Jamie blinked.

"What?"

"You stopped dead," Beth said, picking up her camera bag. He realized she'd walked into him.

"I saw something."

"What?"

"I don't know. Come on, let's see if Franks is here."

Robles stuck his head around the door to Michelle's room. Good, she was sleeping peacefully. The American's shouts hadn't disturbed her. He couldn't have that. Michelle got upset easily, and if she knew someone else was in the house, she would guess it was Elvis. No one ever came to visit, and when he'd told her The King was coming to see her, she'd grown so excited he'd had to sedate her. His daughter was delicate and couldn't deal with too much excitement. He'd let her sleep a few more hours. She'd need her energy for her big date.

"No bloody idea, mate," grumbled Arthur Davies, The Lucky Strike's manager. "I 'aven't 'eard a bloody peep from Franks since yesterday when 'e complained about the bloody food.

"I'm thinking about cutting 'is booking short, as matter of fact. 'e's not turned out to be the draw we thought 'e'd be. Mind you, I thought it were a bloody daft idea to start with. Still, I don't own the controlling share in this place, so what I think don't matter 'alf the time.

"Would you like a cup o' tea, luv?"

"No, thank you," Beth replied.

"Well, what can I tell you, Mr. 'urst? Afraid our 'celebrity' has left the building. Don't know what to suggest, unless you'd like to interview me. I've some interesting stories to tell. Mind you, now's not a good time. To add insult to injury, the stage manager's called in sick, so I got a lot on me plate right now."

Jamie sighed, glad Davies paused. The man didn't talk to you; he talked at you.

"Perhaps Franks has gone sightseeing?" Beth offered.

"Bloody well doubt it. All 'e's done since 'e arrived is bloody complain. About the food, the weather, the town. Bloody Americans—sorry, luv, didn't mean you."

"Who would have been the last person to see Franks?" Jamie asked.

"Oh, Robles, I guess. That's me stage manager, the one who's sick."

"Do you know when he left last night?"

"No, I was busy up here going over last week's figures. Business isn't very good right now. Attendance down—"

"What time does Franks' performance end?"

"'bout eleven thirty.

"Look, if you ask me, Franks probably went off with some bint. Lot of women come 'ere to find a date. Oh, 'e'll probably turn up later on. 'E better."

"What now?" Beth asked as they made their way to the main entrance.

"Wait a minute," replied Jamie. "I've got a hunch."

He walked over to the box office while Beth turned her attention to the framed posters advertising Lucky Strike performers of the past. Wayne Fontana and the Mindbenders. Gerry and The Pacemakers. Other '60s groups. Blackpool wasn't a happening place.

"Okay, let's go," Jamie said, placing a hand on her shoulder.

"Where to?"

"I don't know. Let's go see George Robles, our missing stage manager."

"A hunch or a feeling—one of *those* feelings?"

He nodded.

Darren lay with his eyes closed, breathing shallowly, determined to stay calm despite a rising panic as he knew the call time for his performance was creeping closer.

How was Robles going to get him to make love to the girl? How would he know they were fucking—stand in the corner watching? Probably had a strategic hole in the wall. Fucking pervert. The whole situation was crazy. A blind, crippled girl who had no contact with the outside world and didn't know Elvis was dead. Who thought Elvis actually replied to the fan letters she dictated to her father. Did she honestly believe Elvis was coming here for a dinner date?

Each question posed another, then another. Thinking was giving him a headache.

The sound of music drifted up faintly from downstairs. He opened his eyes.

Elvis singing "Suspicious Minds."

Terrific. Robles must be setting the mood for their "guest"'s arrival.

The way Darren was feeling, tied to the bed, freezing his balls off, was as far removed from romance as it could be.

Beth paid the cab driver since Jamie had nothing smaller than a twenty pound note.

"Tell me," she demanded as the cab pulled away. Jamie had refused to speak once they'd got in the car.

"I can't explain, but I have a gut feeling Robles knows where Franks is."

"He could just be off with a groupie, like Davies suggested. You said that last night when he wasn't at the hotel."

"Yes, but we know he never went back to his hotel room and hasn't been there today. If he was screwing around last night, don't you think he'd want to rest and freshen up before tonight's show?"

"She could be dynamite in bed," Beth said with a smile.

"No." A deep worry line creased Jamie's brow. "I keep getting a sensation of . . . containment, and three times I've had a vision of a white, sparsely furnished room."

"A hospital ward?"

He shook his head and started up the incline leading towards Oak Road, the street on which Robles lived. Beth fell into step beside him.

"What are we going to ask Robles? Isn't he going to think it strange we didn't call first?"

Jamie didn't even hear what Beth said. A buzz of white noise hummed softly in his ears, a preternatural calm enveloped him, growing stronger with each step he took. He'd felt this before—when Alex died, when he entered the apartment building before finding Jessica. On a deep, primal level he knew he was right—Robles was the connection. And whatever the connection was, it was drawing him here like a mouse to a piece of cheese.

He hoped there was no trap.

Robles dropped the dinner plate when the doorbell rang.

Who was it? No one came to visit. He didn't have real friends, he hadn't the time. Looking after Michelle took up most of his life outside of work. The police? How could they know about the American? Had someone seen him removing the laundry hamper from the stage door? So what if they had? He was just doing his job.

Calm down. Probably Jehovah's Witnesses or someone trying to sell him double glazing. Ignore it.

Robles stooped to pick up the pieces of broken plate as the bell rang a second time.

Go away.

He tossed the plate into the rubbish bag beside the mountain of empty cans in the far corner, grimacing as the bell rang yet again.

Go away!

Would the American hear it? He'd better not cry out and disturb Michelle. Robles would have to punish him if he did.

Jamie pressed the bell a fourth time.

Like the rest of the house's exterior, the porch was badly in need of repair. Blue paint bubbled and peeled from the front door's rotting wood. Dry piles of old autumn leaves covered the cracked tiles like parchment, and the ceiling was a tapestry of spider webs.

"He obviously doesn't do yardwork," Beth observed, looking at the overgrown front garden as they waited.

"Or home maintenance," Jamie added, puncturing a paint blister with his thumb. The wood beneath was soft.

"What now?"

"We wait a while, then look around," Jamie said, the psychic static buzzing in his ears. The pressure in his head was starting to make him feel nauseous again.

Darren thought he was dreaming when the bell rang the first time. The second ring convinced him he wasn't having aural hallucinations. His heartbeat thumped in his chest with the third, and a ray of optimism broke through the black clouds of depression shrouding him. Someone was outside the house. Was it worth shouting? No, they'd never hear him, but Robles would. *Don't shout again. I'll hurt you if you do.* He'd use the belt again. Or something worse.

Tears of helpless frustration formed in Darren's eyes.

Please God Almighty, save me. I promise I'll never cheat on Carrie again. I'll give money to charity. I'll go to church—I'll do anything you ask of me. Just get me out of here.

Peering through a gap in the mouldering velvet curtains of what used to be his mother's bedroom, Robles watched the young couple walk back down the path to the front gate. The man wore a black leather jacket, a casual shirt, and blue jeans. The blonde woman wore a black American baseball jacket with the words Rhythm Syndicate emblazoned on the back, and carried a large, tan canvas bag slung over one shoulder. No, they weren't Bible thumpers.

Who were they? What did they want?

Still, they seemed to be satisfied no one was home. They didn't even look back at the house.

Good. Go away. Leave us alone.

He went to check on Michelle. It was nearly time to get his little girl ready for her date.

Robles' detached Victorian house stood on a corner of a t-junction, its garden surrounded by a four-foot-high brick wall. As they reached the right angle where the streets bisected, Jamie guided Beth by the arm down Carlisle Road, so they were parallel to the side of the residence. He peeked over the wall and saw two windows facing in his direction—one upstairs, probably on the landing, and one directly below it, possibly the kitchen. Both had partially drawn curtains discouraging prying eyes. The house held secrets, he was certain. Everything about the place screamed psychic decay.

"What now?"

"We investigate," he said, looking around.

Seeing Carlisle Road was deserted, he linked his fingers together. "Give me your foot."

Jamie boosted Beth over the wall, then followed, ducking down behind a large privet bush next to a sagging wooden shed that looked like it had stood there since the 1920s.

"Let's see what the elusive Mr. Robles is hiding," he said, creeping towards the house.

Darren opened his eyes as Robles entered the room. The man held his white trousers in his left hand. They looked clean.

"Tell me what you want me to do," Darren replied, hoping Robles didn't notice his eyes were red from crying.

"You're going to get dressed and wash up. My daughter deserves the best. The King wouldn't be a slob, would he?"

Darren shook his head.

"And if you try any funny stuff," Robles said, his eyes glazed as his right hand emerged from behind his back, a carving knife clenched in its fist, "I'll kill you."

Jamie's guess was right. The side window on the ground floor looked in on the kitchen, but he couldn't clearly see anything through the dirty glass or the tiny gap in the curtains except a dead plant on the counter.

"Round the back."

Beth nodded.

The rear door was in as bad shape as the front. Weather had worn away most of the ancient paint, and the opaque glass was cracked. Next to it, another window, but this one had a gap in the curtains, like someone had glanced outside and forgotten to make sure to redraw them completely.

They peered in.

"Ugh," Beth groaned.

The gloomy kitchen was a museum of mould. Filthy plates and pots were piled high in stagnant sink water, rotting food lay on the counter, and nearly a dozen large plastic rubbish bags crowded the tiny room.

"Jesus, how can someone live like this?"

Jamie ignored her, focusing instead beyond into the dining room.

"Look over there."

Beth's eyes widened. She pulled her camera from her bag and focused her telephoto lens for a better view.

The room was a shrine to Elvis, walls plastered with pictures of the performer. Some were framed, album covers and a large black velvet painting hanging over the mantel piece, which overflowed with badges, statuettes, and dozens of other Elvis items. Another wall was decorated with a mosaic of pictures roughly cut from magazines and newspapers. The only element in the room which wasn't Elvis-inspired was a heavy old oak dining table and two chairs.

The table was laid for two— Elvis placemats, Elvis plates. Even Elvis salt and pepper shakers.

"Paydirt," Beth said.

Jamie fingered the rotting window frame. The casement moved, the rusty lock probably long broken.

Robles paced the room, pants in one hand, knife in the other.

"You will flatter her. She will be shy, bashful, like a proper young lady. She is, you know. I've brought her up well. She knows manners are important. You'll tell her about Las Vegas, Hawaii, the movies you've made, every story you've ever heard about The King just like it happened to you. She'll want to know what it's like living at Graceland."

Darren kept his eyes trained on the knife as Robles paced around the room. If he'd been scared before, he was terrified now. There was no way the loony-toons son of a bitch was going to let him go alive.

"After dinner you will serenade her with her favourite songs—"Heartbreak Hotel," "Don't Be Cruel," "Treat Me Nice," and "Can't Help Falling In Love." Then you'll get down on your knees and kiss her hand, tell her she's so beautiful that it would mean so much to you if she'd love you."

Robles paused by the window, gazing down into the garden.

"You will—" He stopped dead.

"No!" Robles growled, trembling.

Darren said nothing, his eyes wide with fear.

Robles spun to face him, snarling with rage. He threw the pants at Darren.

"I'll deal with you later," he hissed, rushing to the door.

Jamie took Beth's camera case, placed it on the floor, then helped pull her through the window.

"God," she whispered, wiping paint flakes from her palms and focusing her camera to take a shot.

Jamie picked up a heavy porcelain statute of The King from the mantle. Elvis in the '50s, clean-cut, a guitar slung across his chest, right arm up, hips thrust forward. "You said it," he commented softly. "More than obsessive. *Religious*."

The buzzing in his head suddenly stopped, eclipsed by unnatural calm, every detail in the room standing out in sharp clarity, his senses somehow amplified. Like the moments before Alex died and before he'd discovered Jessica's body. Whatever journey they'd started on when they'd left London was nearly over. But although past journeys had ended in tragedy, this time he wasn't afraid.

Beth's camera flashed.

How did they know?

Robles slowly descended the stairs. He knew which ones creaked and stepped carefully. Mustn't let them know he was approaching, oh, no.

It wasn't fair. Life was trying to cheat him again. Rob Michelle of her happiness. But not this time, he'd see to that. He wasn't going to be a victim any more.

He could hear the intruders moving about in the sacred room. They would die for profaning The King's Temple, they would.

He reached the bottom of the stairs, creeping cat-like towards the door.

"Let's look around," the male stranger said, his soft voice carrying through the partially open door.

Robles reached the wall as the door opened inward.

It happened so fast Beth didn't react until Jamie and the man were already on the floor.

Overwhelmed by photographing the images of Elvis, she didn't notice Jamie was still holding the statue in his right hand and only vaguely heard him say "We need to find Franks."

Then the door creaked and her head spun around. A hand wielding a knife sliced down out of the gloom, the blade penetrating Jamie's jacket at the shoulder. A man screamed as Jamie swung his right arm up in an arc, the statue of Elvis in his fist. But the sound of shattering plaster cut off his cry as his body fell against Jamie and both men fell to the floor.

Jamie groaned as Robles landed on top of him, air rushing from his lungs.

"I'm blind!" Robles screamed.

Beth gasped, a shriek of shock climbing up her throat, adrenalin jolting her body like an electric shock.

She screamed.

The man screamed again.

Jamie swung his right fist again, the broken body of Elvis still clenched between his fingers. The fist hit the man's jaw this time, the force thrusting his body off Jamie's chest.

As he rolled over, Beth saw the man's left eye was torn and bloody.

Jamie sat up like a zombie, his expression blank, the kitchen knife still jutting from his shoulder, and Beth screamed again.

"Shut up," he said calmly, punching his assailant in the face a third time.

Robles went limp.

Beth dropped her camera, a sharp thud echoing as it hit the floor.

Jamie dropped the broken Elvis statue and pulled the knife from his shoulder. He grunted as the bloody blade came free, then stumbled to his feet.

"Stay here. If he comes to, hit him with your camera."

Beth looked at him blankly, her mind unable to comprehend what she'd just seen.

Jamie walked slowly to the stairs and ascended like a somnambulist.

He discovered the girl's room first.

She was anorexic thin. Her pale skin and the dark shadows circling her sightless eyes painting her face like a death mask.

"Daddy? Daddy, are you okay? I heard you cry out."

Jamie grabbed the doorframe for support, suddenly aware of an incredible burning pain running the length of his arm.

"Daddy? What's wrong?" The girl tilted her head, listening.

"Elvis? Is that you?"

Jamie stumbled back into the hallway, his head reeling. The nerves where the knife penetrated his arm burned with pain as he pushed open the door next to the girl's room.

Except for piles of newspapers, it was empty.

He staggered to the hallway's end, falling against the door to the furthest room.

"Darren Franks, I presume," he said to the half-naked Elvis tied to the bed.

Jamie fainted.

October 5th, 1989

The day after a jury found George Robles not guilty by reason of insanity and the judge sentenced him to life in a cozy cell at Broadmoor, Jamie married Beth in a quiet ceremony at Hampstead Registry Office.

Now that the media circus was behind them, they had a lot to look forward to. A new house in Hampstead, bought by the £100,000 advance Collins had paid them for the book rights to their story. Jamie was working on a new novel. Beth had a show at a prestigious gallery in Chelsea. And she was expecting, although they'd already decided on tying the knot before they found out she was pregnant.

The tabloids, of course, had lapped the story up with relish. They hadn't had as much fun since the Joyce McKinney Mormon-in-chains sex and bondage soap opera in the '70s.

STAGE MANAGER KIDNAPPED ELVIS proclaimed *The Sun's* headline.

ELVIS OBSESSION LEADS TO TRAGEDY stated the more restrained *Daily Mirror*.

The lurid details kept the headline writers and gutter journalists busy for weeks.

Indeed, *The Sun* had offered them £30,000 each for their exclusive stories. But concerned he was going to lose the two aces which would ensure a major promotion, Malcolm Jones offered them a joint payment of £90,000. They accepted and Jamie got a promotion, too. Everyone was happy.

Except poor old George Robles, who wasn't, in fact, George Robles.

His real name was Arthur Robles, and this incident wasn't his first violent crime. At age 31, he'd been convicted of manslaughter after killing his mother in a fit of rage—accidentally, he claimed. Diagnosed then as mentally incompetent, he'd spent six years in a sanatorium where none of the doctors deduced the full extent of his illness—he had a split personality. George was the Other, and after Arthur was released, George took over.

The girl, Michelle, wasn't his daughter either. Her name was Alice Brady, an orphan he'd stolen from a home in Doncaster within months of his release and had raised in isolation since she was three years old. She was faring as well as could be expected now in a special clinic, not comprehending the reality of her situation. She wasn't a virgin, a fact *The Sun* had relished, and years of therapy lay ahead.

In sum, Robles' story was a complex web of psychotic delusion, obsession, and sordid tragedy, one which by turns both fascinated and depressed Jamie. At least he'd been able to forget about it while they honeymooned in Venice. But the holiday was over and it was time to return to work.

Jamie sat at the breakfast table reading *The Times* as he sipped his coffee. The news was the same. Thatcher crowed about inflation down to three percent. The Labour Party decried the unemployment figures. The SDP stated the obvious about social collapse in the North.

He yawned as Beth entered the kitchen, a pile of mail in her hand.

"A letter from Darren," she said as she sat beside him.

He smiled. The depth of his love for her surprised him sometimes; what they shared seemed almost unreal. He was lucky after all. Unlike Robles, who'd been abused by his mother and whose desperate need for love had forced him to kidnap a crippled teenage girl.

"What does he have to say?"

Darren had found God after his ordeal and was now a Baptist minister in Atlanta. Jamie could understand. A close call with death at the hands of a psychopath was enough to give anyone religion.

"My Dearest Jamie and Beth," she read aloud. "I have just learned that you wed recently and am overjoyed for you. The union of two fine young people is a wonderful thing. Cherish each other but do not forget to love Jesus Christ, Our Saviour. Only through Him will you know the beauty of God's plan for us all.

"Every day I thank God for delivering me from the sin of idolatry. This world is full of false gods, but there is only One True God—the Father of Our Lord. Elvis was just a man, as am I. And like Elvis, I now sing for Jesus. Do not forget that you, too, are God's instrument, that it was He who led you to free me from sin.

"Your friend in Jesus, Darren Franks."

Jamie smiled, placing a hand on Beth's swelling abdomen.

"Well, I guess we won't name him Elvis after all."

"Who said it's a he?" Beth replied with mock indignation.

"Besides, I thought we could call her Madonna."

Jamie laughed.

—*Atlanta, 1993. For Michael Zulli.*

PONCE DE LEON AVENUE

And nothing to look backward to with pride,
And nothing to look forward to with hope.
—Robert Frost, *The Death of the Hired Man*

The day the world learned Kurt Cobain had blown his brains out, my life changed forever.

I was sitting on the ragged couch in my one-room apartment digesting the news when a loud knock at the door startled me.

If Cobain couldn't cope with the fame, the adulation, the millions of Benjamins he'd made, fuck him. Loser asshole. He'd had everything I lacked—a rising career, money, a wife, and a baby; I was a man barely floating on a Dead Sea of debt, the weight of my credit cards so heavy, no amount of salt could keep me afloat.

I had no sympathy for him, just despised Kurt for the legacy he'd left his daughter.

I'd had to pawn my fax machine to pay last month's rent after I lost my job at the video store—not that the miserable $200 a week I'd been making there was enough to keep me alive. Between rent, utilities, and my monthly IRS payment plan, I was lucky if I had $20 left over for groceries. The phone had been disconnected two months ago. Not that it rang anymore. During the past week my diet had consisted of Ramen noodles and generic cigarettes.

I cautiously approached the door. Squinting through the eyehole, I broke out in a cold sweat. A football player-sized cop was standing on the other side with an ominous piece of paper in his hand. I opened the door.

"Dale Jackson?"

I nodded.

"Sergeant Mallory, DeKalb County Sheriff's department. Bad

news, son," he drawled, his Georgia accent molasses thick. "I'm here on behalf of Strauss Management. Got to give you this."

He handed me the paper.

"But why?" I asked as I read the fine print on the eviction notice. "I said I'd have the rest of the rent money by tomorrow." *If* the money I was owed for a short story sale, all $153 of it, finally arrived.

"Seems you're all out of promises, son."

"But I'm going to have it," I stressed, mentally cringing at the pleading in my tone.

"Management obviously feel you're a liability." The cop gave me a blank look.

"There's a truck an' boys from a moving company downstairs," he continued. "Company're willin' to pay rent on a storage space for a month while you get your life in gear. That's better 'an some folks get."

"*But—*"

He raised a hand as if he were going to slap me.

"Don't have time to argue, Mr. Jackson. Just start gettin' your stuff together. Them boys'll help you."

Two hours later, my minimal belongings shoved into boxes, I drove out of Arbordale Apartments for the last time, following the moving truck to a storage facility on Lawrenceville Highway.

I didn't have much. Abby had taken most of the furniture when she'd moved out at Christmas, and I told them to junk the old couch. Too many memories—some good, but mostly bad—hiding in its creaking springs, the stained cushions. Watching the moving men toss the sofa reminded me of an anecdote an old Hollywood stagehand once told me in Boardner's, a legendary dive bar for Tinseltown's fallen. Actress Elsa Lancaster came home one day to find her husband, the acclaimed actor Charles Laughton, butt-fucking some young wannabe on her favourite chaise lounge. Laughton was appalled his beloved beard had caught him *in flagrante*, but with delicate decorum, The Bride of Frankenstein had said nothing more than "don't worry, darling, we'll just get rid of the couch."

After the paid thugs had buried the bodies of my belongings in a space the size of my old bathroom, I collected the key from the front desk clerk and signed the paperwork.

Then I drove around for an hour, trying to think things through.

Like a homing pigeon, I found myself in Grant Park, pulling up outside Carl's ramshackle house. He was my only real friend in town, his dilapidated shotgun shack my primary refuge other than the dollar movie theatres out on Buford Highway and the bars I frequented in the Decatur area. I was certain I could live on his less memorable couch for a couple of days. My minimalist social life had revolved around Abby's friends, but Carl was my oasis in the desert of her pretentious yuppie social life. Beer and movies were the bricks and mortar which built the Carl and Dale friendship house. But seeing three cars in his driveway and two parked out front, my chest tightened. Two of the vehicles had out-of-state plates.

The front door was open and Carl, clad only in his boxer shorts, lounged in his favourite scuffed leather armchair nursing a PBR.

"What's up?" he said without looking up at me, his eyes glued to the TV set and whatever movie he was watching.

I sat down on the cat-clawed floral print couch, not knowing what to say. Carl's the kind of guy who's difficult to read sometimes. I'd known him for the twelve months I'd been back in Atlanta, returning from three miserable years in Hollywood with my tail between my legs. At least I'd still had some money then, enough to pay my bills and go out every night for a few brews and to shoot some pool, which is how we'd met. Carl tended bar and back then he'd been working at Dooley's over by Emory University. He was a movie junkie. Conversation was inevitable; friendship followed. But sometimes Carl closed up like an orchid, dense and secretive, as if you were a stranger. He had that look on his face.

"You heard about Kurt?" he said, sipping his beer, his eyes glued to Wilder's *The Lost Weekend*.

"Yeah," I replied, then paused. "Look, Carl . . . can I crash here a couple of days?"

He turned to me while onscreen Ray Milland fell apart from

whiskey withdrawal, begging money from the good-time girl whose heart he'd broken.

"Why?"

I explained what happened while he sipped his beer in silence, his eyes locked on the TV. Milland lost his balance down a flight of steps and woke up in the alcoholic ward.

When I finished reading my laundry list of woes, Carl finally paused the video.

"I'm sorry, man. No room at the inn. Gail's sister and her boyfriend are here for a week with their friend Lisa. The couch is taken, so's the floor. I don't have room to swing a cat. They arrived yesterday, and I'm already getting claustrophobic."

"I'll sleep in the bathtub."

He shook his head. "I told Gail to take 'em to Piedmont Park so I could have some space before I go to work."

I felt shitty for asking. His house was a tiny two-bedroom bungalow with a basement, and in addition to Gail, his long-term girlfriend, he had two roommates, Rob the gay violinist, and Steve, the moody skinhead who skulked in the cellar. It wasn't ideal, but Carl made his mortgage payments.

"Guess I'm not going to see that $100 anytime soon." It was a statement not a question. He'd loaned me the money to help pay last month's rent.

"That and the other $700," he continued, standing and heading towards the kitchen and another beer. "$800 over the last six months. I don't mind helping out a friend, but you've only paid back $300. Sure, you've had a tough year, but I'm not the International Monetary Fund."

Carl sat back down, idly scratched his balls, and popped the top on the fresh tall boy. I'd quit drinking at Christmas for both my physical and financial health—and as an effort to get Abby to stay. She claimed I got depressed when I drank; but it wasn't beer or scotch provoking my gloomy moods, it was life in general. I wished Carl would offer me a PBR, but I wasn't going to ask.

"What about your new book?"

"My agent said he couldn't sell a historical horror novel." I replied with a shrug. "He says the market's dead. Even if I'd turned the protagonist into a vampire. We've parted company."

I looked at the floor.

"You can park here and sleep in the car," he said, returning his attention to the movie.

"Thanks," I muttered.

I watched the movie for a couple of minutes.

While a fellow patient had a breakdown, Ray Milland escaped from the hospital and stole a bottle of scotch from a liquor store. Like audiences back in 1945, I'd never liked the film, even though it'd swept the Oscars that year. It was bleak, depressing, the last thing I needed to watch right then. Milland's character was a writer who'd shown great promise but had lost all self-confidence, trying to drown the pain in a sea of rye. Although I'd never hit that low, it still hit too close to home.

I stood up, trying to decide what to do next.

"The paper's on the table. You know where the phone is. Maybe you'll get lucky and find a place you can move into this week," Carl said, sipping his beer.

The conversation was over. Milland going through the DTs in his apartment was more important than me. Onscreen, Milland hallucinated a bat feasting on a mouse. His screams pricked my nerves like hot needles. I picked up *The Atlanta Constitution* and went out on the porch to thumb the want ads.

Five hours, three apartment complexes, and one room in a cobwebbed house later, I pulled my '85 red Honda Prelude into the parking lot of a strip mall on Clairmont Road, fighting the desire to scream, shout, or smash something. I hated rush-hour traffic in Atlanta. Too many cars on roads too small to accommodate them, and too many Goddamn stoplights. The car's engine was close to overheating. Sweat drenched my Blue Oyster Cult T-shirt like a blacksmith labouring over a forge, and the fuel gauge on my hope tank was close to empty. Having a shaky credit rating was bad enough, but the eviction was going to hover over me like an albatross.

None of the complexes would take me because I couldn't pass a preliminary credit check, and living with an elderly gay guy wasn't an option I relished—that's if he even said yes. His favourite phrase was "good references." If he called Arbordale to find out why I'd left, I had no chance.

I found a pool of shade and parked to let the engine cool. A liquor store across the street beckoned, its neon signs tempting me with magic names: *Budweiser, Coors, Rolling Rock, Sweetwater.* "No," I mumbled to myself. I'd been dry for nearly five months.

I hadn't had a serious problem with booze since my marriage fell apart four years ago, and then I'd only increased my intake to knock myself out. I'd been working two jobs during those manic days in New York, splitting my time between anonymously assistant-editing a line of sleazy stroke mags like *Toejammers, Big Cheeks,* and *Moist Mams* (for those with a lactation obsession) and copyediting a downtown fashion trend glossy. Outside of the time I was incarcerated with foot-fetish editors and art-fag critics, I wandered an emotional wasteland, my only companions a constant pint of Jim Beam and a six-pack of Rolling Rock as I sat at my PC writing short stories—thinly-veiled confessions and soul-search monologues that tried to expiate my sense of failure. Most were never finished; those that were didn't sell. Unlike Dylan Thomas, Brendan Behan, and all those others who had used alcohol to lubricate their muse's leathery cunt lips, when spit and jerking couldn't make the creative crown rise to the occasion, I couldn't write shit while exploring my cups. I drank to pass out. Every night for six months. To numb the pain. To hide from the emptiness. To sleep, perchance . . . but not to remember the dreams.

I burned out on the alcoholic abuse fast, about the same time I realized I couldn't read another illiterate letter from a foot fiend relating how he loved to eat the sweat-soaked insoles of his wife's spike-heeled pumps while she had his cock trussed up with clothesline. Then, as if I'd won the cosmic lottery, two weeks after I swore off perverts and sour mash, Fate (if She existed) intervened—a phone call, a plane ticket, and a hotel reservation. The Hollywood Whore, Miss Lady Los Angeles, came knocking at my door, my name whispered on her sweet seductive breath. . . .

I quit drinking cold turkey as soon as I knew the offer was real. Needed to have a sharp mind and a razor wit for all those power breakfasts in the Valley and expense account lunches/dinners at The Four Seasons and Mr. Chow. Right?

That was another lifetime ago. And more fucking fool me.

While I hadn't drunk like that in years, I had imbibed steadily during the time I was with Abby. Only two or three beers a day, wine with dinner—my two glasses to every one of hers—a snifter of Cognac before bed. I was never drunk—buzzed, yes, sir—but I never went a day without drinking, even when money was short. As surely as all that booze was eating away at my liver, the accumulation eroded our relationship as relentlessly as a sandstorm weathers rock.

I started walking towards the liquor store.

Abby stared forlornly at me through the gossamer mist of recent memory as I strode straight for the nearest cooler case, removing a six-pack of Corona. Abby-of-the-mind said nothing, but her eyes sang sad songs. They fell on deaf ears as I maintained a steady pace towards the cash register.

"Pint of Jim," I said as I slapped down a twenty on the counter.

The clerk turned, humming an old Allman Brothers tune. In my pocket, my right hand fingered the other four crisp twenties—my emergency money I'd stashed in a first edition of Stephen King's *The Stand*, natch. One hundred dollars, me, and a liquor store. Whichever way you spelled it—M-O-O-N—it meant trouble.

The Star Bar in Little Five Points was stuffed to the gills at 11 PM as a local, shitfaced cowpunk band belted out a cover of Jason and the Scorchers' "Broken Whiskey Glass." Mine wasn't cracked, but it was empty and that was a crime. Offended by this capital offense, I waved to Tim, the barman, to bring me another Beam—my seventh shot since I'd staggered through the door three hours earlier.

My Jewish mother voice of reason nagged me about falling off the wagon, told me I should've bought a Sprite and headed to a movie theatre to cool off in the air-conditioned darkness instead of fucking Pandora's pussy and opening her box by buying a six-pack of beer. The old punk voice of anguish told her to shut the fuck up as I laid another twenty on the scarred wood and thanked Tim as he delivered my drink.

On stage, the shitty band was now murdering my favourite Merle Haggard song.

Fuck 'em. I'd kill the bastards if they killed an old Kris Kristofferson tune.

I sucked down the shot as the shitbags on the stage destroyed "My Past Is My Present."

Oh, yeah, that was real funny . . .

Next to me a drunken grunge couple were drowning their sorrows over Kurt's suicide. The girl was the kind of whiny pseudo-post-hippie chick who made me puke—pretending to be part Patti Smith with a slice of Joni Mitchell, the illusion ruined by her deliberately unwashed Stevie Nicks hair. And the filthy Afghan coat gave away that she was the cum-stain of stoned hippie parents.

Yet . . . *fuggit* . . . I had to admit, I had been thinking about the bastard all night. Like the other ten million who had snapped up Nirvana's "Nevermind" as they broke big, I'd enjoyed his raspy music, but I could never buy into the whole rock-star-as-messiah rap the media had laid on him, all that spokesperson-for-a-generation crap. At thirty two, I was already too cynical for that shit. My love of contemporary music was fast wearing out like over-played vinyl. Gimme Merle or Kris or The Ruts any day.

The asswipe band finished the set to underwhelming applause. If they dared an encore, I might have to make all four of 'em squeal "SUU—EEEE" like Ned Beatty in *Deliverance*. Meanwhile, whiny Grunge Baby sobbed beside me.

"Why did he do it?" she blubbered into her glass of Bud. Her "sensitive" boyfriend hugged her, tears in his eyes.

"I don't know," he sobbed. "Kurt, why did you leave us?"

Christ! Much more of this and I was going to kill myself.

I lit another cigarette and tried to learn to forget.

The last year, silence was really the only sound I sought. Then the fucking band came back on stage and started to deconstruct The Stones' "Paint It Black."

I tossed my cigarette in Sensitive Boy's beer mug and leaned in to the weepy couple's clinch.

"He was a fucking coward and a loser!" I bellowed over out of tune guitars. "He had no fucking balls. Or maybe that cunt groupie he married had him killed!"

I stormed out of the bar, and that's when the shit began.

I didn't expect Mr. Sensitivity to come after me, but the asshole did, rushing me as I exited The Star Bar.

He laid a hand on me, and I turned. Seeing it was wimpy boy, I swung and punched him in the ribs. The bastard tried to knee me in the balls.

I hit the fucker in the face.

His bitch of a girlfriend came out of nowhere, screaming at me, and hit me in the head. Instinctively, I did something I had never done and would never, ever have conceived of doing—I hit a woman.

I punched the screaming Harpy in the face. Not hard—I think I instinctively pulled my punch—but hard enough to make her head jerk back.

Then the bouncer rushed in. He was a bruiser who could have been Henry Rollins' little brother.

I shoved Mr. Sensitivity into his howling girlfriend, and the two of them went back into the bouncer, then the three of them went down in a threesome of tangled limbs—and I ran for my car.

I pulled out of my parking space and sped up Moreland Avenue. A glance in the rear-view mirror showed the grunge babies and the bouncer were looking for me but didn't realize I'd just driven by.

Then a police car appeared, and I nearly hit a telegraph pole in panic. I dropped speed to the legal limit, barely breathing. The last thing I needed was another DUI; an arrest would mean at least a month in jail, and I didn't think Carl would bail me out even if I had the money to make bond.

The police car shot past me, heading down Moreland. Then a fire truck appeared around the corner with Ponce de Leon Avenue, and its siren went on. Then another police car.

I kept to the speed limit. I didn't want any more trouble. Despite the adrenalin pumping through me due to the fight, I could tell I was too drunk to drive safely.

I turned slowly onto Ponce, my favourite Atlanta street—a heady mix of seediness and splendour—and headed east towards Decatur as if I was returning to Arbordale and my old apartment.

Man, I was fucked up.

I needed to pull over somewhere and sleep off the booze.

Planned by Frederick Law Olmsted as the centerpiece of a neighbourhood with the occult-sounding title of Druid Hills, this section of Ponce de Leon winded in sensuous curves past panoramic parks and stately mansions, dating back to the 1920s or earlier and many designed by Atlanta's legendary architects Neel Reid and Philip Trammell Shutze. I wasn't interested in their glamorous exteriors but rather their long, secluded driveways where I could hide. I found one with an ivy-draped stone wall that looked like it would work and slowly drove in the open wrought-iron gate. The Tudor-style house was dark; two cars, a black Mercedes and a red Miata, parked out front. Whoever lived here had turned in, I hoped, as I pulled under a large oak tree. I turned off the engine and the lights. The Prelude's dashboard clock showed 11:53 PM. My hands were shaking, my heart trip-hammering. But within a minute, I was asleep.

Kurt Cobain was laughing.

"It doesn't matter; no one gets out alive," he said, applying lipstick to his cracked, bleeding lips. He was wearing a dirty wedding dress and looked like a silent movie star. We were standing in the middle of a muddy pasture. The landscape was flat and seemed to go on forever.

"Let me tell you the secret," he whispered.

Somewhere, a woodpecker began banging on a tree. I wanted it to stop. I wanted to hear the secret, but the woodpecker kept banging.

Banging. Banging. Banging.

Kurt laughed and started to run away. I wanted to follow but as I looked down I saw my feet were trapped in mud.

"What?" I cried after him. "I don't understand?"

The woodpecker banged louder.

I opened my eyes, wincing. Disoriented. Bright sunlight stabbed my pupils.

A California surfer was rapping on the Prelude's side window. My neck cracked as I twisted in the seat.

"Out of the car. Now."

Caught between the vividness of the dream and the cold shower of reality, I blinked, mouth open in slack-jawed incomprehension.

Where was I?

My eyes focused on the half-timbered and brick house behind him, and memory kicked in. But my reactions were obviously too slow for this male beach bimbo with his long, blond curls who was now grabbing at the door handle. It was locked.

"Out! *Now!*"

I opened the door but before I could climb out, he yanked me by the back of the neck and nearly launched me into a nearby tree.

"Hey!" I shouted. "I can explain—"

The son of a rancid cunt squeezed my throat, choking the life out of me. I would have punched his mutherfucking lights out, but he had my right wrist locked and was doing some martial arts move on me which hurt so bad I screamed like a little bitch.

"You think that hurts?" he snarled. "Wait until I really put some pressure on you."

The pain was so intense I puked all over the driveway.

Mr. Surfer Muscles jabbed his knee into my ribs. It hurt like Hell. I wanted to kill the cunt, but I was in so much pain I was powerless even to raise a hand or hit the piece of shit in the face.

"Try anything and you'll regret it," he said, suddenly calm.

One hand on my neck, the other still threatening to wrench my arm from its socket, he marched me up the driveway and around the side of the house.

The pain and booze residue kicked in, and I vomited again. One, two, three deep retches—a painful gag of bile and alcohol.

"You disgusting pig!" Mr. Muscles said, then slammed my head against the wall of the house.

He dragged me towards the back of the mansion. I was hurting so bad, he could have dragged me to Hell and left me there.

"I'm sorry," I mumbled. "All I wanted was—"

The SOB kicked me in the ribs, slapping my angry consciousness back into my still somewhat confused head. All I knew was I now really wanted to kill this bastard.

But all I could do was let the piece of shit haul me around the back of the mansion. I could barely lift a hand.

The kitchen door was open, and the deceptively lilting sound of women laughing confused my fragmented consciousness.

As my captor dragged me in, two girls in their early twenties wearing loosely fastened silk robes glanced up with glazed eyes from a long wooden kitchen table. Dawn's early luminescence divided the room into squares of light and shade like a chessboard. A strong scent of weed suggested they were stoned rather than drunk, and a mirror, razorblade, traces of coke, and other drug paraphernalia confirmed the fact that they were high from more than marijuana.

Beach Boy pushed me down into a chair.

"Leave," he said, nodding at the coke. "And take that with you."

"Can't we watch, Mickey?" the blonde one asked, deliberately pulling her robe halfheartedly together in mock modesty. It slid open further to reveal small, perfect breasts crowned with raspberry nipples.

"He's no fun," commented the redhead, taking a deep drag off the joint held between her long, manicured nails.

"Don't damage him, Mickey. He's cute," the blonde giggled, smiling at me as she stood, one hand touching a breast before pulling the robe closed. She sashayed out of the kitchen, leaving the redhead to gather their stash.

In ten seconds, I'd seen more female flesh than in the previous five months. The only pussy that had slept in my bed was my cat, and even Suki had run away. After Abby walked out, I made halfhearted attempts at meeting girls in bars, but the cute ones were taken and big chicks didn't set my world on fire.

"Please . . . take your hand off me," I said, trying not to let my voice crack. "This is all a big mistake. I—"

"Who is he?"

A tall guy in a silk suit which probably cost more than six months' rent at Arbordale stood in the doorway through which the girls had vanished. His jet black hair was precisely styled, but the paint stripes of gray at the temples gave him the appearance of a raccoon. George Hamilton would have envied his hair, and the authoritative tone his body language spoke belonged to a senator. Or a Mafia don.

"Don't know," Mickey Muscles replied

"Search him."

Before Mickey, who belonged in a Steve Reeves *Hercules* flick, could put his plate-sized paws on me again, I stood, hands half-raised. The apologetic position was the wrong move. Mr. Silk Suit's right hand darted under his jacket, producing a gun.

"Wait! It's okay. I'm going to get out my wallet, okay?"

"Don't move. Michael will remove it."

"Okay. *Okay!*"

Mickey—Michael, Samson, whatever his fucking name was—nearly tore the pocket from my frayed jeans, flipping the battered wallet open to my driver's license as he thrust me back in the chair.

"Dale Jackson."

He thumbed through the rest, not that there was much—my social security card, some old receipts, and my last dollars.

"Who sent you?" Silk Suit cocked the gun.

"Hey, hey, put that thing down, will you? There's no need for that." I said.

"Look, I was driving home late last night, but I was too drunk and pulled over—"

Mickey's hand shot across my face.

"Who sent you? Who're you working for?"

I couldn't answer between the pain and the blood in my mouth.

"If you don't start talking by the time I count to three . . ."

"One . . ."

I held up a hand in surrender as I massaged my jaw.

"Two . . ."

Mr. Silk Suit advanced, slipping the safety off.

"John! Where are you? I want breakfast. I want a mimosa!" A woman's voice called out from close by, throwing Silk Suit's arithmetic off.

"John! I want champagne. And *strawberries*."

The voice grew louder, then a glamorous woman with sleep-teased black hair, wearing only a diaphanous negligee which left nothing to the imagination, appeared in the doorway. Silk Suit concealed the gun, annoyance creasing the angles of his face.

"Oh, we have a visitor. Why didn't you tell me, John? Well, don't stand there, fetch some champagne and let's all retire to the lounge."

She wrinkled her nose at the mess in the kitchen. The counters were strewn with empty bottles: Stoli vodka, Cristal champagne, Campbell's tomato juice, and various imported beers. Someone had spilled caviar on the stove. Lifestyles of the rich and unknown.

Maybe. There was something familiar about the woman, a flash of recognition which cut through my pain, fear, and surprise.

She looked to be in her early forties but had obviously tried to preserve a younger image. I knew a nose job and collagen injections when I saw them. The raven hair was pure Sophia Loren, the bee-stung lips Kim Basinger. My three years in L.A. had exposed me to enough boob jobs, butt lifts, anal bleaching, liposuction, tucks, and folds to qualify me for medical school.

Hollywood . . .

There was a connection somewhere, but my booze-bruised brain couldn't find it.

"Michael, darling, please don't tell me we're out of straw-berries," she continued, completely unfazed by my presence and unembarrassed by the fact I could see every inch of her ripe, well-toned, café au lait skin. "If the girls ate them all last night, I'll be mad as hell."

The inflection was studied English, but her affectation couldn't hold water any more than a colander.

"Come! *Come!*" she chirped. "Let's all get comfortable."

"John, a bottle of the Dom, please."

With that she disappeared into the hallway.

Mr. John-fucking-silk-suit gave me a disgusted look, then turned to Mickey.

"Do what she says." His tone was laced with frustration and a touch of humiliation.

As I approached the hallway, he laid a heavy hand on my shoulder, his blue eyes as cold as a morgue slab.

"Don't speak unless she addresses you."

I raised an eyebrow. He said nothing more. Behind us, I heard Mickey open the fridge.

The hallway was long and narrow and opened into a lounge that belonged in a Bel Air mansion. Someone had spent a shitload of money having the interior of the house rebuilt to self-indulgent specifications. But when I saw the framed movie posters hanging above the double-sized Victorian fireplace, my mouth opened.

Could it be? No, it was too big a stretch of the imagination. Yet there was a definite resemblance to the actress whose face looked down on us from the posters—if you added ten years and major plastic surgery.

As I turned, she took off the sunglasses, and my pulse increased. Was I about to drink Dom Perignon mimosas with Lana Hall—*the* Lana Hall who was hot-tipped to win the 1980 Best Actress Oscar for her role in *All That Jive*, directed by Brian G. Hutton, whose career crashed the week before the awards ceremony due to a tragic scandal? *The* Lana Hall who had disappeared off the face of the earth after suffering a complete breakdown following the damning publicity.

Yet here she was, sitting in an over-sized lounge no more than a couple of miles from my old apartment. Unbelievable.

Jesus H. fucking Christ in an Elvis pantsuit! How many times as a teenager had I jacked off to her explicit photo spread in *Qui* magazine? Lana Hall had been my favourite B-movie queen. I adored and worshiped her more than Linda Hayden or the late Claudia Jennings and Soledad Miranda. The woman had fuelled enough teenage erotic fantasies to power two Apollo moon missions. When you're fourteen, don't have a girlfriend and masturbate four times a day, Lana Hall was *the* Goddess I would have readily sacrificed myself on the altar of Teen Want.

"Sit with me," she said, smiling shyly, lightly patting the space next to her. Like a good dog, I obeyed, but faced front, eyes still glued on those posters.

Lana Hall?!

The aroma of money lurked behind her musky perfume—*Obsession*—and I started to mentally salivate. No wonder the Two Stooges had been so rough on me; discovering the whereabouts of Miss Hall made *Lifestyles of the Rich and Famous* locating Betty Page anticlimactic. This was a *real* story.

"I'm sorry, we haven't been introduced, *Mister*?"

The fake English accent and gentile attitude nearly made me come in my dirty jeans.

"Dale Jackson," I replied, taking a mimosa from Mickey the Beach Bimbo.

John Silk Suit continued to stand with his arms crossed near the main hallway.

"And you're here for an autograph, Mr. Jackson?"

I hesitated, looking to Silk Suit for direction, but he was as expressive as Mount Rushmore.

I cleared my throat, took a sip of mimosa, struggling to say something. Was I meant to know who she was? If so, didn't that defeat the disappearing trick?

"What do you do, Mr. Jackson?"

"Dale. Dale's fine."

I dared turn to look her in the eyes, more out of the nervous need to figure out what to say than to be intimate.

"I'm a writer."

Silk Suit visibly bristled at the "w" word.

Lana Hall paused beside me, toying with her champagne glass.

The silence thickened like Georgia humidity, sticky and cloying, and my stomach clenched. Maybe I should have said I was a plumber. But knowing my luck she would have asked me to fix the john.

Mickey saved the moment, returning with a big bowl of strawberries. He gave a slight, obsequious bow, and Lana Hall smiled.

"And what do you write?" she inquired, delicately plucking a fat strawberry from the pile. It hovered over her blossoming lips as she leaned towards me, awaiting my answer. For such a generous mouth, the tongue that appeared to lick the berry's coarse skin was surprisingly small and delicate.

"Fiction. Novels. Screenplays."

The silence resumed. I wasn't going to list my journalistic triumphs—that might push Silk Suit's panic button. Maybe I'd already said the wrong thing. She looked away, staring out the enormous arched window, then snapped her fingers so suddenly I nearly dropped my drink. Mickey came over with a gold cigarette case, removed one, placed it in a black holder and passed it to Lana, then lit it for her.

She asked the question I'd been dreading

"What movies did you write?"

I didn't want to list my credentials. The two screenplays I'd written which actually made it direct to video were so bad I'd changed my credit. I wasn't going to confess to a former Oscar contender that Dale Jackson was responsible for *Strip Bar Slaughter* or *Roller Blade Babes Go to Hell*. Pat Hoby IV wrote those.

"Most of my projects got stuck in development limbo, but I did a number for the majors. Two for Warners. Three for Fox. Scorsese hired me to develop *The Outer Limits* into a feature."

I wasn't exactly lying, just tweaking the truth. I'd only ever been hired once to write a first draft, and that was an adaptation of my first novel, all the other had been "story by" credits and ultimately meaningless since none of the projects made it into the second round of development. All I received were peanuts for the pitches. I had actually met with Scorsese—along with six others—but the project was cancelled before anyone was hired.

Lana Hall said nothing. She inhaled languidly on her cigarette, a Balkan Sobrane Black Russian. I hadn't seen anyone smoke those in years, the rich tobacco aroma tormenting me. Months of smoking generic light 100s was like a prison diet of bread and water.

"Dale. *Dale Jackson*." She turned her full attention to me, carefully examining every line of my face like I was an insect under an entomologist's magnifying glass.

"What novels have you written?"

Before I could answer, she straightened up, her emerald green eyes glowing with fervour.

"You wrote *Mad Dogs*—"

"*And Englishmen*," I interjected with delight. "That's me. It was my first."

Lana Hall placed her cigarette in a marble ashtray and grasped my left hand in hers. What remained of my eternal teenage heart leapt. She'd made me cry with her performance as Blanche in Sidney Lumet's remake of *A Street Car Named Desire* and sent my testosterone level soaring in Bertolucci's *Tropic of Capricorn*.

"I loved that book," she said, breathlessly. "It was a real page-turner. And the sex scenes . . . descriptions don't usually turn me on . . . but those—the scene where Tom and Melissa make love on the mountain. . . ."

Imagine Robert Ludlum written in the style of Jackie Collins. That was *Mad Dogs* and *Englishmen*. But it had taken me to Hollywood and more money than I'd ever seen. Not millions, only a little over $200,000. And between the IRS and my ex-wife, I didn't get to enjoy much of it.

"*What are you laughing at?*"

Lana's face twisted from happy child to wicked stepmother. The accusation was aimed at Mickey, who was trying to stifle a snicker.

"*Get out*. Both of you," she said calmly. Only her trembling top lip betrayed her. "Dale and I have a lot to talk about. Bring more champagne and leave us alone."

Mickey looked at John Silk Suit. His eyes narrowed in Beach Bum's direction. An almost imperceptible nod. Mickey stiffened and went to the kitchen. It wasn't difficult to tell who was the bitch in that relationship.

"What are you working on now?" she asked, her tone that of a fan.

"A screenplay," I nearly choked. "Then . . . erm . . . a new novel."

"Oh, really?" She leaned forward, almost kissing my ear. "Tell me about it . . . please?"

At that point, I almost blew a wad in my boxers.

It was true.

Every. Word.

Only the screenplay was a favour to an old friend who was promising a grand out of his own pocket and planned to shoot it—a post-apocalyptic vampire flick—on Super 16 for $90,000. Real classy. As for a new novel, well, I had plenty of ideas but no faith any of them would sell—especially after I'd been dumped by my agent.

Mickey returned with a second ice bucket containing another bottle of Dom Perignon. Then he and John Silk Suit left us alone.

"You do know who I am, don't you?" she whispered.

I didn't notice it then, but later, as summer's salad days were well beyond their sell-by date, it came back to me, and I realized— *understood*— the fear and confusion behind such a seemingly innocuous, almost embarrassed question. At the time it didn't register. Lana exuded heat—a chemical warmth, pure charisma airborne on potent pheromones. Intoxicating. Irresistible. And her breath—a sweet mélange of strawberries, champagne, and Balkan tobacco. Exotic. Seductive. It was absinthe to my senses.

Swallowing, my mouth and throat suddenly dry, I nodded.

"Let me tell you something," she said, standing and starting to pace the elaborate weave of an Indian rug.

"The stories aren't true; real life isn't the plot of a movie. . . ."

She drifted off into reverie, ceased pacing with the frustration of a caged bird, stared out the windows.

I waited for her to continue.

And waited.

Unable to resist temptation, I plucked a Black Russian from the case. My taste buds began to dance and sing as I inhaled.

"After the investigation . . . I left the country . . . it . . ."

I waited, slowly savouring the cigarette.

Lana Hall rotated towards me, dipped, almost a curtsy, gently took my left hand. Sat beside me. Paused. Then:

"I'm about to make a comeback. I've been trying to write a book, a novel . . . we'll sell it, and the screen rights. A package—book and screenplay. It'll open wide . . . Ovitz and I have been talking. Warners wants it. But . . ."

That delicious-looking little tongue ran across the budding lower lip.

"You *will* help me write it, won't you?"

"It's your book. I don't do ghost work." I said.

"I mean a collaboration."

Her slender fingers caressed the back of my hand as she leaned closer, those lips so near. . . .

Lana Hall tensed, drew back, but continued to hold my hand.

"You can read what I've written. It's not much but—if you like it . . . I'm not a very good writer . . . we can throw out what I've done so far, start all over." The pitch of her voice rose as her childlike excitement grew.

"Well—"

"Say you will. Please."

"I'm kind of busy," I said, savouring the cigarette. "Other contracts—"

"Whatever they're paying you, I'll double it."

"I'd like to take a look at it before I make a commitment."

She dropped my hand, poured champagne, and refilled our glasses.

Everything was wrong with the picture. A former Hollywood B-movie starlet who had almost made it to the A level, living a reclusive fantasy in Atlanta of all places, having a champagne and strawberry breakfast with a washed-up writer who'd passed out in her driveway and trying to persuade him to work with her on a comeback.

It certainly wasn't what you'd call a normal pitch meeting. The two gay minders, the pair of stoned sex kittens, a kitchen overflowing with enough empty booze bottles to have entertained half the Marines at Fort Bragg. And the movie star was pitching the writer. I tried not to laugh. The situation reminded me of the old joke—*you hear about the Polish actress? She slept with the writer.* But there was a story here—not whatever she was planning as comeback, if such were possible—and somehow I had stumbled into it.

"You *will* make a commitment, won't you, Mr. Jackson?"

"I . . ."

She raised her glass in toast. I responded. We drank.

I couldn't argue. This was too good to be true. Goddamn, there was a story here.

"I'll have Michael go bring your typewriter, word processor— whatever you prefer to work on and any books—other things you like to surround yourself with when you work."

"Wait a minute. You want me to move in?"

I put my glass down on the onyx coffee table and looked her straight in the eyes.

"Of course. Until the book is done. We can work without interruptions. I'll see to it your every need is catered for. Your favourite foods, drink—whatever you need to arouse your muse."

Before I could argue, she picked up a small silver bell from the table. It rang like fine crystal, and a moment later Mickey Muscles appeared.

"Michael, be a dear and tell Sunny and Paris to go make up a room for Mr. Jackson. He'll be staying with us for a few weeks."

Mickey tensed at the news, but if Lana Hall noticed, she ignored the fact.

"Once his room is ready, show him up. He'll instruct you where to go to pick up his things, and ask John to come see me when I'm alone."

Mickey nodded politely, his nostrils flaring like a bull ready to charge a toreador.

She turned to me.

"It's so nice to have company—*other company*—for a change. I'm thrilled you're here, Mr. Jackson."

"Dale's fine."

"I take it Mr. Monteleone arranged your visit?"

I looked blank, trying to think up a plausible explanation as to how and why I'd arrived on her doorstep. I didn't have a clue who this Monteleone was, although the name bore a faint familiarity. She took my silence as an affirmative, saving me the indignity of a lie.

"Larry's such a sweet man. I don't know what I'd have done without his support for the last few years. . . ." She drifted off into another reverie. Whether it was champagne-induced or a neurological problem, I couldn't figure. She obviously wasn't firing on all cylinders. Maybe that would work to my advantage.

"Let's start, shall we?" she said suddenly, as if snapping out of a hypnotic trance, and stood. "I'll get the manuscript and you can start reading while the girls get your room ready."

She drifted out of the room on a cloud of *Obsession*.

This was getting weirder and weirder by the minute. I felt like Alice down the rabbit hole or Judy when the world went Technicolor and she woke up in Oz.

A hand on my shoulder made me jump.

Mickey leaned over the couch to push his face close to mine.

"Your room's ready, *Mr. Jackson*."

The hallway leading from the lounge was as wide as my old bedroom, and the walls were crowded with framed photographs— Lana Hall with King Vidor; Lana with Clint Eastwood; Lana at this cocktail party, that event; Lana on a dozen different locations. Holy relics in a shrine to the past.

The hall opened into an impressive entrance lobby complete with curving staircase and ornately carved oak banisters. As we crossed the tiled floor, Mickey looked over his shoulder to see if I was following; his sour expression said I wasn't moving fast enough.

At the top of the stairs, we went to the right, down an avenue of doors. The house had more bedrooms than Mickey appeared to have IQ points.

He stopped, turned, and gestured towards one of them.

I muttered a strained "thanks" and started to go inside, but he suddenly he grabbed me, slamming my back against the wall, one of his blue plate special-sized hands around my throat, the other squeezing my crotch.

"*You don't belong here*," he hissed through clenched teeth. He hadn't been taking care of his oral hygiene.

"I don't know what you're up to, or why Lana wants you here, but don't forget—*you don't belong here*—and I'll be watching every move you make."

Both hands squeezed.

"Got that?"

He let me go slowly. My balls and windpipe were grateful.

"The girls are waiting for you," he said with a lipstick trace of contempt. Whether it was for me or the girls or all of us, I couldn't tell.

And didn't care.

I entered the room.

I wasn't expecting a fully-equipped spa and sauna.

The girls—I guessed *Sunshine* was the blonde, *Paris* the redhead—sat naked on a waterproof massage table equipped with a large hand controlled shower attachment. Behind them was a sunken oriental-style bath. To my right was a pine sauna room and plunge pool.

"I'm glad you're staying," chirped Sunny. "It'll be nice to have a new playmate."

Paris gave me a polite yet unenthusiastic smile, moved her hand from between Sunny's tanned thighs and slid off the massage table.

"Welcome to the house of dick-less men," Paris said.

They switched on the shower and started to wash me down, their experienced fingers teasing sensation from every muscle.

Sometime later—much later—after they had cleaned every inch, every nook and cranny of my sweat-stained body, dried me, massaged my stiff joints, I was as clean as a nun's habit, but my mind was stained like semen-coated sheets.

Then, when I thought it was over, Sunny dragged me to bed.

She sucked me, fucked me, and rode me hard. By the time she

decided she'd had enough of my body, I was hurting, drained.

Shell-shocked, I slept.

The sleep of the Damned.

Someone traced the shape of my cheeks with manicured fingers, drawing me up from the depths of a dreamless sleep. I smiled and sighed, my eyes closed, remembering Sunny's touch as I remained lying face down on the bed. Then something started to probe. It wasn't a finger; it didn't belong to Sunny. It was cold and hard. I gasped, tensing.

My eyes snapped open. John Silk Suit was standing over me, a sardonic smirk on his lips.

"Okay, stud, it's time we talked."

He removed the gun, placed it on the nightstand, and sat beside me. I wasn't homophobic, but his proximity was unsettling considering I'd just received an anal probe from a 9mm weapon.

"I made some calls," he said softly, "and you are who you say you are. But I want to know what you're doing here. How did you find Lana?"

I hesitated. Then I told him the truth. All of it. And prayed he'd believe me, as incredible as it sounded.

After I finished, he was silent for a minute. Then he gave a hollow chuckle.

"Well, for a loser, you just got lucky. At least for the next few weeks. I've discussed the situation with Mr. Monteleone and he's decided you should stay. Thinks you might be able to do her some good."

"How?"

"Work with her on that book she's been obsessing about. Then, when it's done, turn it into a screenplay. Give her something to think about. Maybe try to discourage her from drinking so much. After that, we'll see."

"Is it for real?" I asked.

"The book? She's been trying for months."

"No. The comeback."

"We'll see," he said.

"She's . . ." I hesitated, choosing my words carefully. "Not quite with it, is she?"

"No," he said softly. "She's a lot better now than she was for a long time, though."

His face softened, his tone weighted with sadness.

"Lana's fragile. Even if we could get her to stop drinking . . . there's been a lot of damage done. . . ."

He trailed off, then stood, his expression suddenly hardening like cement, uncomfortably aware he'd let his guard down.

"Now, house rules. One, don't even think of touching her. The girls will take care of that.

"Two, you'll call whoever you need to, tell them you're going out of town for a couple of months. Give them this number if they need to call you."

He produced a piece of paper from his pocket and placed it on the bedside table

"It's a voicemail service. But any calls you make from the house will be under my supervision—"

"But—"

"No buts," he said, picking up the gun.

"Now get dressed and come downstairs. It's time for you to start earning your keep."

"Do I have a choice?" I said, sitting up, pulling the tangled black silk sheet over my groin.

"No. Sounds to me like you didn't have any to start with."

I retired to bed as midnight approached, worn out by Lana's nonstop chatter.

Sunny was waiting for me, dressed in a slinky Twenties-style sequined dress and nothing else. She was disappointed when I declined her offer for a repeat performance—and I was sorely tempted (with the accent on *sorely*)—but she had other options for entertainment and wasn't offended by my refusal.

"If you change your mind later, I'm just down the hall," she said, kissing my cheek as her right hand gave my tender John Thomas a light squeeze beneath the black silk pants I was wearing—one of several gifts already bestowed upon me by my overly generous hostess.

Lana Hall was a woman obsessed with many things, silk being one of them. Aside from the cotton T-shirts and surfing shorts Mickey favoured, standard attire in the Hall household consisted of either leather, lace, or silk, with the latter predominating.

I undressed and donned a black kimono—silk, of course. And propped myself up on the circular bed with the black—naturally—silk sheets, her manuscript beside me. A black marble ashtray and a white ivory cigarette box had been placed on the nightstand during my absence. Fishing inside, I found forty Black Russians. I lit one and looked up at my reflection in the mirrored ceiling. All I needed was a pipe and a Pepsi to complete my transformation into Hugh Heffner, Jr.

I laughed at the absurdity of it all. But I had a hundred serious questions rolling around my champagne-fuzzed head.

What had happened? The vanishing act after the scandal, the crushing publicity, and a shattered career were understandable. Had she been in Atlanta all these years? Who was the mysterious Mr. Monteleone? What strange twist of fate had brought me here?

I didn't believe in destiny, but the probability of me stumbling into her fantasy world was more than my math-deficient mind could calculate.

There was also the fact that in agreeing to collaborate with her on the novel/screenplay package I had apparently made a deal. In return for luxury and a place to live, I had given up my freedom. Johnny Suit hadn't told me that fine print when he'd initially laid down the letter of the law. Not only was it forbidden for me to use the phone without either him or Mickey Muscles present, but also I learned after dinner, I wasn't allowed out of the house without an escort. Even then, my reasons for leaving had been reduced to zero. Mickey would check my post office box twice a week. Mickey did the shopping, be it for groceries, videos, or any other necessities. He was going to remove my belongings from storage tomorrow.

When writing about Ponce De Leon Avenue, local author George Mitchell had described the street as having the character of a southern woman, unusually warm-hearted but tough and gritty. He was writing about the two-mile stretch which started at Peachtree Street downtown and ran to Moreland Avenue, and if his metaphor reflected the cheap hookers who sold their wares there, then the wealthy, curvaceous section of Ponce where Lana lived in her fantasy world was a Prince's courtesan. When the Prelude cruised into the driveway, I'd landed right between her thighs. Now her legs were closed and she had me in a head-lock.

I wasn't hot on the situation, but as John stated earlier, before I arrived here, I didn't have any real choices either.

Picking up Lana's badly-typed manuscript, I pondered fame and success, obscurity and failure. Either extreme could become a prison. Some bad choices on my part had blown my chance of securing solid ground in Hollywood—the wrong agent, insufficient advice, the seductive lure of big money corrupting artistic honesty. Yet so much of success is pure luck, something I'd had little of in my life. Or do we, in true Shakespearian tragedy, sow the seeds of our own destruction?

Lana's attempt at a currently untitled novel turned out to be *Macbeth* meets *The Player*, with a touch of *Blood Simple*. Ambitious executive at top agency, goaded by an even more ambitious wife, murders the head of the company so he can inherit the throne of power, framing a rising actress who's been having an affair with his former boss. The scandal destroys her career, but the executive is then blackmailed by the former gay lover of the deceased CEO, who covets both the ass and the power of the executive. The wife, now paranoid, discovers the plot but is under the belief her husband plans to kill her in partnership with the gay guy. She murders the husband, and writes a damning letter implicating the gay lover. Or something like that.

It went on and on and made no sense. It could be a big page-turner but needed a lot of work. Therapy pieces often do. And Lana wasn't a very good writer. I was definitely going to earn my keep—every cent of the $2,000 a week she'd promised.

Giggles and splashing outside distracted my attention. Looking out the window, I saw Sunny and Paris indulging in Sapphic games in the hot tub next to the pool.

Tired, but not sleepy, I decided to go liberate a bottle of brandy from the bar downstairs.

The house had everything. An indoor and outdoor pool. A gym. A den filled with abandoned pinball and arcade games. A fully-stocked Art Nouveau cocktail lounge. A home theatre containing state-of-the-art equipment. A library overflowing with classics and junk fiction. Judging by the dust coating the serious literature, they were touched as much as the pinball machines.

As I approached the bar, I heard gunfire and screams coming from the theatre where earlier, after dinner, Lana had insisted we watch *Red Wind*, the movie which had broken her out of TV in the late '60s.

I cracked opened the door. Onscreen Eddy Ventura emptied a gun into the body of his film father, as Lana, playing his mother, broke down in the background. It was the climax of *Night's Child*, her penultimate picture. An overheated slice of Tennessee Williams-flavoured melodrama dealing with the incestuous relationship between Lana and her young teenage son, it had garnered the worst reviews of her career. And, as the press had loved to remind the public in the aftermath of Eddy's heroin overdose and his sister's suicide, there was more than a passing coincidence between the plot of that pot-boiler and the events, which took place at 1331 Tupelo Drive, off of Benedict Canyon, the night of May 7, 1980.

Lana dropped a wine glass to the Turkish rug as she started to weep, heart-blood Burgundy staining the deep weave.

The camera panned from the father's corpse—the late Warren Oates—to Eddy's tortured face. Then the thirteen-year-old stuck the gun in his mouth and pulled the trigger.

I quietly closed the door, leaving Lana alone with her ghosts, and continued to the bar. As I selected the finest brandy available, it occurred to me that novel was more than therapy. The autobiographical content could provide me with the key to unlock the secret door to Lana's past. Then the real work would begin. Bottle in hand, I made the library my last port of call and settled down with a copy of Faulkner's *The Sound and the Fury*.

Three pages in, I fell asleep, and for the first time in years dreamed of my dead mother and the Wisconsin trailer home I'd grown up in.

There's Method Acting as taught by Lee Strasberg. Then there was Method Writing as performed by Lana Hall.

It was a week later. We were in the lounge, her preferred place of work, and still re-plotting the novel. I'd thrown out the corny subplot concerning a crusading reporter who had been the accused actress's high school sweetheart, replacing it with that of an obsessive fan who decides to play detective and prove the woman's innocence. The process was taking forever due to Lana's insistence on us acting out each role, every nuance of scene, and the fact she couldn't concentrate for more than an hour at a time. When she was incapacitated by a migraine for two days, I managed to get more work done in forty eight hours than we had in a week.

Currently, we were working on a scene where Clive, the gay blackmailer, interrupts the De Havilands, the protagonists, if you could call them that. Lana and I played a talent agency MacBeth and Lady M. Mickey Muscles was doing Clive, and I hoped when we came to the scene where Clive forces Roger De Haviland into having anal sex, she wouldn't insist on total realism.

"No, no, I think Clive should be direct with his innuendos," she insisted, waving her arms around, champagne in one hand, cigarette in the other. "Your dialogue is too oblique. They won't get it."

"But it's the context of the scene in relation to what's previously taken place—remember?" I protested.

John appeared, interrupting her train of thought.

"Telephone," he said.

"I'm busy!" she snapped.

"It's Larry."

"Oh. Why didn't you say so?"

A call from the mysterious Mr. Monteleone meant the session was over.

Lana tried to exit the lounge gracefully, but the weight of the champagne rocked the boat and she stumbled against the coffee table. The ice bucket crashed to the floor. Mickey rolled his eyes.

It was business as usual in the Hall house.

Days inched into another week. That week slipped into a third.

Paris had become as cold as her namesake city, seemingly jealous of the time Sunny spent with me, which was considerable. I had never met another woman who wanted to have sex all the time. I sensed Lana wasn't too happy about the situation with Sunny either, although she'd said nothing. The book was moving at a snail's pace as she continued to change details every day, disrupting the internal logic of the plot, twisting character motivations to whatever agenda her mood dictated dependent on the amount she drank.

And I, thanks to Sunny, had starting doing coke again after I'd been clean for nearly three years.

It started one night when I failed, despite Sunny's ability to make a dead man walk, to maintain an erection.

Like all addicts, I convinced myself I could just do one line. One became two, two multiplied into four, eight, sixteen . . . until the half-gram was gone, our nasal tissues burned, our sex organs were sore, and our hearts raced like thoroughbreds. Stoned and stupid, we raided the bar and drank and smoked joints until dawn. By 9 AM, the time I was due to start work with Lana, I collapsed.

Fortunately, the incident coincided with one of her frequent migraines, and I was excused duty, the binge escaping her attention. It did not, however, slip past the hawkish eyes of John. He said nothing in his usually discrete manner. Why use words when your body can speak for you? His stiffness left me no doubt he disapproved.

Days became hours; weeks became days. Time accelerated in a haze of champagne and coke, sex, and fantasy. Lana's obsessions had woven a cocoon of silk-lined comfort. I'd always wanted a big house with a pool. Now I had one. I'd always wanted to make love to two women at once, now Sunny and Paris had worn that desire away. Every sexual fantasy had been fulfilled. As for the book, well, it wasn't art, and at the pace we were working we'd be lucky if it was finished by 1999. I didn't really care anymore and had come to consider it a game. Even the questions concerning Lana's mysterious past had stopped nagging me. She was a sweet generous hostess with tenuous grip on reality. What right did I have to destroy her world?

I had Sunny, who gave me anything I wanted and asked little in return. She was flakey as tree bark but as loving and as loyal as a dog, although the constant sex was making me sore.

As for my career as a writer, who was I trying to kid? My two attempts at serious novels had failed miserably. Working on Lana's pot-boiler was about my level. Who cared about fame when you had an endless supply of comfort? After all the years of struggling, I felt I deserved what Lana was giving me. But even though I now had everything I'd aspired to, it didn't make me happy. Neither did the coke or champagne, both of which I continued to consume on a daily basis. At least it dulled the sense of failure.

Around the middle of June, John came to my room while I tried to nap, champagne-induced drowsiness battling coke buzz. At least this time he adopted a softly-softly approach instead of proctology.

"Stop faking," he said when I pretended to be asleep. "The amount of that shit you've snorted, you'll be awake all week."

I opened my eyes.

"It's not what you're getting paid for."

"I haven't been paid yet." Which was true.

After the second week came and went with no check, I'd delicately mentioned the subject to Lana, who asked what I wanted it for. Didn't I have everything I needed? She cut the conversation short with a kiss on the cheek and the promise I'd receive the full amount due when the work was complete.

"You'll get paid," John said.

"I've read some of the latest material. It's good," he continued, an unusual warmth to his tone.

I snorted sarcastically at his obvious flattery.

"Really, I like it. Needs work but—"

"But what? All of a sudden, everyone's a critic around here. Mickey tells me he thinks scenes I've written are 'out of character' for Clive as if he's an actor. I've got Sunny suggesting a secondary subplot involving a lesbian couple and God knows what else."

"He was an actor."

"Who? Mickey? As what, stand-in for the Incredible Hulk?"

"That's unfair."

Hmm. Touched a nerve there. I bit my tongue, but John let it go.

"He might not be too bright, but he means well. And he's very loyal.

"Anyway, Sunny's not going to be a problem anymore."

I sat up.

"I found this in her bedroom," he continued, producing a syringe from his immaculately-tailored jacket pocket. "Know anything about it?

"Heroin?'

He nodded.

"I had no idea she was using."

"The coke was bad enough, but I can't allow smack. I've already made arrangements with Mr. Monteleone."

"What do you mean?" I asked as I got up and donned my robe. "And who the fuck is this mysterious Mr. Monteleone whom no one will talk about anyway?

John ran a hand over his mouth, uncomfortable with the question.

"You might have heard of him. Lawrence Montel was the name he used when he was an actor."

I mentally kicked myself for not having made the connection. Larry "Montel" had co-starred with Lana in *Days of Our Lives*. Like

Paul Newman, Monteleone's passion was racing cars, but a near-fatal crash had shattered his spine, his career, and his dreams of competing in the Indy 500. He was one of those faces who had appeared on a "Where Are They Now?" segment of *Geraldo*. Lawrence Antonio Monteleone controlled lucrative New York real estate, which was owned, it was rumoured, by a very powerful Italian family. It was the Sinatra syndrome. You didn't dig into Monteleone's affairs.

John removed a baggie of white powder from his pocket. "I don't know where's she's getting this shit from. You see any of this around the house, you *will* tell me. Yes?"

I was surprised by his sudden candour and obvious concern. Weeks of him being my head jailer hadn't exactly endeared me to the slick son-of-a-bitch.

"It took us over a year to get Lana clean after last time she relapsed," he said.

"She'd been doing it the night Eddy O.D'd, hadn't she?"

He nodded.

"Were they lovers?"

"Who? Yeah, Larry and Lana were a hot item during the four years they did the show. But Larry was married."

"No, I mean Lana and Eddy?"

John shook his head.

"The only thing Eddy was in love with was his needle and spoon—and Sasha."

"His sister? He was fucking his sister?"

"It was a sick, unhealthy little threesome. I told Lana not to get involved, but she's seldom listened to my advice."

His broad shoulders slumped.

"Where do you fit into all this?"

He looked sad, weary.

"I'm her brother."

John began his confessional. The Hall family saga made the plots of Lana's former soap opera sound simple.

A brother and sister from the wrong side of the tracks escaped small-town Georgia and an alcoholic, incestuous father and headed to Hollywood like thousands before them. But if fate had dealt them a bad hand at the start, luck and Lana's looks turned their fortunes into a royal flush. Within a month she landed a cameo on *Bonanza*. Other TV shows followed rapidly, and six months after they arrived in Tinseltown, Lana was starring in *Days*. When 1967 exploded and Lana's salary doubled, she ate it up. Hippie chicks, acid, every temptation, her appetite for indulgence went wild. Then Larry Monteleone entered the picture, and love blossomed. With Monteleone's support, she cleaned up her bad habits enough to keep working. The soap's rating went through the roof, ignited by the onscreen romance between the young girl from Georgia the trades were calling the next Vivien Leigh and the older, suave heartthrob from New York, and the off-screen reality which gave their scenes added heat.

"When Larry nearly died in that stupid accident, she lost it," John said. "Started drinking heavily, doing coke, which was the new deal, the big thing. Screwed anything she could get into bed. Even winning an Emmy didn't make a difference. She loved Larry, wanted him to divorce his wife—but the family was from, well, you don't get a divorce . . . cheat all you want, but no divorce. When Larry ended up in that wheelchair, Carmen, his wife, gave him payback for all the years he'd been fooling around. Wouldn't let him out of her sight. Lana made a half-hearted attempt at suicide. It took a lot of bullshit to sweep that under the rug."

"What happened?" I inquired after he had been silent for a moment. "I don't know much about Lana's early career, didn't really take an interest until she worked with Bertolucci."

John lit a cigarette and resumed the biography.

With Larry's help, he managed to straighten her out again. No drink, no drugs, just plain hard work and focus. By then, John was both her manager and her agent, and his careful choices were what broke her out of TV and into movies.

"Why are you telling me this now?" I asked as I poured myself a glass of water from the bottle of Evian on the nightstand. "You hate my guts."

"Because you being here makes her happy."

I tried not to laugh.

"Really," he said, clearly responding to the disbelief on my face. "I haven't seen her this way in years. You've given her hope."

"But there isn't going to be a comeback, is there?"

"She's not well enough." He sighed. "My sister is damaged goods."

"But you're helping her by reinforcing her delusions? What happens when we finish the book and the screenplay? You're not going to submit them, are you?"

"Then you'll write another one. Write your own books on your own time. Do whatever pleases you. Paris'll take care of you. Sunny's got to go. But no more drugs."

"Do I have a choice?"

I wanted to laugh

"No," he replied, standing. "But look at it this way: you're doing something more meaningful than just writing a book."

He paused.

"Lana's dying. She has a brain tumour. They've operated once but it's incurable."

John's statement shocked me into silence

"How long does she have?" I finally asked after seconds of silence seemed to turn into hours.

"Maybe three months."

"Does she know?"

"She's in denial."

Going cold turkey was a cunt. Coming down off the coke left me with a crushing depression and anxiety no amount of booze could calm. With Sunny gone, I felt empty, and I realized I had fallen in love with her. But it was too late for love. It seemed too late for anything. Outside of trying to work with Lana, I tried to turn my attention to a novel idea I'd had for some time—a "literary" piece about spiritual redemption in South America—but it wouldn't come. My words were as empty as the champagne bottles cluttering my room.

Through the haze of tumour-induced delusion, Lana sensed my

unhappiness and tried diligently to improve my mood. She even invited me to join her and Paris in bed.

I declined. I couldn't make love to a dying woman.

One morning at breakfast, she gave me a gold Rolex. I thanked her with a chaste kiss, and after an abortive hour of working, returned to my room and placed the watch in the desk drawer.

Time had no meaning.

July came, and with it my birthday. I didn't mention it. There was nothing to celebrate.

Struggling with my writing didn't help but only depressed me further. I'd never been good at anything else, yet what kept me alive was suffocating me as surely as the tumour was killing Lana.

Years of frustration, of being fucked over, of fighting to make it work.

I drained the third bottle of Dom Perignon and staggered to the john. The bedside light split the room in two. I didn't recognize the face in the mirror before me. Shadowed, bloodshot eyes, unruly hair, a forest of dark stubble.

It was the ghost of someone I thought I once knew.

That's when you took the cold shower, trying to wash the image, the memories, away as you muttered lines of Yeats. . . .

I, being poor, have only my dreams . . . tread softly, for you tread on my dreams. . . .

Dressed, you walked on down the hall like that old song and found silk-fucking-suit's gun hanging on its holster beside his bed.

And went to the room where your hostess slept.

And shot her in the temple, eradicating tumour and deluded dreams in an orgasm of bone, blood, and cancerous brain.

When you appeared in the hallway, Paris screamed, ran back into her room, bolted her door.

It took one shot to smash the lock—two to shut her the fuck up.

Her empty eyes said "thank you."

Cranial matter sliding down your cheeks like the tears that couldn't come, you shot John Silk Suit as he ran up the stairs, treading on his twitching wrist, stumbling as you crossed the lobby, making for the outdoor pool.

You always wanted a big house with a pool, remember?

Now you've got it and enough 9 mm currency to buy the fucking farm as well.

Mickey Muscles, wet from his swim, cried when you thrust the gun against his balls, begged, pleaded . . . sobbed like a baby.

You shut him up.

Brain sizzling like an egg in the desert. The humidity makes the silk robe cling to your body like a spent lover's embrace.

Somewhere in the night, a scream erupts. And keeps shrieking its metallic harpy wail.

Shut up. Shut up.

So tired. You just want to sleep. . . .

Sleep, perchance to dream again.

Squeezing the trigger's so eas—

STILL LIFE WITH PECKERWOOD

Written with Anya Martin

Once a month my dearest friend comes to visit. Tonight I sense his presence although I cannot see him. Due to circumstances beyond our timeless abilities, his magnificence is shielded from the eternal gaze of my eyes. And yet, I always know he is there, my constant companion, *the Moon*, even on nights like this one, shrouded in clouds of darkest pitch. Sky as black as the feathers of my bête noire—my once, or so I thought, friend—*that poet's raven*.

I know he is there, for I have counted the days since his last passing and know it is time for him to visit me again.

My compatriot, the Moon. Full as a wheel of cheese, yet pearly white like the perfect secret of an oyster, the fine, melancholy lustre of his rays far preferable to my mood than the burnished gold of the Sun, whose damnable brilliance would dry me out, crack my oily skin. The Sun, whose blinding rays have streamed unmercifully through the window beside me for hours, drenching the far wall of the room and fading Her image if not Her memory.

Emilia, whose skin once gleamed like fine alabaster with cheeks of the most subtle pink and now lies dull and chalky like too many layers of powder trying desperately to de-age an older woman's face. Emilia, whose piercing green eyes once bewitched this poet's heart. Emilia, whose tresses cascaded like a thousand scarlet rivulets upon such dainty shoulders. Emilia's waist, so tiny my fingers and palms touched each other when I held it. Such lovely shoulders. Tiny fingers, tiny feet, a sweet trill of a giggle—like a little girl.

Sometimes, They would remember to close the curtains to shield her. Or so some of Them would for a time. Recently, though, They have been younger ones, more forgetful. Although They did buy a special set of curtains for the strange woman, the hideous mangled thing that resembles a child's experiment with triangles. And for the ghastly, tasteless painting that looks like somebody spilled their dinner and never rang for the maid. But mostly They just place the works They say are special on my side or in the more shadowy corners beside the bookcase on the far wall to my left.

At first, it was just family until the Grandson started to collect. He and his wife talked of moving me, too, putting me away in the attic once, but his younger son, Harry, said he liked my expression—*it was spooky*—and the skull I bear in my fingers. Old "oooh-ooh," he dubbed it and would come by and ask it questions as if it were a fortune-teller who could predict Christmas presents and the victorious team in boys' sports tournaments. When my benefactor grew into a man, the collection grew stranger, and his wife wanted to take me down—*that grim-faced old geezer*—but he remains steadfast and will not allow her. The familiar faces have almost all disappeared though—*upward, I suppose*—until it is just me, Her, and the marble bust of Admiral Nelson, to whom Harry's wife claims to be related.

Pity. I often wonder if I would have liked the attic. At least it would have afforded me a different view. One hundred and fifty years of staring at mostly the same sights is more time than any man, even a poet, desires to muse alone with only his thoughts, her fading eyes, and a side-glance view of that scoundrel's acclaimed literary volume on the mahogany coffee table to keep him company. For it is Emilia whose curse is responsible for making me more than an image, and the canvas across the room is merely that. It does make me periodically giddy to think that Her loveliness is now mere bones and dust. And it is Edgar who was responsible for reducing the legacy of me, Milford Nathaniel Peckerwood, into a forgotten image on the wall of some distant relative's gallery.

And so I ponder, weak and weary of the endless tedium, as the old grandfather clock in the hall strikes midnight ever more. And then the silence, the perfect silence, the damnable sound of nothing descends again. I wait for the small dong of twelve-fifteen. If someone forgets to douse the hall lantern, I can watch the hands of the clock progress through the small oval window in the gallery door, my only "eye" into the rest of the house. On cloudless nights, I can track the time also in the expansion and contraction of the moonbeams on the floor and onto Her. Tonight though I am denied even that solace. Another night in a never-ending expanse of eternity drags on.

It was to be a Crow. *Crow, more.* Cannot anyone see the improvement in the cadence? Remember my poem was published one month before his. It was so thoughtful of that celebrated poet to take the time to correspond with a fine Alabama lawyer whose true passion lay in the art of crafting words into melodic verses. Why does everyone believe that lying, pompous. . . .

One o'clock, chimes the clock. Hickory dickory dock. Fee diddle dee dee. I thought of her first, my Emilia Lee, whom I loved as a child and would grow to love me, whom I would bury rather than see love another, but who instead buried me alive in oil.

Tap.

Something has hit the glass on the window, I suppose. An acorn perhaps, dropped by an overeager squirrel. One of my games is to ponder the origin of all night noises.

Silence again.

I miss the boy. He is not half as much fun all grown up, a musician They said he was, but the sound that erupts from beneath the house where he is said to practice does not sound like any music I have ever heard, just noise fit to shatter the eardrum. I had wanted to tell the boy so many things, like the skull was an old Indian skull dug up by a friend, a wealthy landowner, in north Georgia in the old Cherokee territory. He presented it to me because he thought my manner was somewhat morbid, which even made Emilia laugh. Her father had the right idea to marry her to a wealthy lawyer rather than that brash young lieutenant from Charleston who had no money in his family and more looks than any type of talent or intelligence.

Tap. Tap. Tap.

The sound is not loud but repeats itself in a quick sequence. It could not be that damnable raven again. *Go away.*

Tap. Tap. Tap.

Leave this old man alone. Is it not enough that instead of this true poetic genius, your master received the glory for your creation?

Tap. Tap.

The sound ceases as suddenly as it had begun, and I feel a stupid, senile old man. Of course, there is no raven. I have seen stranger things, like a woman's evil heart imprisoning love in the stagnant confines of a canvas, but the sheer audacity of me to believe He whose name endures would be at all concerned with tormenting another poet completely forgotten. No, that would be too much of a compliment. He is in the ground, as are all my friends and enemies, languishing in the sweet eternal peace that only I am denied.

A sharp creak pulls outward suddenly, and a single beam of light hits the floor. The Moon returns and floods up from the floor onto Her face, brighter than daylight onto Her green eyes.

I do not want to gaze at those eyes anymore.

I prefer the darkness after all. It hides the memories. If I could only close my eyes and sleep. If I could only die. If I could cease this miserable existence and progress to another place, be it Heaven or Hell. I would prefer to dwell with the Lord in His kingdom of light, but I no longer care—just to quit the painting!

At that moment, I realize that I am mistaken. The light is not my old friend Moon but a torch of some kind. It glides from one end of the room to the other, careful to avoid the glass of the door's oval eye and back onto the bookcase. And then it revolves onto me. For a moment I am blinded, and then it glides onward to the other side of the window, and I see two trim figures completely covered in queer, tight-fitting, black garb. One is a woman. I can tell by the unseemly revelation of the contours of her body against the torch held by the other, a man with a chest so brawny that it indicates physical activity of some sort.

He guides the torch while she opens the drapes covering the ugly woman and removes the frame from the wall, loosens the painting with a gloved hand, and gently—with, again, only the slightest tap—lowers the frame to the floor. Then she takes the torch as he begins to detach the canvas from the boards to which it is adhered with what appears to be a sharp-toothed instrument not unresembling the mouth of a serpent. The wood is laid beside the frame, canvas quickly but carefully rolled, and placed in a large duffel bag.

Then the torch scans the messy one, and again the ritual begins. Frame off the wall, picture removed, canvas gently disengaged from its wooden inner frame, meticulously rolled and stashed into the bag. And the thrill of freedom rushes over me like a gale wind. The thrill of a trip to someplace else. Anyplace else. I have heard Them speaking of a new world out there, a world full of wondrous machines called "cars" that take you from here to Atlanta in one hour. And things called "airplanes" with magnificent wings that transport one to California in a few hours more and occasionally crash, but usually just make your ears "pop" due to a circumstance called "turbulence." And plays that one can see without actors being present called "movies." They are always speaking of "which movie did you see last night?" or in the place called the Mall, where you can shop or eat at a Scottish restaurant which also serves French-fried fare. Will I see any of these wonders? I would be happy just to walk in the park and smell the fresh scent of spring azaleas and daffodils in the crisp night air under my old friend the Moon. I have been dubbed a cynic by my dear Emilia and others, but I have always felt a soft spot for the unwavering beauty of that most graceful orb.

They are now rolling up a blue dog I have never seen before because its image was on the same wall as me but beyond the window. And then the man lowers another painting and points it in my direction as he removes the boards—a nude woman with skin as pale as Emilia's sprawled like a Sabine temptress across a sapphire love seat. I cannot tell the color of her eyes because the torchlight is too dim, but they appear gay and inviting, and I remember when Emilia's were such, on a spring day under the dogwood behind the back terrace of my Southern home, Villa Persephone, named after the tragic, beautiful Greek goddess who agreed to marry Hades.

Emilia, who at first was such a kind and generous wife, bringing me tea under the tree when I was so engrossed in the creative process as not to desire a break in my thoughts. Quiet evenings of cards in the drawing room or clutching my arm at the Opera, her slim form bristling with excitement at the wondrous range of heavenly voices. Knitting as I read from Coleridge or Longfellow or my own works. If only that brash young suitor had really been killed in Texas fighting the damnable Mexicans and had not, wonder of wonders, returned home to steal Her heart away from me.

I first spied them kissing under that same dogwood tree when they thought I was taking my habitual afternoon nap. It was but a brief kiss at first, the blond lieutenant pressing lips to Hers and She drawing away, knowing it was wrong. And then the transformation, he starts to leave like a gentleman would and She, the whore, pulls him back and pressing Her lips long and hard against his.

I knew that Fanny dabbled in some form of magicks. She and my manservant, Taylor, were my only slaves, but other city slaves would come knocking on the back door, and I would watch Fanny measure out crushed herbs and roots to heal blisters, bring luck, or attract a lover. It was part of some queer, dark religion they brought over with them from Africa. Some of them may be God-fearing Christians, but I had long suspected that Fanny had some other religion on the side. I was never afraid of the Black Arts. Indeed, they fascinated me, the simplicity of casting a spell and manipulating the will of God to my own whim.

I burned the potion Fanny gave me along with a few strands of my Emilia's lover's hair, and within a day, he grew ill, very ill with scarlet fever. Of course, She ran to his bedside—"just a friend," She said— but within two weeks he was dead, and She was again my Emilia.

Everything returned to its normal routine. Cards and knitting, me reading to Her a new novel by an English gentleman named Dickens. I tried to ignore the sad look that now stained Her lovely eyes. And then She told me She wanted to paint me, and I would sit for hours in the drawing room clasping the old Indian skull as She laboured. A perfect likeness was what She had said She wanted to create. When the final brushstroke was complete, She pulled me over finally to look at it. Imagine my surprise when I saw that the man in the painting She had laboured upon so long and meticulously had no face. It was then that Her eyes began to change and I first began truly to see Her as the vile creature cackled with laughter, chanting in an arcane language I could not understand. As I went for Her throat—the screech of Her voice so grating and horrible to my ears—I found myself dragged instead away from Her and into the portrait.

She hung me over the fireplace to watch as my lifeless body was proclaimed dead by the coroner. My will had clearly stated that I wished to be buried under the front steps (to prevent Her from ever bringing another suitor across them), but She gleefully told me that she had had the church declare that last wish ungodly and I had been buried in the town cemetery instead. Mute for eternity, I could only listen and watch as She never remarried but paraded countless lovers into the drawing room to make me watch them seduce Her and then carry Her upstairs in their arms. My one solace was to see Her grow old and cracked until no lovers would come anymore. Until the day when the men in black suits and women in black dresses arrived to declare that She had finally died, alone.

My memories are interrupted as I notice that my two night visitors are not rolling up any more paintings. They are perusing the bookcase with an intense sense of purpose. She pulls out one book, and he shakes his head. Then she points at the coffee table, and he nods. The torchlight hits the cover: *The Complete and Unabridged Poems of Edgar Allan Poe*—the first edition that has haunted me for over a century. They pause as she hands the book to her accomplice, and then he hands her the torch and begins to peruse the pages carefully, lovingly.

I want to scream: "No, the real poet is *here*." I want to point them to the thin, forgotten volume in the far corner of the bottom shelf, to the poems that He stole from me so shamelessly. For Him to say that He sent me His works in friendly correspondence, and I was the thief! My cadence is so much more lush, only the deaf ear could truly believe otherwise.

But, of course, I sit silent, only staring at the intruders, a lifeless work of art, a likeness of a long-forgotten relative. No value for a thief. They will leave me. The walls are empty now, except for me and Her and Admiral Nelson. They will leave me alone with Her and the dour-faced English naval hero who is too heavy to be lifted by any fewer than two men.

"Come on, Stan, we've got to hurry," the woman whispers, the first words passed between them. "You can gush over it later when we're safe in Cancun."

"Sorry, Carla," the man whispers back. "It's just you know how much I've wanted to get hold of this, how much money it's going to get us. Good ol' Edgar!"

He pulls a thin, slippery cover out of the bag, carefully drapes the book, and eases it inside the side pocket so as not to damage the rolled paintings.

"Okay, let's go," Carla whispers.

They start to crawl out the window, but then suddenly Stan steps back inside. His eyes dart around the room, the light with them, as if he thinks he has forgotten something. Unexpectedly, they lock on me.

"Wait a minute," Stan whispers. "We forgot about him."

"We've got to get out of here," Carla urges, sounding worried.

"No, this is that guy who says Poe plagiarized his work," Stan adds softly. "Remember that guy I told you about? What was his name, Pecker-something? Yeah, I almost forgot that his picture was here, too. Poor old fucker. Must've eaten him up, that Poe first edition across the room from him on the coffee table."

"Stan, we've been lucky this long," Carla goes on, her voice rising ever so slightly. "Let's go."

"No, I want to take him along," Stan says, his voice dropping as if in warning to her. "As a memento of the last great heist. Poe's volume will bring us a fortune, along with the Picasso, the Renoir, the little Jasper Johns, but no one's gonna miss this guy. I kinda feel sorry for him. I think we owe it to him, babe."

"All right," Carla whispers impatiently, stepping back into the room. "But make it quick."

With that, he lifts me off the wall and removes me from the frame, turning my back toward Her for the first time in over a century. It tickles when he removes the nails from the board. He cannot use the serpent teeth because my nails are older, heavier, unlike the odd metal prongs used to connect the younger paintings. Then, with a sudden tingle, I am rolled up and clutched in his hand, and he carries me out the window.

My vision turns to pitch, but I can smell the fresh night air, a scent I could not forget. At least I am not in the bag. I do not have to rub shoulders with that damnable tome. This thief does remember me. *Somebody remembers me.* And now I am to rest in the place of honour in his home. What difference does it make that it is a home bought with wealth obtained by the sale of stolen possessions? I finally will be granted appreciation.

From the motion, I infer that these thieves—my liberators—run a short distance from the house. How I wish to see my old, dear friend Moon and to gaze at the façade of the place of incarceration! Stan, however, keeps me rolled and holds my canvas with a reverence, for which I am grateful. I hope their abode will be a magnificent place and that they will hang me somewhere with a splendid view. *Ah, to be remembered!* I, a poet, cannot find words superlative enough to describe the sense of elation I feel.

They slow then, as I seek those elusive words, and the sound of a door opening distracts me from my jubilant reverie. Stan's gentle hands lay me carefully on a leather surface, and I am aware that the duffel bag is placed beside me. Darkness lessens somewhat as my canvas unrolls a trifle, allowing my ever-open eyes to detect the alabaster luminescence of my constant companion of so many years, now peeking out from the clouds.

"We've done it, Carla! This is it! Man, I can't fuckin' believe those stupid bastards were only using that antiquated alarm system."

"We're not out of the woods yet, hon," Carla replies. "And don't forget to change clothes."

"Jeez! You're right. Where would I be without you, babe?"

"Wasting away in Riker's probably."

"Sure as shit, sweet pea."

The sounds of fabric slipping from young, adventurous bodies follow their exchange, and I decide I like this couple, despite the fact that young Stan has the manners and vocabulary of a guttersnipe, for he yet has taste enough to take an interest in me. Miss Carla, I sense, loves her brash, larcenous beau fiercely, and the knowledge makes me yearn for my long-lost youth.

"You ready?" asks Stan.

"Just a sec. Okay."

"Love you, babe."

The sound of a kiss follows, then a click, a whir, and the roar of some infernal machine. We are obviously in one of those horseless carriages they call "cars," and I wish I could see more. In fact, I am quite giddy—and perhaps, a tad fearful—at the thought of being transported in such a machine. But then we are off and the sensation is surprisingly pleasant.

"You know how much that Picasso's worth?"

"Half a million," Carla replies.

"One-point-five, baby. One-point-five."

Silence descends then, and I wonder what painting they are referring to. Surely not that hideous triangular woman? One could hardly call *that* art.

My liberators continue to guide our travels in quiet for a little while, and any trepidation I had fades like the colours of Her portrait. The sensation is most pleasing and lulls me into a reverie. Words which had eluded me earlier now flow forth unbidden. If only I could write them down!

Then, as I am measuring the beat of a line, refining to the precise dictates of iambic pentameter, Miss Carla's sudden urgent tone derails my inspired train of thought.

"Slow down, Stan. You're going too fast."

"More likely to attract attention at this time of night if I stick to the limit like some drunk pretending to be sober."

"Slow down! I think I see something blue up ahead," she stresses.

"You're imagining things."

"No. There—in the median, hiding in the bushes."

"Fuck. Well spotted. Probably just the state patrol doing their job. Old Joe Cop's snacking on a doughnut, waiting to slap down a DUI," Stan laughs.

Our motion slows steadily, and I wonder what they are talking about, the nuances of their slang escaping me.

"Damn, he pulled out," Carla snaps. "He's following us."

"No, he isn't. It's just a coincidence. If he was, he'd have those blues going."

"Slow down."

"Honey, I'm going five under the limit."

Then a sudden, high-pitched banshee wail assails my ancient ears, and the horseless carriage lurches forward.

"Shit!"

"Oh, hell," Carla cries. "Maybe they're only checking for insurance."

"I don't think so! Damn! There must have been a secondary alarm."

A sudden, frantic spurt of power tosses my rolled form backward, thrusting me up against the duffel bag as a terrible roar descends from somewhere in front.

"Try and catch me, you dirty pig!" Stan laughs.

The roaring increases, the devilish wail retreats somewhat, and a peculiar affliction assaults my stomach. Then it dawns on me—I am feeling sick, a sensation that I had long forgotten.

"Slow down! The road bends ahead!" Carla, ever the voice of reason, shouts.

"I can't! We've gotta lose him!"

"Stan! No!"

"Hold on, baby!"

"Look out! He's over the line!"

Nothing could prepare me for the sudden motion which hurls me over and over as my night-time escape from Her dead eyes turns into a rolling barrel ride, a terrible, unearthly bellowing like a Spanish bull slain by a toreador roaring around us. A most dreadful crashing, smashing cacophony explodes, and my new friends and I are flung violently to one side. But the torment continues as Miss Carla screams and Stan cries out in terror. Sailors at the mercy of a cruel sea are we, tossed and turned and—

Then I am free, flying through the night air.

NO! I want to cry. No! No!

My portrait glides slowly, with such unexpected gentleness in contrast to the terrifying violence, and as I float to the soft embrace of a grassy embankment, my canvas unrolls, allowing me to see what has happened.

Stan's horseless carriage is a gnarled tangle of metal and broken glass lying on its side. And there, not more than a stone's throw away, is another of those infernal contraptions. It, too, looks like it has been smote by the hammer of Thor, the Norse God of Thunder. Behind the wreckage, a third vehicle approaches, seemingly the source of the harpy's screech, a fact confirmed when it comes to a stop and the noise ceases. Only the satanic red and bright blue of its lanterns persists, painting the dark countryside with rhythmic splashes of primary colors. Then poor Miss Carla begins to scream, and from my vantage point on the embankment, I see why.

Tongues of fire lick at the back and belly of the metal beast.

"Run! Get out!" I shout in my eternal silence. "Save yourselves, my friends!"

A tall man in some kind of uniform I do not recognize steps from the vehicle of flashing lights and dashes toward the rapidly spreading conflagration. Then an explosion, the likes of which I had never imagined, splits the sky asunder more violently than any lightning storm I had witnessed as a young man in Florida. The sound deafens this poet's ears and is followed by a hot wind of dragon's breath which snatches me from my grassy resting place.

Up, up I go, rolling, then tumbling down, down toward the road. But no, it is not to be. A spring breeze decides at that very moment to chase the fiery wind, and on I go, borne aloft by invisible arms. As

I float over the other smashed carriage, I see a young man, bloodied and beaten, struggle to free himself. Then he is gone as the blessed breeze snatches me away from the tragic scene.

Oh, my poor friends! Dear Stan of the profane mouth. Poor Miss Carla. How right you were. And now my freedom is empty, for I shall never hang on the wall of your home and watch your two lives in the making. Once again, I feel the truth of the pronouncement: "the wages of sin are death."

The breeze exhausts itself, and I flutter down to hook onto a bush.

I am cold and wet despite the sun's steadily warming rays, for it rained before dawn, a deluge of biblical proportions. Some of my oil has run, and I feel most queer. My left eye, I fear, has drooped a little and now my perspective on the radiant countryside is askew. It promises to be a fiercely hot day, and it is not yet noon. Will it hurt as I dry, Her brush strokes flaking as the elements undo Her artful work?

Yes, I will soon be released, and I pray the Good Lord will lift me with open arms into His place. I will endure the pain, for certainly that will come as nature's forces consume me, and in fact I welcome it. After one hundred and fifty years of numbing confinement, it is wonderful to feel something. And at least I have the scent of blooming flowers and the hedgerow song of birds to stimulate the higher senses.

I will be free, but who will mourn for me?

Dedicated to the memory of Dr. Thomas Holley Chivers, "the Lost Poet of Georgia," who did, in fact, accuse Edgar Allan Poe of plagiarism and, later in life, according to local legend, request to be buried beneath the doorstep of his home, Villa Allegra, so that his lovely younger wife would never remarry.

LOVE SELLS THE PROUD HEART'S CITADEL TO FATE

Love is a breach in the walls, a broken gate,
Where that comes in that shall not go again;
Love sells the proud heart's citadel to Fate.
They have known shame, who love unloved.
—Rupert Brooke, "Love"

Van Helsing's Journal, September 14th, 1861.

It pains me so to commit shameful details to vellum, yet I cannot help but believe perhaps some significance lies in the reoccurrence of these terrible dreams, these night-shadows which haunt me such that I awake trembling with disgust. Yet my occult studies have proven much can be learned in the dusty recesses of a man's mind.

For the fifth night in succession, the phantoms of memory have come to vex me like a succubus, though never in my forty years have dreams elicited a sense of dread so strong, so devastating to the soul. I wake a man whose very moral fibre threatens to shred.

This night's black agent was of the most negrescent stripe, and by far the most heinous a man of my standing could tolerate. It began, as always, by finding myself exiting Piccadilly Circus in the direction of The Strand. The smuts, as ever, hung thick enough to induce a heaviness of the lungs, a sluggishness of step.

There, on the corner of The Haymarket, stood a Mother Midnight, her reddened lips smeared by what I do not wish to think about. Like many of her ilk, she had with her a daughter for trade peering with the startled eyes of a wounded lamb.

"What's yer fancy, sir? Me, or something younger?"

As the drab concluded her proposition, she pushed the child forward. In the half-light cast from the doorway of a Mollie House I saw she was no older than six; all in rags, dirty, barefoot and hollow-cheeked. The child had suffered a severe beating, and her body, which showed through the torn cloth, was covered with bruises. The child's filthy countenance could not mask the true look of such distress, hide such hopeless despair on her face. My heart thudded with anger in my chest at such a sight, and filled my soul, too, with such despondency I could neither speak nor move away from this terrible vision of innocence so defiled. The child shook, and kept shaking her tousled head as if arguing about something, gesticulated and spread her little hands, and then suddenly clasped them together and pressed them to her little bare breast.

I turned away, my heart and mind in such moral turmoil, for I desired nothing more than to raise my walking cane and smite the leering face of this mackerel who call herself a mother. On, then, I strode as fast as my sleep-guided legs would carry me, away from this perverted Madonna and her damaged child. Somehow, with that peculiar reason only felt in the dreaming state, I next found myself on the south side of Soho Square, approaching Oxford Street to the north. It was there, as I bisected the finely manicured lawn of the tiny park, that temptation accosted me.

"Would you help me, kind sir?"

The voice was young, surely no older than thirteen years. Female and underwritten with an Eastern European accent far thicker than my Dutch-English. It came from beside a bush heavily curtained with shadow, for here, in the middle of the park, the sulphurous tallow of the sparsely placed gas lanterns could hardly reach. As I approached the voice, I could faintly make out a shapely figure, high and rich of bosom. Surely I was mistaken? The voice belonged not to a child but a young woman of at least her twenty-first year.

I asked what aid she was in need of, and as I did so, a hand reached out for mine. Not the hand of a woman, but that of a young man. Yet before I could rectify that which my dream eyes and ears had mistakenly led me to believe was a damsel in distress, the cold, male fingers touched me, attached themselves to my skin like some terrible human leech. The sensation disturbingly stirred my blood, and as the gamine stepped forward into the orange glow shed by the nearest lamp, I felt a stiffening in my loins. As the toothless mouth opened, the lips rounding in a perfect circle, a mocking travesty of the kiss, my body betrayed my spiritual repugnance at the vision and what it promised.

Two hours have passed since I awoke, like Lazarus, from that terrible state. Yet unlike Lazarus, I do not have the solace of the Lord to comfort me in my resurrection. The state of my awakening so shameful, I removed the sheets from my bed and soiled nightgown and burned them in the fireplace. Heaven forbid poor Marta, my devoted maid of this past year while I have been living in London, should have to deal with the betrayal of my body. I partook of a cold bath to flagellate my corrupt flesh until I shivered like a Russian bathing in an ice-brook. Yet, still the dream pursued my waking state, and my nerves were such that my hands shook so I could not put pen to this paper. Much as I despise the habit, I drank a small draught of laudanum to ease my vexation.

Dawn has now arisen with all the rich hues of a bonfire night blaze as a vibrant sun fights the smuts of the infernal smokestacks and coal fires which choke this teeming city. Deep in my soul I yearn to return to Haarlem, to breathe fresh air and bicycle through tulip fields of passionate red and soothing yellow. Duty, however, calls; I have another six months of teaching at the Royal College of Medicine. My heart, though, is heavy, for there are other reasons I must stay in this manmade Hell. And I must go to them now.

A brougham waits, and I must away to Bedlam.

Van Helsing hissed in disgust at the stench rising from the cobble-stones outside his chambers in Holland Park, for even here in this more salubrious area of west London, feces both human and animal ran thick in the gutters. Treading wearily, he entered his carriage, the door held open by Mr. Tobias Flemyng, his driver. A man afflicted at birth by a port wine stain which smeared the right side of his face like some terrible jest performed by children playing with a pail of paint, and cursed with weak, degenerate teeth, of which few remained in his head at the young age of twenty-nine years, Mr. Flemyng, despite his disturbing appearance, was a man of good heart and solid moral character. Besides which, in all his years either living in or visiting the cesspool of London, Van Helsing had yet to find a more knowledgeable or safe brougham driver who could navigate the dangerous streets of the teeming metropolis.

Once his dear patron was comfortably seated, Mr. Flemyng took the reins in hand and they set off towards the rising sun—east, and to that most troubling of places, the hospital of St. Mary of Bethlem, known to all in Britannia as "Bedlam."

Founded at some unknown date in the fourteenth century, St. Mary of Bethlem was, from the very beginning, devoted to care for those sick in mind. Over the centuries, this once noble, but now shameful, establishment had come to epitomize the city as a great madhouse, populated as it was with so many afflicted and distracted souls. Such was the moral, psychic, and physical decay of its hapless inhabitants, and the attendant effects upon their keepers, that Bedlam had fallen into such a state of physical desolation, the hospital had been moved and rebuilt twice since its founding, and now resided in the borough of Southwark, the traditional nursery of prisons and other such forbidding institutions.

Tobias Flemyng made careful haste, guiding his dear patron and passenger through the chaos of swarming Oxford Street to Holborn, to the Blackfriars Road, then south, over the bridge and into the borough of the melancholy mad, the dismally deranged, and the condemned.

The current institution was as grand as its predecessor in Moorfields—the façade an impressive portico decorated with Ionic columns, topped by a formidable dome. Like a prestigiator who charms the eyes with his finely manicured hands while palming a tarnished coin, Bedlam's exterior hid the unvarnished, sullied truth—the hospital had become a circus, a morally degenerate entertainment for a paying public who came to see tales acted by those who were now mad, fragmented versions of those life experiences which had driven them into the abyss of insanity in the first place.

Van Helsing dismounted from the brougham, tipped Mr. Flemyng and informed him he would be no longer than ten minutes, then strode with the purpose of a Higher Power into this purgatorial place.

Entering the vestibule, he glanced at the two sculpted giants, known popularly as "the brainless brothers," a pair of bald-headed and semi-naked figures named "Raving Madness" and "Melancholy Madness" by the sculptor, Cibber, who had been commissioned to create them for the previous incarnation of St. Mary's. Calling to a steward, Van Helsing requested an immediate audience with Dr. Christopher Hughes. A shilling slipped into the man's hand quieted his protestations that Dr. Hughes was "busy, and cannot be disturbed, sir."

Van Helsing waited for no less than a minute before Dr. Hughes, a rotund, ruddy-faced fellow crowned by a mop of baby-fine blond hair, appeared.

"I must see Susannah," Van Helsing said.

"Her condition is, I am afraid, very fragile, and I do not think—"

"I do not pay you to think! I pay you to take care of her! Take me to her now," Van Helsing hissed, his customary sign of emotional distress.

Like a ruffian, he grasped Dr. Hughes's arm and pushed him in the direction of the stairs which led to the rear of the asylum, away from the public galleries where the curious and salacious took sport in the theatrics of the inmates.

"I have done . . . everything that I am able for Miss Susannah," Dr. Hughes bristled. "But I fear your own state of mind when you see how her condition has worsened since your last visit three months ago."

Hughes's remark stabbed Van Helsing like a surgeon's scalpel slipped deliberately between his ribs; he did not want to admit to himself he had busied himself these past weeks to hide from the terrible truth—Susannah was rapidly dying a most dreadful death.

"The spiritual pathology of Miss Susannah has degenerated to such a state, I fear she will no longer recognize you," Hughes mumbled as they mounted the stairs.

"*God in de hemel!*" Van Helsing hissed under his breath. "I do not need you to remind me! Whiles I am a taxed man, Susannah is of utmost importance to me."

Van Helsing clenched his iron jaw, his bushy eyebrows knitting together in consternation as he halted suddenly, drawing Hughes close to his chest.

"I expect you, sir," he said slowly, his voice firm yet hardly more than a whisper, "to take very good care of Miss Susannah in her last days."

"Y-y-yes, Dr. Van Helsing. I understand. But I fear she is close to succumbing to *Locomotor Ataxy* and the end is very near."

Van Helsing hissed again with indignation and continued to march Hughes up the grimy stairs.

The private cell, far removed from the carnival of Bedlam proper, measured eleven feet by eleven, and contained nothing more than a wooden bed, a filthy sheet, and, as a concession to comfort, a soiled pillow on which Susannah sat, muttering incoherently to herself as she obsessively ran her right index finger over the unyielding stone of the cell's floor, writing indecipherable hieroglyphs with her bloodied digit.

Van Helsing rubbed a hand over his now sweating face as he peered into the dingy compartment. Dr. Hughes unlocked the door and stepped back.

Van Helsing's Journal. September 14th. Evening.

Today's visit to my dear, darling Susannah was almost as disturbing as the night-phantom which compelled me to call upon her. The vile ravages of syphilis have turned this once beautiful, albeit haunted, young lady into a rotting crone who resembles some hag dreamed by the Bard; and like the hags who vexed the Thane of Cawdor, she plagued me with remarks which, I dread, are signpost to future tragedy.

Yet this I know; for my beloved Susannah—child of the night, former daughter of darkness—the end is near. What burdens a heart so is that she denies mine very existence and no longer knows her Benefactor: I, who saved her from the life of a harlot and guttersnipe.

All the poor girl would say to me was: "the man in black will come to test you; he will take someone you will come to love away from you." Then she sang a strange ditty and turned to face the wall.

"Such antic and such pretty lunacies,
That spite of sorrow they will make you smile."

So heavy was my heart when she punctuated this cryptic comment, I could not linger.

Dr. Hughes promises he will do all he can to insure Susannah will be taken care of; however, at this delicate stage I must be bold and resolute. The Good Lord will take Susannah away, and I must make good my promise to take care of our little Lily, her precious child.

Death is a release for those incarcerated in the prison of flesh; it is the living who serve out their days under a far worse penalty.

However much my visit to that damnable place increased my sense of foreboding, the journey to the strawberry fields of Hammersmith to visit young Lily raised my spirits a little—until Baroness Lewis came a-calling. As often, I am getting ahead of myself. We do not depart for Bath until the morrow; for now I need to record the pleasure of seeing my Lily.

As always, the journey was bittersweet like fine Dutch chocolate for the yoke of guilt lay heavy, as it often curse me, on my shoulders. But I am in no state to house a five-year-old child and be a suitable surrogate father for her. It is impropriate for a man of my age and unmarried condition to raise a little one in such a heated atmosphere of the sacred and profane, for when Bulwer-Lytton and A.E. Waite and other supplicants in their order come to meet here, I send Marta away; such is not an environment for impressionable women-folk, be they child or spinster. Thus, Susannah's Lily has, with great providence (and my workings and coin), had good fortune to be raised in a fine household. When I saw her this morning, the child was radiant with a life only a Beneficent Being could bestow upon one so young. However, I deduce Mr. and Mrs. Davis, the shipping clerk and his fair lady wife, now become abject when I visit their humble abode. Ma'am Davis is with child and filled with moods. Yet I suspect the difference in social standing infects them with this barely concealed resentment of my visits. So be it; Lily is in good hands.

The child was at play when I arrived unannounced, and, thus, I did not disturb her; merely observed from the casement window. Like her name, she is pure, and any vision of her brings to mind those inspiring words from Matthew 6:28—"Consider the lilies of the field, how they grow . . ." From the top of her golden crown of hair, the color of which brings to mind visions of freshly scythed wheat, to the tips of her tiny pink toes, the girl is a painting of such promise I ache to hold her. Sensing Lily's "family" were discomforted by my presence, I made my leave reassured she will not suffer the fate of her mother.

With considerable relief, I returned to my chambers despite the growling of my empty stomach, for only then did I realize I had not taken a repast since my supper of the previous night. Concerned for my well-being, kind Marta hurried to the kitchen to prepare a salad of cold herring and potatoes. Alas, before I could dine, the Baroness arrived.

September 15th.

Van Helsing and the Baroness escaped the bricken wilderness of London on the 10:30 morning departure of The Great Western, flagship steam train of Brunel's Great Western line which connected the capital at the recently constructed Paddington Station to Bristol Temple Meads, one hundred and forty miles west. With his customary loathing of Industrialism, the journey was an unpleasant one for Van Helsing for many reasons, not the least of which was the company of the Baroness Arabella Lewis herself.

Pulchritudinous of breast and tiny of waist yet with loins girded by powerful childing hips, she resembled less an hourglass than a tightly compact figure eight. A petite five-foot-and-one-inches tall, her figure, porcelain skin, lips the natural inclination of which were to pout, and leonine mane of long red hair had a tendency to turn men's heads. She was a God-faring woman, albeit a progressive thinker, being a Unitarian—both of which were characteristics Van Helsing found appealing—and indeed, it was their mutual Unitarian beliefs, particularly in the realm of social reform, which had brought this odd couple into their respective orbits. However, regardless of her stout moral nature, her appearance shouted "libertine." So much so, gossip a-plenty danced in the drawing rooms of London that the Baroness had been the death of her late husband, the far older Baron Horace Lewis. For Van Helsing, who preferred to go about his business as discreetly as possible, being seen in the Baroness's company made him feel like a beacon in the darkness. Then, there was her maddening—and unbecoming, in the Professor's mind—habit of smoking small, stinking cigarillos imported from Mexico as she was doing now in the hermetically-sealed compartment.

The journey, conducted nonstop at The Great Western's maximum speed of an un-Godly—or so Van Helsing believed—sixty seven miles-per-hour, took less than two hours to reach its destination—a journey which, the Professor thanked Providence, had passed in silence due to the Baroness's absorption in Mr. Dickens's latest work, *Great Expectations*.

But as the train exited the Box Tunnel, through the smoke-begrimed window, a vista of unprecedented aesthetic delight captured Van Helsing's eyes. Like Rome and Jerusalem and many another, the city of Bath—named *Aquae Sulis* after the goddess Sul Minerva, the Roman Goddess of Wisdom, of Arts and Sciences, and of War—was said to be built upon seven hills, though in fact, it was founded not on a hill but in the valley of the river Avon.

A carriage met them at Bath Spa Station and took them—at a speed seemingly only slightly less than that of The Great Western, much to Van Helsing's consternation—to the Baroness's pied-a-terre at the Royal Crescent, where the Professor was relieved to escape the fog of his companion's cigarillos.

Van Helsing's Journal. September 15th. Early evening.

I am tired, but 'tis early, for the sun has not yet set. Traveling in that a-cursed locomotive has, I fear, wearied me, for God did not mean for man to journey at such speed. There is, however, work to be done, for time is of the essence. Again, alas, I get ahead of myself.

The Baroness, whom I know through our mutual work with Mr. Chadwick, spoke only for a few minutes when she came to visit my chambers before I agree to join her on this journey to Bath. We share a mutual concern for the plight of the young, and when she tell me of the disappearances of little ones, for she is a mother, and have two children by her late husband, I could not say no to her request to accompany her.

These "disappearances" appear no simple case of the children of the lower classes, the sons and daughters of working men and women, gin-besotted, who allow their offspring to wander and fall prey to Fate or the machinations of ruffians, or are smite down by their parents in fits of drunken rage, then the consequence of which are hid from the eyes of Justice under the pretence of an accident. No. Those who have disappeared are the sons and daughters of well-to-do families who vanish from their beds after saying their prayers. For six months this has occurred in this fair city; twelve children in all, two a month, boy and girl, none older than eleven. The Baroness, who has many social connections, learned of this through the vexation of an old friend, a former paramour of Lord Cadbury, who now resides in Bath. This poor woman, recently widowed like the Baroness herself, is one of those who has lost a little one. Furthermore, rumour has now spread like the Great Fire which cleansed London, and fearful parents speak in hushed tongue of some Evil which is stalking the young of Bath; an Evil which seeks to destroy the next generation of Bathonians.

Experience has taught me that rumour which take root and

becomes powerful like superstition often mirrors a social hysteria which spreads like the plague. Yet for all groundless superstition, often-times the cause is a grain of sand which chafe like the particulate which lodges inside the Oyster and eventually grow into a pearl: hard, unyielding, resolute—and real. In growing, it become not a substance of beauty but a black malignancy, reflecting the nature of its origin. Knowing of my occult interests, my study of secret societies, and arcane lore, the Baroness, who, for one of woman-kind show good intellect aside that curse and blessing of all who are of the fairer sex—often wild "instinct"—has conducted something of an inquiry into the disappearances which have made fearful the people of this fair city.

(And fair it is because it does not depend on the Industrial scourge for its well-being, being founded by the Roman conquerors as a resort renowned for its healing waters which flow in hot torrents from one of the most potent natural Spas in the British Isles and make it long a destination of the wealthy and famous. Surrounded by the lush farmlands of the county of Somerset, it is a rich center of produce to be sent to London and nearby Bristol, that western port city.)

But I digress when I should be speaking of the hushed voices which whisper of degenerate behaviours orchestrated by one Lord Manfred, a recent habitué of the city, and his social circle which encompass many lower members of European royalty.

Bath, the Baroness informs me, also has long held a reputation as a site of indulgence for those of money and power. Yet for all this city's bounty and seeming grace, a darkness flows in the waters which bubble and froth from deep inside the Earth. Bath, from that which I have learned from a hasty reading of materials gathered with speed from the British Museum, is a haunted place filled with spectres and phantoms, a nexus of timeless energies that seem to attract those who harbour dark desires.

The Garrick's Head Public House, for instance, which sits alongside The Theatre Royal on Barton Street, is well known to house a mischievous spirit who will often-time hurl a tankard of ale from the bar to the nearest wall. Along the Newbridge Road, built atop an ancient Roman thoroughfare, many a local has seen a division of spectral Roman Legionnaires marching westward in formation—and many others beside. Ancient entities do not die here, nor do they fade as sunset into the arms of eternal night. Some strange force keeps the dead here as Un-dead. This is not new to me for I have witnessed many things in my travels which defy the will of God and make the mind of scientific reason mad with contradiction against the law of Nature Herself.

The clock chimes seven. I shall write more later, for it is time to make my toilet and dress for Lord Manfred's Masquerade at the Pump Room. Baroness Lewis has made provision for us to attend this gathering in honour of the Mayor. Her belief is this soirée is a prelude to events more akin to the proclivities of Sir Francis Dashwood of High Wycombe and his "Monks of Medmenham," those corrupt libertines who caroused through the ruins of that old Abbey along the Thames over one hundred years ago.

Van Helsing partook of a cold bath, despite the protestations of the maid who thought him mad, and dressed with customary haste for he loathed to waste time. Yet it was more than impatience with the ritual of dressing well which stoked his fires; the Professor's curiosity was aroused, but he was driven by the consideration that children were at risk and had fallen prey to something far more insidious than human evil.

On the stroke of eight o'clock, Van Helsing and Baroness Lewis departed the grandiose sweep of the Royal Crescent in a fine brougham which slowly navigated the cobbled street, affording them a view of acclaimed architect John Wood the Younger's masterpiece of design and building with its one hundred Ionic columns supporting a continuous cornice over two hundred yards long. Their carriage dipped down into the eastern corner of the Royal Victoria Park towards the Upper Bristol Road, then left towards Queen Square and Milsom Street and down to the Abbey and the Pump Room, the focal point of the city's social life since Richard "Beau"

Nash had transformed the crumbling, walled Medieval fortress into a glorious expanse of revelry in the early eighteenth century.

Gas lamps guttered as the brougham made its way towards its destination, the ornate confines of the chambers situated alongside the Roman Baths, where the wealthy afflicted with various diseases came to drink the mineral waters which ran beneath the streets, and thus named the Pump Room.

Van Helsing's observant eyes drank in every detail of the breathtaking Palladian architecture with which Wood the Elder and the Younger had transformed the city into a remarkable vista of Georgian splendour. "Beau" Nash, who reigned as "King of Bath" for fifty years, had turned the city into the queen and casino of the west. Under the hand of the man who invented his own rules for society, especially in the realm of civic entertainment, and sometimes pushed those rules beyond all reasonable limits, the city became a center of fashion. But that was the eighteenth century, and this was now 1861, the twenty-fourth year of Victoria's reign, not Nash's. The town—for its size, it had always been a town rather than a true city—had returned to a place to live in rather than a meeting point of gay birds of passage. Those who remembered the wild days of gambling, cockfights on the Abby Green, and masked balls at which behaviour unbecoming gentlemen was rife, now considered Bath a provincial municipality peopled by superannuated celibates of both sexes—admirals and post-captains, generals and majors, lawyers and clergy. Which is why Lord Manfred's parties over the past six months had caused such turbulent ripples on the calm surface of this genteel retreat from the grime and hurly-burly of London.

The brougham came to a halt at the corner of Union Street and Cheap Street and waited behind a line of other carriages waiting to enter the square in front of the Abbey. Drawing close to the entrance to the Pump Room, the driver opened the door. Van Helsing, in his adopted persona as the Baroness's personal physician, alighted first and took her hand, gently coaxing her from the carriage to the flagstones. Then, ever-present battered brown valise in hand, they entered Lord Manfred's den of iniquity.

Van Helsing's Journal. Entry undated (loose pages found in the back of the book).

Whiles my professional life often times entails social gatherings, I far prefer my own company or that of close friends, for true friendship must never be taken for granted as life itself should never be. For the sake of friendship with the Baroness I was here; and for the sake of those children who, I had no doubt, had fallen into the hands of some malign agent.

The Pump Room proved an aesthetic delight, a most harmonious assembly of antique furniture and Georgian design. Lord Manfred spared no expense on his personal decoration. Thousands of candles illuminated globes of fine Venetian glass which remind me of the light inside Notre Dame de Paris when the devout burn many, many votives. Garlands and bouquets of flowers from all over Europe, including the beloved tulip, festooned the walls and tabletops, their rich scents mingling in the warm air. A smorgasbord of exotic fruits and vegetables complemented an array of meats to make the butcher proud: watermelon from the Americas, mangoes from the Caribbean, star fruit from Asia. A small ensemble played Mozart from the tiny stage as, masked in the style of the Venice carnivale, Lord Manfred's guests mingled.

The face may don a disguise, though sometimes reputation is too grand to hide beneath a simple covering. Floating close to our host in a manner which denied his size was a figure I immediately surmised as Monsieur Boullan, the Parisienne sorcerer and compatriot of Eliphas Levi, practitioner of dark arts whom I had met once through Bulwer-Lytton. What strange company you keep, Lord Manfred.

As if reading my mind, our host removed himself from a tête-à-tête with a rotund individual I subsequently discover was Mr. Oliver Gaye, the Major of Bath, in whom's name this charade had been arranged.

"Your Ladyship," Manfred said, taking the Baroness by the hand, bowed and kissed her fingers with a flourish I can only describe as both theatrical and of the feminine manner, a touch I found both surprising and distasteful, for the Baroness had not inform me

Lord Manfred was a habitué of the Mollie House. I tryed not to flinch when he limply took my hand for I find the activities of sodomites an abomination in the eyes of God Almighty. "Doctor Van Helsing, how good of you to escort your patient and allow her to attend my little soirée. 'Tis an honor, sir, to have a physician of such standing join us this evening; I have heard much of your work in anatomy at the Royal College." This also surprise me, for I had no inkling this degenerate member of British aristocracy was to know who I am. Yet before I could question him on this account, a young lady whose deportment could not hide her true nature, approached, whispering in his ear, and Lord Manfred excused himself to speak with another guest.

Like the cuckolded husband, I saw then the truth behind the lie; social decorum is but a fancy curtain drawn to conceal the baseness of certain human natures. Behind this façade of eccentric gentility stood moral corruption like the voyeur who peer out from a dark recess. Gathering my wit, I realized that many of the gentlemen guests were older and single, their corpulent frames draped by the attentions of young women who, like the harlot who guided Lord Manfred away, were professional companions—not the gutter Mackerel I had become so accustomed to see on London's foul streets, but "ladies" who live in fine houses which discreetly administer to the base needs of wealthy married men.

I asked the Baroness if she knew of whom the revellers were. "That is Admiral Ducket with the petite sparrow; that is General Kitchen in conversation with those girls I believe are twins. Like many who now reside in Bath, they are retired and are either widowers or have never married, such as the General. They say he was married to his troops," she informed me.

"I fear you have misled me, friend Baroness; I did not know you were so familiar with either Lord Manfred or so many of the burghers of Bath," I said.

"Professor, my dear sir, for once your reason has deserted you. How can a woman of my social standing, a frequent visitor to this fair city, not have encountered its most prominent citizens?" she reply. But before I could quiz her further, Lord Manfred returned and took her by the elbow. "Forgive us please, Doctor; I must have a word with your 'patient' and introduce her to someone," he said before guiding the Baroness away from me to stand alone.

I felt then like the foolish fly who finds itself trapped in the web of the spider, for no doubt now resided in my mind the Baroness had deceived me, though for what purpose I could not then guess. But, as often, I am getting ahead of myself, and it is only through Grace of God I am here, back at my chambers in Holland Park, barely able to recount this tale for my hand does shake.

Feeling himself obtrusive and vulnerable so close to the center of the Pump Room, and not wishing to invite the unwanted attentions of the bordello girls, Van Helsing withdrew to a corner table where he accepted a glass of wine from a masked waiter. Giving the room close scrutiny, the Professor was disturbed to find that Monsieur Boullan had disappeared from sight—no mean feat for a man who stood close to seven feet tall. If Boullan's presence troubled him, Van Helsing was disquieted by the fact the Baroness Lewis, judging by her relaxed manner in Lord Manfred's company, knew their host so well. Why had she deceived him? And more importantly, why had she brought him here?

The Professor tried to recall what little he knew of Lord Manfred. Aleister Manfred was a lower member of British aristocracy, related to the throne on Prince Albert's side. Other than that, all he knew the Baroness had told him. That Lord Manfred had been expelled from Cambridge University, where he had been studying philosophy, for some scandalous incident, the details of which no one would dare speak. Apparently, the incident in question had so upset Lord Manfred's father that the old man passed away suddenly, just days before, or so it was rumoured, according to the Baroness, he planned to disinherit his wayward son and sole heir.

Rumour, Van Helsing thought, was an English disease that afflicted many of the landed class, slithering serpent-like through the drawing rooms and salons of London. Several leading Unitarians, a small cadre of those who, like himself were committed to social reform, shunned the Baroness's good works with the poor and children of the workhouse. For Baroness Lewis, too, had been the sources of some rumours, which painted her in a less than flattering light. Van Helsing had heard, but dismissed, gossip that Arabella Lewis was responsible for the passing of her husband; that she was a woman of boundless appetites and had worn the man into an early grave. All of which sounded like poppycock to the Professor; the late Baron Lewis had been forty years' Arabella's senior, but that was hardly surprising in Victorian society as many a member of the landed gentry who were gaining in years and had no heir took younger, robust women as their wives. And it was no secret that the late Baron's first wife had died during childbirth many, many years ago. The occurrence had so broken the Baron's heart that he had spent the next thirty years living alone, reclusively in the family estate in Kent. Then one day, seeing his mortality facing him on the horizon, beckoning him towards a dusty death, the Baron decided to take another wife and father an heir.

How, exactly, Arabella, the daughter of an Essex magistrate, had met the late Baron, Van Helsing did not know. Nor did he care, as such social matters were of no importance to him. What mattered was that he considered the Baroness to be a fine, upstanding woman—a little headstrong perhaps, and not without her eccentricities—but a selfless soul who devoted much of her fortune and time to those less privileged. Yet now he wondered if he knew her at all.

As he sipped his wine, the thoughts which vexed Van Helsing began to fade, for he was suddenly overcome by a terrible tiredness, both physical and mental, which fragmented his silent questions, shattering them like the glass which slipped from his fingers to break on the Pump Room floor.

Van Helsing dreamed.

The nightmares that had pursued him through his troubled sleep of the past week had left him shaken to the core on awakening; this dream, this lurid vision which now enveloped him, both disgusted and aroused him to an unprecedented level.

He found himself guided into a sumptuously furnished room filled with plush red velvet cushions piled upon ornate rugs from Morocco and the Orient, but the décor's accent was predominantly Greco-Roman. And like ancient Rome during the reign of the Emperor Caligula, a sea of writhing flesh undulated before him, grasping hands lapping at his feet—his bare feet, the Professor now realized, as he appeared to be dressed in some kind of toga, his flesh naked and vulnerable beneath a thin layer of sensuous silk. He sought to avert his eyes, but everywhere he tried to turn his heavy head his vision was assailed by this cornucopia of copulation as old, bloated, gout-ridden flesh pushed itself against young, smooth, alabaster skin. Somewhere in the midst of this river of wanton behaviour, this bacchanalia of breasts, buttocks, and genitalia, he thought he spied the Baroness's red hair, a wig floating on waves of flesh. Van Helsing felt sick to his soul. Yet worse was to come.

His eyesight dimmed, and as one sense retreated, his other senses became more acute. Smell, touch, taste, hearing—all four faculties were suddenly so sharp the sensations danced on the threshold of pain. The rich, heavy aromas of incense and myrrh assailed his nose, inducing a feeling of suffocation; hands, many hands—tiny hands—caressed his skin, causing his blood to race and rise. His lips were parted, his mouth opened, and a heavy, sweet wine flowed down his throat like nectar, the taste so seductive to the tongue he drank deep, deep draughts of Bacchus's bounty. His ears ached to the infernal, overwhelming sounds of voices reduced to grunts and sighs, moans and groans, cries and whispers, as if he were surrounded by Dante's damned, writhing in one of Hell's nine circles. His senses overwhelmed, the rhyme of his reason reduced to hedonistic doggerel, and Van Helsing, too, cried out like a lost soul as his body betrayed him once more . . .

Slowly, like a tentative winter sunrise that struggles to push back the chill of a frozen night, Van Helsing escaped from the clutches of the phantoms that cursed him. But when he awoke, what he saw nearly drove him mad.

He stood in a large, sepulchral underground chamber decorated with the remains of ancient, worn Roman statuary. Broken columns adorned a number of jet black doorways which appeared to lead away from the chamber in a measured geometric formation, but the columns, too, were mere ornamentation, as Van Helsing could tell the chamber was a natural geophysical formation adapted by and not made by men's hands. The air was fetid, humid, cloying with the heat that rose from the deep, dark green pool situated in the center of the chamber. The water swirled and bubbled, and Van Helsing fleetingly realized he was somewhere underneath Bath, that the pool before him was fed by the natural spring which wormed its way upwards from deep within the heated rock miles beneath his bare feet. Six bloodstained slabs radiated out from around the pool, each one angled so the end nearest the water was lower than the farthest tip of stone. On each altar, for he immediately realized that was what they were, lay the body of a child no older than nine or ten—boy, girl, three of each, all deathly pale, unconscious, unmoving, as blood trickled from cuts in their hands and feet to dribble into the pool. The professor's stomach churned with anger and his digestive system tried to expel the noxious pollutant of drugged wine which held his body in its sluggish state.

"Two thousand years this temple has remained hidden from the eyes of the unworthy," a voice said from behind him. "But for two thousand years there have been those who have been blessed to know its secrets."

Dressed in a ruby red toga, Lord Manfred appeared beside the Professor on his left side.

"Why?" Van Helsing managed to speak despite a numbness in his tongue.

"Why are we doing this? Or why are you here?"

"Because She Who Lives Beneath The Waters needs sustenance if She is to grant us her boon," said a female voice to the Professor's right.

Van Helsing turned his head as far as his drugged muscles would allow. Baroness Lewis smiled lasciviously as he laid eyes upon her.

From the periphery of his vision, Van Helsing saw another four toga-clad figures enter the chamber led by Monsieur Boullan. Each took up a position behind an altar.

"You are here, Professor, to bear witness," Lord Manfred said. "And because I take great delight in bringing torment to others. You are a man of God—the Christian God, the false God—yet now you will have the honour of gazing upon the face of a true Goddess."

Van Helsing stared helplessly at the dying children, their life's blood flowing into and staining the water.

"You are evil," he managed to say, despite his inability to fully move his lips.

"There is no Good, no Evil; just the natural order of things: those who serve, and those they serve; those who feed to survive and their prey. Those who serve will be blessed. Now, watch!"

The pool's previously placid surface began to roil, a churning turbulence like a bubbling pot of murky green stew. Something stirred beneath the surface, a dark, reptilian shadow. Then, slowly, regally, a head emerged from the water. The head of a beautiful woman with golden eyes and olive skin framed by a slick of jet-black hair.

"Behold the Lamia, wife of Poseidon, granter of eternal life!" Lord Manfred whispered forcefully into the professor's ear.

Van Helsing stood like the temple statuary—broken, immobile, frozen by the abominable sight.

The Lamia placed two webbed hands on the lip of the pool and raised herself up from her watery womb. The creature's breasts were perfectly shaped like those of the Venus de Milo, but there her resemblance to womankind ended. As she reached out a hand towards the nearest child, Van Helsing saw in abject horror that from the waist down the creature was pure serpent.

"Watch! Watch!" Lord Manfred urged.

If Van Helsing believed he had seen evil in the world, nothing he had witnessed before this day could prepare him for the sight of the Lamia as it began to feed.

News Item from The Pall Mall Gazette, September 20th, 1861
PROFESSOR RECOVERING.

Professor Abraham Van Helsing, the noted Dutch Lawyer and esteemed Physician who has been Guest Lecturer in Residence at the Royal College of Medicine for the past year, has been diagnosed as fully recovered following a most unfortunate incident which occurred while he was visiting the City of Bath last week.

The Professor suffered a serious blow to the head when attacked by ruffians while taking a late night stroll through Bath's much acclaimed Royal Victoria Park, and has been confined to bed since returning to London on Thursday.

(continued Page 7)

Van Helsing's Journal: September 17th.

I cannot sleep nor can I close mine eyes, for every time I do so the most terrible images flicker in front like some infernal daguerreotype. The horrors I have borne witness to are such that my sanity scream like the inmates of Bedlam. Yet there is worse I must bear than the memory of ancient evil. That which I saw, I cannot bring myself to write about, in part because I cannot fully make sense of all which has befallen me since I awoke in a hospital bed seven days ago; but more so because my heart is broken, and a melancholy weigh me down.

The Good Lord has taken my Susannah and freed her from this mortal coil; that is the best of news even though it pains so. Dr. Hughes informs me she pass peacefully in her sleep the first night I was in Bath. But there is more, much more—news which once received a day after I returned to London nearly drove me back into the arms of unconsciousness.

My little Lily has been stolen away by a thief in the night. Gone. Disappeared. Vanished as breath to the wind.

I know who is responsible, and that terrible knowledge is harder to carry than the fact of her abduction. I can only pray what fate has befallen her has been swift and painless. Yet feeling so impotent, and the realization that I cannot act—for I can prove nothing and have no mapped avenue to follow—fills me with both despair and righteous anger. Yet anger must be the tonic for my soul if I am to survive and grow strong and illuminate the darkness so we, as men, may better define the light.

I will not crumble like the sea wall that is worn away by the ocean—in this incidence, a sea of evil.

I shall not write of that which I recall following Lord Manfred's masked soirée; in part because my recollections resemble potsherds uncovered by the archaeologist: tarnished, incomplete. And more so because what I do recall is shameful and disturbing, and to dwell upon these recollections will only confine me to a cul-de-sac of regret, shackled by guilt and hopelessness.

This I know: I have been a pawn in an evil game designed to eat away at my faith in God, to break my sanity and spirit.

I was found, in the Royal Victoria Park, at dawn the morning after the party, by a delivery boy, seemingly attacked by a thief, for I was bereft of money and my gold watch. Two days I lay unconscious in Bath's finest hospital before I awake. Confused, I did not contradict the theory of my state proposed by the Bath constabulary. My requests to have the Baroness visit me came to naught as, according to her local maid, she suddenly returned to London on receiving news her son had taken sick. Attempts to locate the Baroness at her Belgravia house proved equally fruitless; the abode was empty and shows no sign of having been lived in for some time. As for the burghers of Bath, they claim no knowledge of Lord Manfred's whereabouts save that he, too, departed the city for "a destination on the continent" the day following the ball. When men such as a mayor and his powerful friends have been compromised as I suspect, they have secrets which impede truth; I shall find no help there.

As the Lord God Almighty is my witness, I shall not rest until I have brought them both to justice. Not Man's justice, for as a lawyer I know only too well there is one law for the rich, another for the poor; no, the justice of Van Helsing.

I know now the path I must follow. As I have long suspected, in part supported by my occult studies, far stranger things walk on Earth than we dream of in Heaven and Hell. The evils men do are, in the main, petty evils, but evils nonetheless; mine eyes have seen the testimony of a greater Evil which feeds on the little evils of men, encourage those evils, cultivates the soil in which dark blooms grow.

Why did they let me live? To torture me? As Manfred says "to corrupt the Good"?

The arrogance of Evil!

This proves he is a fool.

Evil is an absence of love; a desire to erode our moral fibre, to bring unnecessary pain and suffering to our condition so that we may despair of God and lose our faith in a Higher Purpose. A desire to destroy that which is Good, to corrupt and break and trample into the dust the Lord's greatest gift: Love. If I have sinned, my sin has been weakness—a cowardliness which held me back from love, for those who do not love fully do not live as God intends. I loved Susannah as a father, but as a father I should have loved little Lily. Even so, had I taken her into my house would she be safe and sound now, sleeping the innocent sleep only children are afforded? I cannot say. All I know is I will never know because I was weak, and afraid of mine own weakness.

No more.

Where there be monsters, I shall smite them down. Where there is darkness, I shall be the beacon of light. Where there is absence of love, I shall be sustenance.

Evil beware.

A MOTHER CRIES AT MIDNIGHT

He stared at me sadly over his steaming cup of coffee, and I saw then how the terrible weight of his responsibility had crushed his spirit. Instead of fathering hope and life, instead of saving lives, he had given birth to the most destructive force known to mankind. There had been no irony when, as Fat Man exploded, he had said, "I am become Death, destroyer of worlds." For eight years he had tried to deal with that terrible knowledge.

"How are things at the Bureau?" my friend J. Robert Oppenheimer asked, pulling his pipe from his pocket. "How's Trevor?"

"Quite well. He asked me to send his best," I replied, watching him pack the pipe bowl with a pungent tumbleweed of Balkan Sobrane tobacco.

The waitress suspiciously eyed the back booth in which we sat. Not because of the cloud of thick, sweet smoke now pluming above Robert's head, but I sensed it was my presence that made her uncomfortable. Even though we were only a few miles outside of Roswell, New Mexico, and since 1947, shortly after I moved away, the locals had grown used to strange sights, and even stranger goings-on, having a large, red creature seated in your diner was certainly unusual. Beneath my duster, I tightened my curled tail lest it slip below the hem. Some women, I have discovered, frequently found the tail to be more than they could handle.

"They've taken away my clearance. I'm persona non grata," he said into his cup. "But I can't be a party to it anymore. They're not going to stop. It's all about bigger and better bombs. And they don't want me as a conscience. My opinions are uncalled for."

His angular features were pinched. You didn't need to be a rocket scientist to see he was in pain.

"But that's not why I asked you to come . . . I'm acting as middle man. Do you remember Jamie MacDougal?"

I nodded.

I remembered him well. A spry Scottish-American research scientist. MacDougal and Trevor Bruttenholm had spent many an evening playing chess during the year we lived at Roswell. As I had come to look upon Brutteholm as my father, at that time Jamie MacDougal had been like an uncle.

"He's here, stationed at Los Alamos. Very hush-hush. Now I'm considered a liability, I can't have any contact with him. But somehow he managed to get a note to me, requesting I contact you to see if you'd come." Robert puffed slowly, savouring the rich aroma.

"I'm here. So what's the problem?"

"His son's disappeared."

A half-crescent moon rode high in the sky like a severed quarter as I walked the arroyo running parallel to the road where young Malcolm MacDougal had last been spotted. I was five lonely miles outside of Los Alamos, heading southwest into the foot hills of the Jemez Mountains. I was searching for a stream, for there I hoped to find a woman who would lead me to the boy.

"They believe he's dead," Jamie MacDougal had said earlier that evening. "He's been gone a week. They called off the search on Monday—said it was a waste of manpower—that he must have perished because no seven-year-old could survive the night temperatures.

"But I know," he said, pouring himself a generous glass of single malt. "I'm his father, and I know in my bones he's still alive."

I hadn't seen Jamie in nearly eight years, and the river of human time had eroded his once-full head of red hair and reshaped his features like a rain-washed statue. He looked closer to sixty than his fast-approaching forty-seven. It was his birthday next week. I had remembered en route to Los Alamos from Roswell. Robert had stopped the car outside Santo Domingo so I could buy a gift. The

Anasazi pot sat on Jamie's dining table, ground zero between the two of us.

"Go slow, old friend," I said. "Start at the beginning."

Jamie took a hearty swig of his malt, and sighed.

"Lucy—his mother—died a year ago. Car crash. Almost a month to the day," he added, wistfully staring into his drink. "So the base provided us with a housekeeper, a nanny of sorts who could take care of him. Dona's her name. Local woman of Zuni extraction. But of course he took it hard. We both did. And a seven-year-old wants his mother, not a stranger."

He was right. All boys need a mother. Even a Hellboy. I, however, had no recollection of a mother, or a father. Or of anything before I appeared in the ruins of an old church in East Bromwhich, England nearly ten years ago.

"Yes," I said, "go on."

"Dona's a good sort. Takes excellent care of him—or did until she let him wander off.

"The last couple of months have been very hard, what with the anniversary coming up, and I've been working long, long hours in the lab.

"I should have been there for him," he suddenly exclaimed, slamming a hand on the table top, almost spilling his drink and knocking over my pot.

It took a while, and another drink, to calm him.

Malcolm, I learned, had taken to wandering away from the base over the last few months. There was nothing unusual in that. Boys will be boys, and with so many ruins to explore, the summer-kissed landscape surrounding the cold, uninviting barracks-style housing could be a place of endless wonders to the over-active imagination of a seven-year-old. Summer was gone now though, swept aside by an early, harsh fall, and the nights came cold and hard at this elevation. Still Los Alamos was a safe town, perhaps the safest in the United States due to the secret nature of its inhabitants' work, and Dona had thought nothing wrong in letting the boy play outside after sunset. But that all changed when he met the woman.

CITIES OF NIGHT

There was a good reason why New Mexico was called The Land of Enchantment, for there are arcane energies here, powers present which defy national explanation. Was it coincidence Los Alamos became the Secret City, birthplace of the atom bomb, or that Fat Man's explosion happened at Trinity Site? Why not Nevada, or some other desert state with even more wide-open spaces? Why did a supposed extraterrestrial craft crash at Roswell? Trevor Bruttenholm believed this state forms a nexus of paranormal energies, and when the US military insisted on relocating me from England so I could be studied at Roswell, he was only too happy to accompany me. During the time we lived here, he immersed himself in the myths and legends of New Mexico and took me along on frequent investigatory trips. One of my first memories was of our visit to the Santuario de Chimayo which was nestled in a secluded valley in the Sangre de Christo foothills. Like the pilgrims who had trekked there over the centuries, predominantly the sick and enfeebled, we went to experience the mysterious healing powers of its magical soil. Bruttenholm was convinced it cured his arthritis. All it did was make me itch.

I had so many other stories and experiences during that early period in my life that perhaps it was no surprise I decided to follow my adoptive father's line of work. We spent nights in the ancient mission of Isleta Pueblo, hoping to see the restless corpse of Father Padilla and his cottonwood coffin rise from beneath the altar, as he had done so on numerous occasions over the past two hundred years (he didn't). We spent days camping on low mountain slopes, sitting up through the night in case a fireball-riding bruja passed by overhead (we never saw a witch, but I saw my first shooting star).

New Mexico was like the Navajo rug Bruttenholm bought as a gift for me before we left Roswell for the East Coast and the BPRD headquarters in Fairfield, Connecticut. It was a simple rug, just two rows of white, rectangular clouds outlined in black against a light blue background. But the rug had a deliberate line woven through its lower border, a "spirit line" worked into the weave in case a soul became trapped during the weaving and needed a way out. New

Mexico itself seemed like a spirit line, a gateway between realms, and some of what sought freedom here was of a malevolent stripe. Then there are those forces which are a reflection of the souls of the beholder, neither good nor evil, merely a mirror to our needs. She was one of them—the one known as La Llorona, The Weeping Woman.

A particular manifestation of New Mexico and its Hispanic heritage, La Llorona's story had many variations concerning her origins and nature, but I knew she was more than a myth. I knew because I met her.

Back in early '47, a few months before the Roswell crash and our departure for the lush New England green of Connecticut, Bruttenholm had taken me to Santa Fe where he was visiting Fray Angelico Chavez, the renowned historian and restorer of ancient churches. Fray Angelico had been researching the recorded appearances of Fray Padilla, and he invited Trevor to read the first draft of the paper he was preparing. Although I had only been on the earthly plane for a couple of years, I had already reached adolescence and was suffering restlessness as a youth. So, as the day waned and the magical spring twilight bathed the Sangre de Christo range ruby red, and as Bruttenholm and Fray Chaves continued their impassioned discussion, I walked out into the streets of Santa Fe.

Since I was still wary of the reactions of others to my unusual appearance, I walked away from the bustling plazas, sticking to narrow side streets lined with sleepy adobe homes squatting behind hand-carved wooden gates, half-hidden by gnarled cottonwoods or softly hued hollyhocks, and made my way down to the banks of the Santa Fe River. It was peaceful there, and it calmed my troubled thoughts as I followed the water eastwards.

Maybe it was the onset of adolescence and the need to understand who and what I was. Or perhaps it was the natural questioning of an orphan concerning his parentage, but for weeks I had lain awake at night tossing and turning, wondering and wanting answers to an enigma—the enigma of myself. Seeing the other children who lived on the Roswell base play ball with their fathers, go shopping with their mothers, made my heart heavy. Trevor Bruttenholm was a kind, compassionate, and thoughtful mentor, as fine a father figure as a Hellboy could have. Yet when sleep would not come, I would lie in my room wondering what it must feel like to lose one's self in a mother's embrace or to rage at my inability to remember where I came from before a magical rite summoned me to this world.

Did I have a mother? Did she mourn for the loss of her son?

The thoughts vexed me daily, but that evening as I walked the river bank, the preternatural calm of Santa Fe soothed my soul, and my mind turned towards more intellectual ideas. Albert Einstein had visited Roswell with Oppenheimer the week before and spent hours with me explaining his theory of relativity. Trevor was intent on providing me with the best educational opportunities, and who better to explain physics than Einstein? I savoured the time we spent together, even though the deluge of knowledge he unleashed threatened to sweep me away. So it was with a head full of equations and formulae that I wandered into the dark, barely aware of the distance I had traveled or the fact that night had almost completely descended in its diamond-studded velvet glory.

At first I thought the sound was that of an animal. But as I listened more carefully I realized it was a human sound, a sorrow-filled lament. Then, maybe two hundred yards ahead, I saw a figure standing on the bank where the river curved. It was a woman clad in a long gray dress, her head and shoulders cocooned in a black woollen shawl.

The wail ripped from her lips with a terrible strength, a power born of great emotional pain, and I realized she was about to fling herself into the water.

Again she cried out: *"Ayyyy, mis hijooooosss!"*

I didn't understand what she was screaming, but her intentions were clear.

I started to run as she threw herself into the river, shedding my long coat like a second skin as I dove after her. The chilly waters made me gasp, shocking me like an unexpected slap to the face, but I doubled my efforts as her head disappeared beneath the surface. It was instinct, pure and simple. I had no time to think, only moments to act. The undercurrent was surprisingly strong considering the seemingly slow momentum of the surface, and at the bend I saw sudden turbulence as the now speeding water rushed over jagged rocks. If I couldn't reach her in time, she'd surely be smashed to a pulp against their sharp peaks.

An Air Force sergeant at Roswell had taught me how to swim, and I put every ounce of strength into a fast crawl which would have made him proud. And not a moment too soon; I grabbed her hand as she went under a third time, trying to halt my forward momentum in the midst of frothy whitecaps a dozen feet or so from the bend. Somehow I managed to pull her now-limp body towards mine, but I couldn't fight the flow. Turning, cradling her against my chest, I managed to spin around so my broad back hit the first partially submerged boulder. The impact felt like a mule kick. And then we were moving again, leaves in a hurricane, tossed from one boulder to the next.

I don't remember seeing the low-lying branch or grabbing it. Suddenly we were in stasis, surrounded, pummelled by the river's wild waters, but not moving, not at its mercy. Not completely at least. The fact the branch didn't break, and amazingly, that I was able to pull us up and out of the bank one-handed—well, I guess those Charles Atlas exercises Trevor encouraged me to do on a daily basis paid off. I saved us through dynamic tension.

Chest heaving, lungs aching, I lay on my back on the muddy bank beneath our benefactor, the tree. She lay beside me, conscious now, sobbing softly. In English this time.

"My children. My children . . ."

Placing a reassuring hand on her shoulder, I stood, swaying slightly with adrenalin-driven vertigo, my equilibrium still spinning like gyroscope after the dervish dance of the rushing waters.

"It's okay," I mumbled. "It's going to be all right.

"I'll get my coat. Need to keep you warm."

Stumbling through the scrub, my mind still a tilt-a-whirl, I don't remember hearing the sudden silence as her sobbing stopped.

Scooping up my full-length duster, I turned towards her and—

—she was gone.

Vanished.

Into thin air.

Later, seated around a roaring open fire in the rectory of Loretto Chapel, Fray Angelico explained I had been blessed by encountering La Llorona, and that my selfless act would bring good fortune.

"La Llorona is ancient; her true origins go back, way back before the time we have recorded. She was a part of this landscape long before the Spanish came. She even predates the indigenous Anasazi people."

"I've heard tell—"

Fray Angelico waved a hand to silence Trevor. "Listen. And learn. If not for your own sake, then for Hellboy's—for this special child has been blessed.

"She is not always so forgiving. Nor is she so vulnerable to the eyes of others. One might hear her sorrow. One might see her struggle with her pain. But to see her in such naked despair . . . That is highly unusual."

Felicia, Fray Angelico's housekeeper, brought me a mug of steaming hot chocolate. Its warmth revived my shivering senses, and I listened intently to the legend of La Llorona.

"There once was a girl," the priest began, "who was said to be very beautiful. Because of her looks, people didn't treat her like others. And the more beautiful she became as she blossomed into womanhood, the more people shunned her. Even her own family felt ashamed for not being able to provide for such a beauty.

"One day a stranger came to the pueblo. He was well-dressed, obviously a man of wealth. Generous, too. And his largess made him very popular with the locals.

"The stranger soon grew tired of the pueblo and was preparing to move out when he laid eyes on the beautiful woman, and he was entranced. How did such a woman come to be here in a poor pueblo surrounded by nothing more than cacti and dust? He had never seen such fine elegance and decided to stay to court this ravishing woman. When he proposed marriage, her family encouraged her to say yes, for this fine man could provide for her, give her the future they believed their beautiful daughter deserved.

"They wed, and the match seemed Heaven-made. The stranger was given the respect of a mayor, and the beauty found happiness beyond her imagining. Soon they had a child. The beauty's joy was such she could barely believe it. But as time passed, the stranger grew tired of the sleepy village. Even his devoted wife bored him, and the child had eyes only for its mother. It was not what he had expected. His money was running low, and he thirsted for adventure, for the temptations of the big city. And so one day he left without saying a word.

"His beautiful wife waited. Each night, after she had put the child to bed, she would light a candle by the door. Each morning she would awaken the child with a kiss, then blow out the candle. Days turned into weeks. Even though her husband's disappearance worried her, she never gave up hope. Weeks became months. No one came to visit. Not even her family. They were sure she had somehow chased the stranger away with her formidable beauty. She started to go crazy not knowing what she had done to turn everyone against her."

Fray Angelico paused, as much to savour his snifter of Benedictine brandy as for effect.

"The weather changed with the seasons, and the monsoons began building. The heavy air exacerbated her already fevered imagination. At night, the winds picked up, and mesquite thorns rubbed against the windows. The heavens opened up. It was as if the sky was crying a torrent of tears, soaking their adobe home. Mud seeped into the house, bringing with it the smell of the grave. The beauty could stand it no longer. She grabbed her sleeping baby and raced out the door into the storm.

"Driven mad by the desertion of her husband, her family, she raced to the river. She had lost all reason. And there, standing beside the overflowing river bank, she threw her child into the raging waters. And in that terrible instant, she regained clarity of mind—albeit for a painful second—and let out the most agonizing cry. Unable to accept the horror of her obscene sin, she threw herself into the storm-swollen waters.

"It was the worst deluge anyone in the village could remember. Few people could sleep that night, for cries too terrifying to describe were heard all over the valley.

"To this day, when rivers fill and flow fast, some say they see a beautiful woman walking the banks. Should you get too close you may hear an eerie cry, and some say an elegant hand may even touch your shoulder."

Fray Angelica set down his glass. He looked me deep in the eye. "You, dear boy, did a very noble act. You touched her. I am certain the beauty will not forget."

"But there are other variations of the legend, aren't there?" Bruttenhom interjected.

"Yes," Fray Angelico nodded.

"Often times she is seen by the side of a road. Those who stop to offer her a ride either find she disappears as they approach, or she scares them away."

"How?" I asked.

"Instead of being a beauty, she is either a hideous hag or has the face of a skull." He chuckled a dry laugh. "Those who see her this way are often adulterous lovers returning from or going to an illicit rendezvous. It seems she does not appreciate unfaithfulness."

"But I've also heard she protects children," Bruttenholm added.

"Indeed. Those foolish enough to play by rivers after dark are known to encounter her."

This apparently was what had happened to Malcolm MacDougal, I learned from Dona. But instead of scaring the boy, La Llorona had entranced him.

Dona was working in the kitchen, preparing a late dinner for Jamie. She was so absorbed by her task she lost track of time. Then, when she realized it was past nine and the boy hadn't returned home, she started to panic. She had gone but a few yards from the house when she found him wandering, dreamy and distracted. He told her he had been to the river, and there he had seen a beautiful woman who told him his mother loved him and that she was well, waiting for the day they would be reunited. At this, Dona scolded Malcolm and told him to never, ever go to the river at night. Sometimes, of course, forbidding a child from doing something was the worst advice an adult can give, as the young are naturally curious about things they should not do.

The next night, Dona insisted Malcolm stay home. Surprisingly, the boy agreed and read in his room. Relieved that he calmly accepted her request, she went about her household chores not thinking anything was amiss. But when she went to call Malcolm for his supper, she discovered the bedroom empty, the window wide open.

Jamie was beside himself when he heard the news, so distraught the base commander refused to allow him to join the search party. Besides, it seemed straightforward. A technician driving in from Jemez Springs reported seeing what he thought was a young boy by the side of the main road. He had stopped to investigate, but the figure disappeared into the woods a mile from the river. However, a night-long search proved a failure. Malcolm MacDougal had vanished into thin air. There was no stopping Jamie the next morning.

Every stream and tributary was searched, and the section of river where Malcolm had told Dona he had seen La Llorona was dredged. A week later with the hunt for the boy dissolved, I was Jamie's last hope.

Coming out of the arroyo, I headed in the direction of a lush sloping pasture and the forest beyond. Half an hour later, I located a stream and sat down to wait, hoping my instincts were right.

At midnight, my suspicions were confirmed, my patience rewarded. The sound started low, mournful at first, then rose steadily in pitch. To the unsuspecting, it could have been a coyote call, but I had heard that soul-wrenching cry before. It was impossible to forget. For a moment, the years slipped away, pulling me back to the banks of the Santa Fe River. Then, suddenly, it stopped. The silence following felt eerie, almost suffocating in its intensity.

I waited, my eyes trying to penetrate the jet-black shadows cast by the trees. Nothing moved.

When the hand touched my shoulder, I nearly leapt out of my red skin.

I turned. There, beside me, stood the Weeping Woman. My first encounter had been hectic, fraught with frantic actions; I had never gotten a clear look at her. Now, I saw her beauty was remarkable, almost too painful to gaze upon. To try to describe this ethereal creature would be foolish. Besides, the deep, dark olive of her haunted eyes drew me in, made me a fellow prisoner of her sorrow.

"The boy," I said softly, barely a whisper. "Please, take me to the child."

La Llorona took me by the hand, leaning me away from the stream and into the stygian secrets of the forest. She remained silent. I didn't know what to say. What could I say to this spirit?

We reached a clearing. Although Old Man Moon's light was largely obscured by the towering oaks, spruce, and Douglas firs, I could make out a stocky hill ahead. She led me around it and, on the opposite side, stopped before a thick tangle of bushes. Those sad eyes stared at me a moment before she stepped forward. Since she touched me she had appeared solid. Now she dissolved through the bushes, letting go of my hand, freeing my arms to fight through the undergrowth. Behind them was a small cave mouth, and I stopped to enter.

Instead of pitch blackness, the cave was softly illuminated, and it took me a moment to realize she was the light source. La Llorona glowed from within. The cave floor sloped down, and she took my hand to steady me as we descended. The natural rock walls narrowed, the ceiling lowering, forcing me to bend. The tunnel curved before opening into a subterranean chamber.

Malcolm MacDougal lay on a bed of leaves beside an underground pool the size of a goldfish pond. His eyes were glazed, feverishly delirious. His left leg was broken and lay at a painful angle. How had he come to be here? Had she carried him?

"Mother," he said. "Don't leave me. Stay with me. I don't feel well."

She said nothing, but a strange smile crept across his dirt-smeared features. He had his father's mouth, his mother's eyes. I sensed something pass between them.

"I'm here to take you home," I said.

The smile faded.

"Yes, Mother said it's time to go now," he mumbled.

I scooped him up as carefully as possible, and as La Llorona led, we made our way back.

His head felt hot, his body thin and fragile. The water had kept him alive, but the boy was famished and the fever had drained him. As I navigated my way through the trees, I sensed she was no longer with us. Turning, I saw she had faded in the night like breath on a cold day. She had done her part, and now I had to finish mine. I hoped my luck would continue; perhaps we'd run across a passing motorist who wouldn't crash at the sight of a large red creature carrying the body of a small boy.

Malcolm murmured in his delirium.

"Mother . . . don't leave . . . me. . . ."

His condition was worse than I first thought.

I wanted to run. I needed to get him to the hospital in Los Alamos. Every step seemed to rattle his bones. Sudden movement was out of the question. I hoped for a car or truck. Otherwise, all I could do was take it one step at a time. His breath came in short dry wheezes.

One step became another. Keeping my eyes on the ground, my mind wandered. Halfway across the meadow, I realized I had left the forest behind.

And realized Malcolm was dead.

Tears of frustration spilled from my eyes. I lowered myself to the ground cradling the small corpse. Too late. I had failed.

"We're cursed," Oppenheimer had said as we drove to Los Alamos. "I believe those of us who made the bomb, or continue to work on the program, will never be forgiven for what we've done. Whatever your faith, whichever God you believe in . . . it doesn't matter. We're cursed. We committed the greatest sin against life. We create to destroy. Women create. They create life. We only destroy it."

Those words echoing in my mind, I looked down on Malcolm's urchin-like face. In death, his features more resembled those of his father. Poor Jamie. What could I say to him? In helping to father weapons of destruction, he had lost sight of the life he had helped create, unintentionally pushing the boy towards the arms of a delusion.

A tear fell from my face and ran across Malcolm's cheek, wiping away a smudge of dirt. It looked like he, too, was crying. A tear of joy, for I hoped he was with his mother now.

And I wondered, in that unguarded moment, who would mourn for me?

From deep in the woods, I heard La Llorona let loose her painful lament.

UNEARTHLY POWERS

OVER MULHOLLAND

Like Raymond the butler in *Citizen Kane*, I knew where the bodies were buried.

I eased the vintage 2010 Mercedes E-class Coupe out of the fortressed iron gates of my house on Mulholland Drive, heading east towards the Cahuenga Pass and the rebuilt 101 Freeway. There was no traffic on the road as I guided the car like a long-term lover along the snaking, sensuous curves. My wheels had caressed the tarmac here for close to forty-two years. If El Pueblo de Nuestra Senora la Reina de los Angeles had been my spiritual wife for over half my life, then the drive which rode the Monroe-esque ridgeline of the Santa Monica Mountains was my true mistress.

"Slow down!" Paul cried as I took a turn a tad faster than I should. *"You'll get us killed!"*

"You told me that's what you wanted, you dumb fucking cunt," I chuckled as I turned up the theme from *Shaft* on the sound system. Old habits die hard, and I loved to drive with soundtrack music and twentieth-century funk tunes pounding out loud enough to almost damage my digital hearing aids. There was nothing like a dose of Isaac Hayes to get my old body movin' and a-groovin' in the morning, and since this was my death day, I was bloody well going to go out happy.

"Jesus! Look out!" Paul screamed as I deftly manoeuvred the Coupe around the carcass of a coyote straddling the centre line.

I pulled over at the tourist spot which gave an unhindered view of the San Fernando Valley spread out like a soiled carpet beneath us.

"Sobered you up enough have I, old son?" I frowned at Paul Pope. "Enough beating around the bush. It's time to tell tales and spill the beans, Sunny Jim."

The Pope of Perversity told me an inane tale which rivalled the plot of a Ray Dennis Steckler movie from the 1960s; it made no sense but I couldn't care less. His wife had died. His mistress had left him. And Wendy, who he thought was his daughter, had stopped speaking to him and had apparently disappeared. I had been keen to get out of the house and do something on the day of my death so found all this rather amusing. Indeed, do something which might actually kill me, because, honestly, as much as I had a feel for certain future events, I could never see the actual line on the horizon where life and death intersected, as had been the case with my late brother whose fatal rampage of self-destruction had inspired my first award-nominated novella.

Then there was Blackpool and the events which led to my first failed marriage. I had loved Beth with such an intensity that when she left me for another man I nearly died. Nine months of intense drinking and drugging and fucking any snatch I could pull in to bed . . . shit, self-destruction didn't work. I didn't realize it then, and a life misspent should have taught me that trying to kill myself just wasn't going to work either. But I wanted to be reunited with my beloved Tess. My soul cried out like Frank and Jesse James or Butch and Sundance jumping off that cliff or Pike telling the Gorch Brothers, *"Let's do it."*

I wanted to die.

And if Paul wanted me to kill him, I was going to blow his brains out with a revelation, not a gun.

Truth is the sword of us all.

Words could be weapons, and I was about to sharpen the knives.

"She's not your daughter," I said.

"What?"

"She's mine."

"What?" Paul bleated.

"She's not your daughter! She's mine! I fucked Angela nonstop for eight months, you idiot!"

In ninety-three years I had never seen someone go from stark white to apoplectic beetroot in twenty seconds. Paul literally went red with rage.

Paul Pope and I had been friends for six months before he betrayed me. Then screwed me over. Paul subsequently spent twenty years badmouthing me, sabotaging business deals because he resented my successes, envied my talent. For a decade, I languished in work-for-hire Hell, either as a journalist or as a fledgling fiction writer while he won comic book awards, directed a couple of crappy music videos and went to Hollywood, riding the coattails of a mega-millionaire who had sold a stupid cartoon concept which made more money than *Barney The Dinosaur*.

But success *is* the best revenge, and that I had in spades.

His career languished. I had screwed his wife. I had fathered "his" daughter when he couldn't get it up...

Pope then had a cardiac arrest.

He died within a minute as we passed the Hollywood Bowl exit. Once I reached North Highland, I opened the passenger door and pushed his body out.

On the day of my death I had no regrets, no worries or concerns.

My daughters were safe in other parts of the world: Cassie in New York, Cali in London. Wendy, Paul's "daughter" was in Maui, probably drinking a salty margarita at the Hollywood Hawaiian Motel she loved to stay at.

As I turned west onto Sunset Boulevard to head towards the Pacific Ocean, the Big One hit. Beverly Hills and Bel Air rippled. The ground beneath my favourite old car crumbled.

It was more spectacular than that silly Emmerich movie from decades ago.

As Mother Earth swallowed me up, all I could think was, *Tess, we will be together again.*

For eternity.

There would be no more dreams.

—*Atlanta, January 28, 2010*
(For Jayson "Lobster Boy" Palmer.)

We are dust that dreams.
—Henry Miller

ACKNOWLEDGEMENTS

This book would not exist without the vision of Brett Alexander Savory & Sandra Kasturi and CZP.

Thanks to artists Erik Mohr and Mark Maddox for making it all look so good.

Debts to Anya Martin and Helen Marshall for cleaning up my messes.

And a thank you to my screenwriting students (Class of 2009) for pushing me to think about narrative design—especially Barbara Barth, Michael Brady, and Jayson Palmer.

The book was fuelled on Guinness, Sauza Tequila, Echo & The Bunnymen (very LOUDLY), and Monty Python.

And as the Pythons would say:

"Now piss off!"

COPYRIGHT

ABOUT THE AUTHOR

Philip Nutman is a man of many hats (literally, he has a very cool hat collection). He is a multi-award-nominated novelist for the seminal apocalyptic zombie espionage police procedural novel, *Wet Work*. An internationally acclaimed journalist who has written over 2,000 articles, he was *Fangoria* magazine's British Correspondent for over 10 years. He is an award-winning screenwriter and producer (*Jack Ketchum's The Girl Next Door*). And he has written and edited over 70 comic books. In 2009, he also became a brand of coffee (we're not kidding; Philip Nutman's *Wet Work* "coffee that's a shot to the head" is available from www.coffeeshopofhorrors.com).

An English ex-patriate, Nutman has made Atlanta his home since 1993. For more about his work, go to www.philipnutman.com.